Here's what reade
about the 'Phoe

"Phoebe Wren books make me read faster" – Ella, age 11

"Exciting!" – Jamie, age 13

"Couldn't put the book down" – Catherine, age 43

"I love these books, they're definitely on my 're-read' list"
– Kathryn, age 17

"This author knows how to grab the readers' attention and
never let go" – Ian, age 60 something

"Best books ever . . . on my top ten best book list!"
– Benjamin, age 12

"Books to be read by the whole family" – Debbie, age 30(ish)

"Brilliant! I just can't read these books fast enough!"
– Caitlin, age 13

"Absolutely riveting, couldn't put it down!"
– Donna, age 40(ish)

"I'm don't read an awful lot, but I really enjoyed the
Phoebe Wren books" – Jack, age 16

"I can't wait for the next adventure!"
– Abi, age 11

"Excellent!" – Dylan, age 14

"Brilliant books! Love the storylines and characters"
– Jamie, age 13

Phoebe Wren

AND THE
MYSTERY OF
DARKEN ABBEY

Britain's Next
BESTSELLER

First published in 2015 by:

Britain's Next Bestseller
An imprint of Live It Publishing
27 Old Gloucester Road
London, United Kingdom.
WC1N 3AX

www.britainsnextbestseller.co.uk

ISBN 978-1-910565-40-7 (pbk)

~ DEDICATION ~

To Marty, Caitlin and Ella

You are my sunshine and my story

I love you

xxx

~ THANKS ~

By its very nature, writing can be a solitary activity, but the road to publication has been far from lonely. I am deeply grateful to so many people, and am delighted to have this chance to say thank you to...

♥ Every single supporter listed in these pages, and to those who chose to remain anonymous – you know who you are, and I know who you are... I am so thankful for your support and encouragement.

♥ The team at Britain's Next Best Seller – thank you for this opportunity! And especial thanks to Murielle Maupoint whose vision, drive and *'go get 'em'* attitude to life is inspirational.

♥ Everyone at Carrick Primary School, Lurgan, Lurgan Junior High School, and Emmanuel Church, Lurgan – there is something incredibly uplifting about *en masse support*, and that is what you have given me; I am indebted to you all.

♥ My newfound 'family' of BNBS authors – how lovely it has been to meet you, and find kindred spirits in you all. My particular thanks go to David McCaffrey and Andy 'Editor-In-Chief' Males – your cheerleading skills and tireless support have been humbling and very much appreciated.

♥ My indefatigable family and friends for believing in me; especially my parents, George and Kaye, for unconditional love, encouragement, support and still more love; Suzanne for always seeing the best in everything and everyone; my wee sister Kathryn and her tribe for lending me their support and their names.

♥ And my own Atoner, on whom the character is loosely based – because You cannot be confined to my imagination or the pages of this book . . . I owe You everything...

~ ENDORSEMENTS ~

'Phoebe Wren And The Mystery Of Darken Abbey' is an engaging and daring adventure that stimulates the imagination while stirring the soul through redemptive themes of love and justice.

Alain Emerson, 24-7 Prayer Ireland

Julie Timlin has once again crafted a wonderfully magical novel, and proved that she is an author to watch out for. The character of Phoebe remains charming, the storyline engaging and the pace thrilling. One of the most imaginative and original books of its genre, the world of Phoebe Wren will leave every reader desperate to spend more time there.

David McCaffrey, author of *'Hellbound'*

How refreshing to read a novel of this genre that exudes more light than darkness! *'Phoebe Wren And The Mystery Of Darken Abbey'* is a brilliantly crafted work of fiction that leaves you wondering, *'What if..?'*

George Emerson, Lurgan YMCA Chairman

~ SUPPORTERS LIST ~

Alice Priday, Hazel Hendron, Becky Ellis, Donna Toye, Lydia Emerson, George & Kaye Emerson, Marty, Caitlin & Ella Timlin, Lisa Kernoghan, Cherith Abraham, Julieanne King, Janet English, Sandra Crymble, Paula McConville, Diane Burrows, Catherine Burns, Suzanne Sloan, Andrew Agnew, June Agnew, Benjamin Watterson, Debbie McDowell, Norma Cousins, Kathryn Bateman, Jack Bateman, Jamie Bateman, Abi Bateman, Sarah Dowey, Elaine Dickson, Hazel McCready, Jacqueline Harrison, Lauren Tolmie, Nina Hubbard, Andrew Males, Laura Walker, Patricia Burke, Karen Emerson, Rhonda Armstrong, James Sleator, Yvonne Calvert, Frank, Kathleen, Madeline, Pamela Turkington, Nathan & Jessica, Helen Poots, Karen McKay, Ellen McIlwaine, Sophie, Emma Kerr, Rick Preston, Eden Wilson, Julie-Anne Myers, Bekki Pate, Andrew Robinson, George Emerson, Alpha Quarry, Allison Chambers, Robert Wilson, Jill Hutchinson, Arlene Verner, Ian Thomson, Philip Emerson, Stephen Dunn, Victor Pickering, Jenny Williams, Kate Cunningham, Brenda Mussen, Gordon Dickson, Brian Bradford, Linda Matthews, Gillian Stewart, Sharon Yearl-Wallace, Ken Rowe, Gayle Woods, Caroline Allen, Phil Stone, Anne McCullough, Helen Hamilton, Carrick PS, Lurgan, Phil Mcevoy, Joanne Wilson, Dermot Toye, Joanne McKinley, Fionnuala Black, Linda McMullan, Sandra Crymble, Stephanie Maguire, Christine Holmes, Laura Jago, Leigh Livingstone, Heidi Heasley, Joanna Gordon, Gillian McCullough, Stephanie Wethers, Kenneth Emerson, Zara Crooks, Kathryn McCready, Shirley

McClelland, Noreen Graham, Tracy Archer, Laura Wheeler, Zara Baird, Eden Rachel Greer, Ernie Knox, Rosie Knox, Noreen Graham, Julie Hewitt, Paula Hutchinson, Keely Mosley, Sabine Ayeni, Erin McCandless, Naomi Bennett, Eleanor Thomson, Becky Hefty, Dillon Morris, Jim Austin, Darren Liggett, Julia Wood, Stephen Doe, Ruth Blevins, Lisa Sleator, Marlene Tapscott, Diana Stewart, Lise Buckley, Josephine Hughes, Ann Hughes, Benjamin Sawyer, Becky Ellis, Sarah Quigley, Jan Woods, Karen Hamilton, Heather Willis, Laura Arcikiewicz, Alisha Brown, Mel Wiggins, Lilly Shirlow, Julie Haines, Elizabeth Wilson, Ruth Allen, Ellen Faloon, LS Kingsley, Miriam Collen, Sarah Todd, Dylan Watters, Colin & Beverley Emerson.

CHAPTER 1

THURSDAY 26ᵗʰ AUGUST 1909
DARKEN ABBEY, IRELAND

BROTHER Thadius Bennett hurried silently through the secret underground corridor that stretched from the monks' quarters above ground to the stone altar at the front of Darken Abbey. The faithful old monk moved as quickly as his arthritic legs would allow, and as he ran silent tears of righteous anger and frustration streamed down his wrinkled cheeks – tears for lives destroyed, tears for goodness corrupted, tears for light usurped by cruel darkness. For more than half a century Brother Bennett had served the Atoner in this glorious abbey, and for it all to end this way pained him greatly. He had asked himself over and over again if he could have prevented the events of the last few months. Should he have been more vigilant? Maybe he ought to have kept a closer eye on the younger monks, especially Brother Byron and Brother Ernest? Was it his fault for trusting them so completely when perhaps they had not been ready for the pressure of being entirely responsible for themselves? Time and again, however, Brother Bennett had concluded – and found solace in concluding – that he had not stepped outside of the Atoner's will but had done his utmost to oversee the running of Darken Abbey with integrity and uprightness. Yes, evil had found its way into the midst of the monks, and the corruption and destruction that followed had been absolute, but Brother Bennett knew that the schemes of the Enemy were always underhand and sneaky, and Brothers Byron and Ernest had fallen foul to the Enemy's dirty tricks.

Darken Abbey had always been a special place where those who entered found themselves in a thin place, a place where communion with the Atoner was facilitated and encouraged. By its very nature then, the abbey was a spiritual place, and Brother Bennett had always been entirely aware of the dichotomy of the realm of the eternal. He and his fellow monks had sought at all times to bring light to the people of Ireland, pointing always to the Atoner and promoting goodness and hope. But where there is light, darkness is never far away, and Thadius Bennett knew full well that his battle had never been against flesh and blood, but against the principalities and powers of darkness in the realm unseen. He believed – because he had seen for himself – how the spiritual forces of darkness operated; Brother Bennett knew that evil had found the chink in the abbey's armour, and once the dark forces had secured entry, they did not rest until invasion was full and total. The thoughts plagued him as he ran, and he shook his head as if in so doing he could change the reality of Darken Abbey's catastrophic demise.

Brother Bennett knew that he did not have much time, whatever he was about to do must be done quickly. He rounded the final corner of the long narrow corridor, his sandaled feet moving nimbly for a man of his seventy years. Up ahead, he could see by the light of his lamp a small trap door that opened up at the front of the stone altar. The hatch blended well into the floor in the Great Hall above, and could not easily be seen unless one knew that it was there. An old wooden ladder was propped up with the top step resting against the rim of the hatch, and Brother Bennett wasted no time in scaling the uncertain looking rungs to the top. He slid the latch open and pushed his right shoulder against the hatch; the door had not been used in many years, and

Brother Bennett had to lean heavily to persuade it to move and allow him through.

Behind him along the underground corridor, Brother Bennett could hear movements, and knew that his whereabouts had been discovered. He was being followed, but the sounds echoing along the stone corridor told him that it was not mortals who were on his trail. Where one could have expected to hear footfall, there was instead the scratching, whooshing noises of talons on stone and large leathery wings brushing against the sides of the narrow cloister. Brother Bennett did not wait to see who – or *what* – would appear around the corner, and wasted no time in hoisting himself up through the narrow hatch and out into the Great Hall of Darken Abbey. It took a moment for his eyes to adjust as he clambered out of the gloom of the underground passageway and into the bright light which was streaming into the Dark Hall through twenty exquisite stained glass windows, all three feet wide and some twenty feet tall. He blinked and rubbed his eyes, acutely aware that there was not a moment to waste, his heart pounding so hard that it felt as if it may burst out of his chest. Brother Bennett clambered to his feet and dropped the trapdoor shut behind him with an ominous clunk that reverberated around the Great Hall. He reached into a clandestine pocket which he had sewn into the hem of his habit when he began to suspect that all was not as it seemed in Darken Abbey, and pulled out a small leather bound book – his journal.

Brother Bennett had always been an avid scholar of the written word, and these last few months as things had begun to unravel in the abbey, he had kept a meticulous record of events and peculiarities, which he felt sure would be crucial, if not during his time, then for whoever would come after him. Despite his steely resolve, Brother Bennett's sinewy hands trembled as he knelt in front of the stone altar, and ran his fingers along the decorative stonework. What he was looking for was so well hidden that even he, who had designed this secret hiding space, had trouble finding it. Although it seemed like an eternity, it was in fact only a few seconds before Brother Bennett's fingers found what they were looking for, and he pressed firmly on a small smooth stone, releasing a little square of rock just below it which slid deftly inwards, revealing a space just big enough to hide his precious journal. He slid the well worn leather book into the secret chamber just as the trap door through which he had moments earlier ascended lurched and heaved against a great force which was pushing on it from below. Whatever was following him through was obviously relying on brute force to break through, and had neither the patience nor the wherewithal to loose the latch and simply lift the door open. Brother Bennett was thankful for the ignorance of the pursuing dark creature, which afforded him the time to securely reseal the secret cavity in the altar, locking his journal safely away from evil prying eyes. He arose shakily to his feet, and was about to begin his escape towards the abbey's anteroom when the trapdoor behind him finally gave way to the beast underneath it and seemed to explode skyward with a tumultuous crash, although in reality the small but solid door did not even bend its hinges.

Brother Bennett held his breath as yellow vapour billowed through the opening in the floor, then gasped in horror as a hideous head appeared, bulbous red eyes flashing with fury. It was Schnither, feared captain of the Dark Army.

During the last few weeks, as Brother Bennett had uncovered the extent of the interference of the Enemy in the abbey, he had encountered Schnither firsthand. Indeed, he had almost lost his life to the fiend, who was apparently bent on his destruction, whilst returning from a supplies run to the local village just a few evenings back. But this was different. Now, the Enemy had actually *infiltrated* the abbey, intent on taking up residence there, and the usurped monks had been forced to flee. As Schnither pushed his way up through the trap door, he had obviously overestimated its size, and his giant frame became trapped fast, granting Brother Bennett a few vital moments to make his escape. The monster behind him had not witnessed Bennett placing his journal in its secret hiding place, and for that he was extremely thankful. There was nothing more he could do now to redeem the fate of Darken Abbey, but at least he could help those who would come after him to win it back from the clutches of darkness.

As Schnither writhed and struggled in his prison, inching painfully but interminably closer to his emancipation, Brother Bennett seized his chance and spun round in the direction of the anteroom. He was only a few feet away from almost tangible freedom, when a tall shadowy figure stepped out from the relative gloom of the anteroom, blocking Brother Bennett's escape route. As the figure moved into the light, Thadius Bennett instantly recognised the pale face with its thin pink lips and squinty green eyes – Brother Bartholomew Clarence. The old monk stopped dead in his tracks. Behind him, Schnither had finally squirmed free, and was standing there, wheezing and panting as though he may keel over and die at any moment. Brother Bennett glanced over his shoulder at Schnither, whose foul breath was warm on his back, then he fixed his gaze resolutely on Brother Clarence whose face was an eerie mask of evil intent.

"So, Brother Clarence – or should I say, *Craven* – it has come to this," Brother Bennett's voice was steady and strong, and his eyes displayed not a single trace of fear, although the old monk must have been afraid. He refused to be intimidated by the beasts surrounding him, because he knew that *his* Master, the Atoner, had ultimate authority over even these most fearsome of creatures.

"Yes, *Thadius*," hissed Brother Clarence, and even as the word slid from his thin lips, his form was changing and metamorphosing like the dark antithesis of a butterfly emerging from its cocoon. Craven – for that is who he was – shed the human form of Brother Clarence like an old coat, until there was nothing left that resembled anything human, and he stood before Brother Bennett in all his serpentine vileness.

"You could not stop us, *Brother Bennett*," leered Craven. "Oh you tried, you tried very hard indeed, and your efforts were... well, *almost commendable*. But did you really think that you were more powerful than us? Than *me?*" Craven was unashamedly boastful and proud, and it was very apparent that he believed entirely in his own abilities.

"I could not stop you in my own strength, Craven, no. About that much you are correct. But neither you nor any of your cronies can stand against the might of the Atoner. Your eternal fate has been sealed!" Brother Bennett's wrinkled face seemed somehow fresh and alive and his eyes flashed as he shouted this truth defiantly at the two demons he could see, and those he couldn't but who he knew to be there, listening from the rafters.

"Enough!" Craven bellowed at the old monk. "I will not hear it!"

"You *will* hear it, Craven, and some day you will acknowledge that your fate has been sealed and your doom awaits you!" Brother Bennett shouted back, straightening his back and standing up to his full height. "You cannot win this war! You may have taken Darken Abbey, but even that is temporary! The Atoner will take it back and you will be banished!"

"Nooo!" Craven was enraged, hissing and frothing from his mouth. "How dare you defy me! Schnither," he roared. "*FINISH HIM!*"

Schnither was poised, just awaiting the word to put an end to this annoyingly righteous old monk, and on Craven's angry command he pounced like a preying cougar, limbs outstretched and his gaping mouth revealing three rows of deadly teeth. Brother Bennett was motionless, apart from his lips which were twitching in fervent prayer. If this was his sacrifice, then so be it. At least the journal was safe, and the key – these ignorant buffoons would never find his section of the Key of Esse. It was sewn into the hems of the old monk's robes where it lay hidden until such times as he could find a secure and more permanent hiding place. Only Brother Eli was privy to the fact that Thadius Bennett had the key on his person, but would never reveal this knowledge to another soul. Brother Bennett closed his eyes, accepting and awaiting his certain fate, when suddenly a light blazed through the Great Hall, so bright that it illuminated through Brother Bennett's closed eyes. The old monk's eyes flickered open as he heard the furious screeches of Craven and Schnither and a hundred other black creatures, and there before him was a myriad of radiant angelic beings, all dressed for battle with bronze breast plates and devastatingly powerful swords in their mighty hands.

"Thadius Bennett!"

One of the Heavenly Host thundered to Brother Bennett from the furore. "Go, *now!* You must take the key and commit it to a safe place. It cannot be found – *must not be found* – until such times as the Atoner stipulates. Do you understand?"

Brother Bennett nodded his understanding to the great warrior, who stood at least eight feet tall, and whose golden eyes sparked and flashed like lightning. The angelic combatant did not repeat himself, but returned at once to the battle, his sword thrusting and slicing with deadly effect.

Brother Thadius Bennett did not waste another second; he grabbed his habit around the knees, and hoisted it up just above his ankles then ran with all the might he possessed, out through the abbey's anteroom, out through the small side door and into the light. Shading his eyes from the glare of the sun, he ran down the winding pathway and out through the abbey's gates, his pace never slacking despite the burning and aching in his old knees. Brother Bennett ran on, with the supernatural pace of a man half his age, never once looking back, until Darken Abbey was nothing more than a speck on the horizon and an image emblazoned in his memory.

CHAPTER 2

BROTHER Bennett's first face to face encounter with Captain Schnither had occurred a few days previously, while the old monk was returning from a supplies run to the local village. Thadius Bennett had made the comfortable journey to and from the village a thousand times, and the well trodden path was very familiar to him. He had always looked forward to this unhurried time when he would walk down into the village, stopping with every local he encountered for a chat, then calling with the farmers who supplied Darken Abbey with food and provisions. Brother Bennett had always been glad to be able to trade with the villagers, and it had given him a sense of pride to know that the monks' presence in the area had generated welcome revenue for the locals. Now, however, all that had changed. The relationship that had been forged over time between monks and locals had been hideously marred, and the ultimate demise of Darken Abbey had been set in motion. The downward spiral towards ruin had commenced in earnest, and it was with a heavy heart that Brother Bennett had traversed the path into the village just a few fateful days earlier.

Despite having already instigated plans to evacuate all of his fellow monks, Brother Bennett had resolved to remain at Darken Abbey until the bitter end with Brother Eli, a young monk whose intentions were honourable and whose integrity was beyond question. Brother Bennett had become a mentor

⌐ the earnest young monk, and found in him a trustworthy helper and loyal companion.

On the evening in question – Monday 23rd August 1909 – Brother Bennett had walked into the village, as he had done many times before. On this occasion, however, he had not been able to enjoy easy repartee with the locals as had been his normal practice, but was acutely aware instead of angry glances, turned backs, and whispered complaints. Thadius Bennett had sourced the necessary supplies, and had not raised an eyebrow when he was charged over twice what he would ordinarily have paid for what he purchased. '*The people are angry,*' he told himself. '*And with good cause. They have been let down, they feel that we have failed them – worse, we have cheated them. I cannot blame them for that.*' He had graciously resigned himself to the overpayment and commenced his return journey to the abbey, his face downcast and his soul heavy.

As he made his way back up the hill towards Darken Abbey, Brother Bennett had become aware of a peculiar aroma; he imagined it to be something akin to sulphur, although he could not say for certain, but the scent was bitter and repugnant to his nostrils. An uneasy sense of foreboding had begun to grow in the old monk's belly, and despite his best efforts at reassuring himself, the unease just would not go away. Brother Bennett had quickened his pace, clutching the heavy bags of food and supplies tightly to his chest so that he would not let them drop and be forced to stop unnecessarily. His gut was telling him that he was not alone, and in his fifty four years of service to the monkhood, he had learned above all else to trust his instincts. The evening was drawing in, and he had been almost back inside the abbey grounds when a low rumbling growl had caused the hairs on the back of his neck to stand on end. Brother Bennett knew then that he was not alone, and realising that he probably could not outrun whatever was pursuing him, he had stopped, set down his purchases, and slowly but resolutely turned around, squinting into the dusky fading light. He could not say that he was entirely surprised to find that he was being followed, as he had suspected for a while now that there were things seriously amiss at Darken Abbey.

"Who's there? Who is it? What do you want with me?" Brother Bennett's voice had held steady, although his stomach lurched alarmingly and his aged knees felt as weak as water. Whatever was out there, Thadius Bennett was fairly certain that its origins were not human... but nothing could have prepared him for the vision that assailed his senses as his pursuer stepped forward from a small but dense copse of oak trees. Brother Bennett worked very hard to keep his reactions minimal, but he could not stop a quick and audible intake of breath at the heinous sight in front of him. Schnither, Captain of the Dark Hordes – for that is who it was – snarled and bared three rows of rotting teeth at the old monk. The creature was over seven feet tall, with a muscular body and piercing red eyes that glowed in the early evening light like fiery coals.

"I have been watching you, *Brother Thadius Bennett*," snarled Schnither. "I am Captain Schnither – and you would do well to show me the respect due to me."

Brother Bennett's suspicions about Brother Clarence's duplicitous nature flooded at once into his mind, and in that moment he knew beyond a shadow of a doubt that his worst suspicions were confirmed – Brother Clarence was not who he had claimed to be and should never have been trusted.

"It is our intention to take Darken Abbey," Schnither slurred menacingly, his imposing form inching closer to Brother Bennett in the most intimidating of ways. "Indeed, the ground work has been done, the rest is merely formality. But I assure you, old man, you would do well to step aside and make the process easy for yourself and your pathetic brothers. We are willing to spare your lives and let you go – but we will *not* tolerate resistance, make no mistake."

Schnither's scarcely veiled hatred for the old monk was almost tangible, and despite his mouth being dryer than cotton, Brother Bennett defiantly straightened his back and looked the devilish captain squarely in the eyes.

"Brother Clarence..." Brother Bennett's words were not a question but a statement of fact, which seemed to please Schnither as his face contorted into a jagged grin. "He is one of your ranks.... A shape-shifter, unless I am very much mistaken."

"Ah, you are not as stupid as some of your fellow mortals," Schnither jeered, apparently pleased that his prey was formidable rather than puny. "Your observations are accurate for indeed Brother Clarence is one of us – a shape-shifter as you so eloquently put it. I am loathe to admit it, and he will certainly never hear me utter the words, but Clarence – or Craven, as I know him – is one of our best. And I am glad to see that he has carried out his task with great effect..."

"No," Brother Bennett interrupted Schnither, the clear defiance in his voice unexpected yet unmistakable. "No, he has not *carried out* his task – he may have tried to quench the fire of good and justice that burns in Darken Abbey, but I believe that time will show that he has served only to fan it into an even greater flame."

"*How dare you contradict me!* Have you lost your senses old man?" Schnither roared, stretching his neck forward so that his hideous face was only inches away from Brother Bennett's visage. "I will not tolerate such impudence, and certainly not from a puny mortal! Prepare for the end, *brother*..."

Schnither unfurled enormous black leathery wings which expanded to such an extent that they seemed to blot out what remained of the dying evening light. He reared back to his full height, red eyes flashing and yellow vapours mixing with the frothed saliva that was escaping from the sides of his mouth.

"No!" Brother Bennett voiced his defiance once again, his tone clear and resolute. "You cannot take my life, for it is not yours to take! The Atoner Himself created me and He alone will decide my fate!"

Whether or not Schnither agreed with Brother Bennett was not clear, but the monk's plucky assertion seemed to knock the dark captain for six, and Schnither reeled back in stunned silence for an instant, his jaws snapping shut as if they had been bound by an invisible cord from which he could not break free. A fleeting look of shocked bewilderment shot across the demon's face, but was banished almost as quickly as it had appeared, and was replaced by a mask of sheer malice and fury. There could be no doubting Schnither's intention to silence the plucky old monk once and for all.

"Brother Bennett! *Thadius!*"

A third voice took precedence in the momentarily paused scene and Brother Bennett spun round to see his trusted comrade Brother Eli racing towards him from the direction of Darken Abbey. At thirty years of age, Eli was much younger than his teacher, and was a fearless and devout soul who, like Thadius Bennett, was far from unaware of the schemes of the Enemy.

"Brother Bennett, this way, follow me - *quickly!*"

Eli had witnessed the exchange between the old monk and the heinous Captain Schnither unfolding, and as he reached Brother Bennett he grabbed the old monk by his shoulder. Schnither snapped out of his astounded reverie and appeared somewhat bemused by the arrival of the brave young monk, and almost laughed as he commenced his valiant rescue efforts.

"So Brother Bennett," Schnither jeered. "You had to roll out the *children* on me did you? Is this puny whipper snapper the best defence you have to offer?" Schnither was enjoying the moment; making little of the faithful old monk pleased him enormously. "No matter," he snarled with barely disguised glee, "I will just have to finish you *both* off, it is of little consequence to me."

"You will *not*, fiend," declared Brother Eli with an unhindered defiance in his voice. "Brother Bennett is correct – you and your dark kind have no authority over us. Your powers may be impressive, but they cannot touch us!"

Captain Schnither, who had been proportionally good natured until now, suddenly erupted in a violent outburst of fury. "I *cannot touch you?*" he screamed. "Are you *entirely* devoid of any common sense? I will not tolerate such impudence!"

The Dark Captain's hacked voice boomed through the autumn evening sky, tearing the silence asunder as he deftly drew a serrated black sword from the scabbard slung across his broad back. "This ends *now*."

Without a moment's hesitation, Schnither swung the ferocious looking sword with all his might, and had the blade found its intended mark, both monks would have lost their lives – and probably their heads – with the single blow. But the sword did not complete its deadly arc. Just as the blade was about to make contact with Brother Eli, Schnither stopped, a look of utter confusion etched on his hideous face. The two monks had braced themselves for the apparently inevitable impact, and when it did not come they looked at each other in questioning wonder, then glanced back at Schnither whose own face was a mask of rage and confusion. Captain Schnither drew back his sword arm another time, and swung the mighty blade with every ounce of energy he had within him, but again the sword was halted just inches away from

Brothers Bennett and Eli. Schnither's sword seemed to slam into some invisible barrier and bounce back, rendering his parries frustratingly ineffective. He tried again and again to inflict certain death on the two monks, but each blow was deflected away and no harm befell his stunned targets.

Whatever the invisible barrier was which seemed to have sprung up between the terrified monks and Captain Schnither, Brother Eli could not tell, but he wasted no time on trying to finding out. Brother Eli grabbed the opportunity and, pushing Brother Bennett ahead of him, the two monks took to their heels and ran towards the relative security of Darken Abbey. They could hear Captain Schnither screeching with rage behind them, as his sword clunked against whatever invisible barrier had been placed in supernatural protection around the monks. Eli and Thadius burst through the main doors of the abbey and landed in the Great Hall, puffing and shaken, but very much alive despite Schnither's best efforts.

"What... was... *that?*" gasped Brother Eli, who had sunk to the floor in a genuflect position that reflected the gratitude he felt at being alive.

"*That*," replied Brother Bennett after great consideration, once he had regained his breath, "*That* was our Enemy, the one who seeks to overthrow Darken Abbey and use this place of light as a source of darkness. *That* was Schnither, captain of the armies of darkness. Eli, many of our brothers have been compromised already, I am afraid that the Enemy has secured a foothold. All we can do now is get our fellow monks to safety and ensure that although the Enemy might win this battle, he will never win the war. Come, we must act now and make the necessary preparations. We will resist to our last breath, but I fear that the outcome is inevitable, and it will not be long before Darken Abbey is usurped from us."

CHAPTER 3

THURSDAY 26th AUGUST
DARKEN ABBEY, IRELAND
PRESENT DAY

FIFTEEN year old Phoebe Wren could not believe the sight that assailed her eyes as the terrible events unfolded in Darken Abbey. She looked from her best friend Ella's pale, wide eyed face to Malva's dark, eyeless guise and back again. Ella was quaking, her entire body shaking so violently that Phoebe was sure she would collapse in a crumpled heap on the floor if Malva loosened his grip at all – although he certainly did not look as though he had any intention of doing that. Phoebe felt as if all the air had been sucked out of the Great Hall; she was struggling to breathe, she could barely think straight, and her trusted friend Demetrius did not seem to be faring much better. He was standing beside her, rooted to the spot, a look of horrified disbelief etched across his face. Phoebe could think of only one thing to do – cry out for assistance from the angelic warriors who had thus far seen them through. But even as she drew in breath to call for Cosain and his fearsome comrades, Malva raised a bony hand in warning and began to speak. His raspy voice emitted foreign words which neither Demetrius nor Ella could understand, for the language he spoke did not belong to any realm on Earth as far as either of them could tell. But Phoebe understood. Somehow, while her friends were hearing nothing but terrifying guttural sounds, Phoebe understood Malva's every word as if he was speaking them to her in her mother tongue.

"Phoebe Wren," Malva's harsh voice cut through the atmosphere, and Phoebe held her breath as she awaited the monster's instruction. "Do not dare cry out for your ridiculous angelic guardians. You know that I could snuff out your little friend's life with a mere scratch of one of these," he jeered, flexing his treacherous talons. "These little blades of mine aren't what you would call *mortal friendly* you know. And if you make so much as a *sound*, I won't hesitate to use them, believe me..." The eyeless creature ran a spiky talon lightly across Ella's throat, and jeered at the helpless teenagers before him, leaving them in no doubt that despite his ocular shortcomings, he was in no way disadvantaged. Although the creature's face was devoid of eyes, he was entirely aware to whom he spoke and where in the Great Hall the frightened teenagers were standing.

Phoebe recalled a conversation she had had with Neam, one of the angelic warriors who had battled with Malva in the past, and remembered his warning that Malva's claws contained a toxin deadly not only to humans but to angels as well. She knew that Malva was not exaggerating about the ease with which he could end Ella's life, and she did not dare irk the ugly beast.

"W-w-what is it you want?" Phoebe worked hard at sounding indifferent, despite the urge to wretch violently at the demon's stench and horrifying appearance. Her mouth was watering and she knew that it would not take much for her to be sick.

Malva's reply was simple, instantaneous and sure. "*The Key of Esse*," he drooled as if the very words were tantalising his taste buds. "For the Geata Gate. I want the last piece of that key, and I want it *now*."

"But... I... uh, we..." Phoebe stammered, unsure how to answer the vile creature without riling him. When she finally worked out what to say, her response was starkly simple and pertinent. "We don't have the key."

There was no point in pretending that she did not know what Malva was talking about, so Phoebe decided that faltering honesty was the best policy, even in this inconceivable situation.

"I know that, *pathetic human!*" Malva roared, the sound and stench of her captor causing Ella to close her eyes tight in terror and scrunch up her nose in disgust. "Of course I know you don't have it! If you had it, I would simply have *taken it from you* – by whatever means necessary. But you will have to *find it!* And when you do, you will bring it to me. Because if you don't..." He paused, a malicious grin twisting slowly across his face. "If you don't, you will never see this scrawny little mortal again."

Malva lifted Ella off the ground, squeezing her ever tighter with four of his six powerful wings, until Phoebe feared that he might squeeze the life right out of her friend here and now.

"Okay!" Phoebe yelled, desperate to distract Malva from crushing her friend's bones. "Okay. We'll find the missing piece of the Key of Esse! We'll do whatever you want! Just don't hurt her, okay? Please..."

"Are you *bargaining* with *me?*" Malva looked bemused, but he lowered Ella back on to terra firma nonetheless. "Well, it would seem that you although you have no sense, you've got guts, I have to give you that."

Phoebe held her gaze steady; she was terrified, but she would not let Malva see that he frightened her. She wondered whether he actually *could* see her, despite his lack of eyes, and so she resolutely stared the monster down.

Eventually, Malva conceded. "*Yes-s-s*," he hissed. "Yes, I will agree to your paltry terms. You bring me the final section of the Key of Esse, and I will let your little friend go, she's of no use to me anyway. But you're not getting her back until you have something to swap her for! Those are *my* terms, and they are non-negotiable."

Malva's face contorted into laughter, and the arrogance and impertinence of this act was one step too far for Phoebe. Overcome with anger and defiance, Phoebe willed her leaden legs to move and made a sudden dash in the direction of the imposing demon and his trembling prey, which surprised her almost as much as it amused Malva. Almost before Phoebe had taken a step however, a swirling undulating vortex of storm clouds and lightning appeared up from the ground and with a nimbleness that contradicted his size, Malva leapt backwards into its all encompassing darkness, with Ella screaming in fear in his vice-like grip.

"*Ella!*" Phoebe's cries went unheard by Ella and her diabolical captor, and as quickly as it had appeared, the dark vortex snapped shut behind them, leaving not even a trace of its existence. Demetrius, who had also made a bolt towards Malva, put his hands on his head and sank to his knees.

"Phoebe," he cried. "Where have they gone? How will we get Ella back?"

"*Don't be afraid.*"

A gentle yet entirely authoritative voice spoke from the direction of the altar. Phoebe and Demetrius turned in the direction of the familiar voice, and there before them was Cosain, the Captain of the Heavenly Host, and their trusted envoy.

"Cosain!" Phoebe could not hold back her tears as relief mingled with deep distress flooded her soul. "It was Malva! He took Ella! We don't know where they went or how to help her. Please Cosain, we need you!" Phoebe paused before voicing the words that had just occurred to her. "We *needed* you..."

Several more huge angelic warriors materialised beside their Captain, all looking with deep concern at the distraught teenagers. The mighty combatants were clad in robust breast plates and carried hefty swords at their sides. All appeared imposing and ready for battle and yet their eyes carried a softness and a gentleness that looked to be bruised by the distress of the two teenagers before them. These ethereal giants were no pushovers, but it seemed they were capable of the tenderest of emotions towards those in their care.

"Why..."

Phoebe hesitated, unsure even in the midst of her angst whether or not to ask the question that she desperately needed answered. She looked up at Cosain and although his face was solemn, his golden hued eyes assured her that it was alright to voice her query, granting her unspoken permission to proceed.

"Why did you not intervene?" Phoebe's question cut the air like a knife, and pained her and Demetrius with its starkness. "You were right outside, right? Why didn't you smash through and stop Malva? Surely you could have fixed this before it got out of control? You've looked after us this far, Cosain, how could you..." She paused again, aware that the next words she spoke could cause Cosain great pain, then voiced them regardless. *"How could you have let us down?"*

"Phoebe," Cosain answered gently, ever aware that she was just a mortal, and a youngster at that. "There is always a *bigger picture*, more than meets the eye. For us to have swooped on Malva may have meant that Ella evaded capture for now, but we would have alerted the Enemy to our presence, and many more mortals would have suffered as a result. Ella will be alright, we *will* find her, you must believe it. Trust me. But there is much for you and Demetrius to do..." The gentle giant's voice trailed off, then he refocused and asked, "You found Brother Bennett's journal, yes?"

In the midst of the furore and confusion, Phoebe had temporarily forgotten about the elusive journal. She nodded at Cosain then moved to the front of the stone altar, where the secret cavity was still exposed. "I think so," she said weakly. Phoebe knelt in front of the altar, and put her hand into the void. She was surprised that the area hollowed out of the stone was much deeper than she could have ever imagined, and was obliged to stretch her arm in just past her elbow. Phoebe was beginning to think that the search had been in vain, and perhaps there was no journal after all, when her fingers fumbled across a soft leather clad book. She clasped her fingers around it, holding on to the thin strips of leather which were bound around the book, then gently wiggled it free from its stone tomb and pulled the little book out into the light. Brother Bennett's journal was an unexceptional looking book, and Phoebe turned it over in her hands, examining the soft brown leather and rubbing her finger down the length of its worn spine.

"This is *it?*" Phoebe said with a note of disappointment in her voice. "This is what they want so badly? *This* is what we just lost Ella for?"

There was an undeniable anger rising in Phoebe's belly, and as she stood shoulder to shoulder with Demetrius in front of their angelic guardians, she no longer felt the need to politely suppress it.

"Yes, that is exactly what the Enemy wants," answered Ernan, the imposing first lieutenant of the Heavenly Army, and second in command to Cosain. "But it is not *just* a book. Brother Bennett's journal will contain all the clues and information you will need to locate the third part of the Key of Esse, and when you find it, Phoebe, you – *you* – will have the power to rout the Enemy from this abbey, and goodness can prevail in this place once more. Darkness will be banished, and Darken Abbey will stand once more as a beacon of light and hope."

"And what if I don't find this Key of Esse? What if Brother Bennett was actually just an old fool whose scribblings send us on a wild goose chase, eh? What then, Ernan? Do we just forget about Ella and go back to our lives as if none of this ever happened? Do we just put it all down to experience and leave Ella *wherever* that monster has taken her?"

Frightened and frustrated, Phoebe hung her head as more hot tears of annoyance overcame her. Demetrius came alongside his friend and put an arm protectively around her shoulders. Phoebe buried her head against his shoulder and wept silently for a few moments before gathering herself and wiping her face angrily with her hands.

"I'm sorry, Phoebe," continued Ernan quietly, "I'm sorry that this is such a burden on you. But you have been *chosen*, Little One, *handpicked* for this task. There is no-one else who could do it. And that is why we need you to be strong."

"If I'm honest, I just find that so hard to believe. I mean, what's so special about me? If *I* can do this thing, then surely *anyone* could do it?"

Phoebe had regained control of her emotions and the logical side of her was wondering why on earth Cosain and his comrades had singled her out from the millions of souls far braver than she. She furrowed her brow so tightly that it hurt, and shook her head in bewilderment. "I don't know, Ernan, maybe this is all a big mistake – like, mistaken identity or something? Maybe it was never meant to be me..."

"It is no mistake, believe me. But... you can opt out Phoebe; we will not force you to go on." Ernan was definite with his words, but gentle as he offered Phoebe her way out.

"Oh *please!*" Phoebe's voice was raised now and her outburst shocked Demetrius as his usually reserved best friend looked Ernan boldly in the eye. "I can't opt out any more than *you* can! My best friend has been taken... to *who knows where* by Malva. I can't just walk away from *that!* Besides," Phoebe seemed to physically stand down as she resigned herself to the situation at hand, and her affection for her angelic guardians was apparent despite her frustration. "I've gotten used to having you guys around, and I have no intention of letting Malva or Schnither or any of their horrible goons get the upper hand here. You told me once, Cosain, that goodness will always triumph over evil – I believe it, and I want to be a part of that victory! What do you reckon Demetrius?"

Phoebe looked round at her friend, who had been standing quietly for the last few minutes. Demetrius had never been one to shoot his mouth off, always opting instead to gather all the information he could, mull things over, and reach a considered conclusion in due course. Today was no different. Demetrius's face did not betray what he was thinking, and he gritted his teeth momentarily before he replied, causing the muscles in his jaw to jerk and twitch.

"I'm in," he said simply. "I've always been in. I didn't move my entire life from Africa to Ireland to jump ship now. Cosain told us from the start that we had a job to do Bird, and nothing has changed, except that now it just seems that bit more important that we do it well."

Phoebe inhaled deeply and held her breath for a moment before exhaling slowly, deliberately. She nodded her head in agreement. Of course Demetrius was right. His level headedness was contagious, and Phoebe felt her soul settle as she allowed herself to absorb his simple truths.

"Then it is agreed," said Cosain softly. "We will pursue the darkness with all our might and set things right."

Phoebe and Demetrius nodded their heads in agreement. They knew that Brother Bennett's journal was the instruction manual they would need for the adventure on which they were about to embark. Phoebe untied the leather binding from around the diary with faltering fingers, and opened the ancient book. She gently thumbed through its fragile pages until she found Brother Bennett's first diary entry, and in a quiet, almost reverent, voice, Phoebe Wren began to read . . .

CHAPTER 4

THURSDAY 10ᵗʰ JUNE 1909
DARKEN ABBEY, IRELAND

"I, Brother Thadius Bennett, have taken the decision to keep a journal as a means for me to record conditions and circumstances within Darken Abbey, if only for my own reassurance and peace of mind. It has not escaped my notice that things have been . . . *changing* within the abbey during the last period of time, and I intend to monitor this and investigate the source of the change of which I speak.

It has been almost two months now since the enigmatic Brother Clarence arrived in our midst at Darken Abbey. The changes in the abbey during this time, although subtle at the start, have been remarkable and have been, I reluctantly admit, in the best interests of the abbey and all the brothers. Brother Clarence definitely has the wherewithal to get things done, and I cannot pretend *not* to be impressed by his ability to present me with solutions rather than merely highlighting problems. And yet... There is something about this young monk that unsettles me, although I cannot put my finger on exactly what it is, but I am sure that it is no coincidence that the changes in Darken Abbey coincided with his unexpected arrival. There is a soul disturbance within me – that is the only way I know how to describe it – and I cannot be more precise at this point. I think it may be the effect that Brother Clarence has on the monks, especially the younger brothers, that unnerves me. In particular he would seem to have some sort of (I am reluctant to use the term, although it certainly fits) *hold* over Brother Byron and Brother Ernest, although again I cannot say for sure exactly what it is that I am witnessing. These young and impressionable monks hang on Brother Clarence's every word, and I do believe that they would do his bidding in any matter he would choose to bring to them. I sincerely hope that I am merely being overly cautious, and that Brother Clarence is simply the breath of fresh air that, admittedly, we all needed. But something tells me to err on the side of caution. His arrival at Darken Abbey was unannounced, unexpected, and his history remains a mystery to me... He was not recommended to me by anyone, nor did I request his secondment. Where then did he come from? Who, if anyone, sent him? And why did he choose Darken Abbey?

With these queries as yet unanswered, I will keep careful watch on Brother Clarence and his day to day life in the abbey, in the hope that I am wrong in my assertions about our mysterious brother."

* * *

FRIDAY 18th JUNE 1909
DARKEN ABBEY, IRELAND

"The days since my last journal entry have been relatively unextraordinary, and I am glad to be able to report thus. Brother Clarence has busied himself – as has been his way since he arrived here – with assisting in the everyday tasks of the abbey, and his willingness to volunteer and serve over and above the call of duty continues to render him an unofficial favourite among the twenty four brothers here in Darken Abbey – of course, we do not encourage the favouring of one brother over another, and yet by his very nature Brother Clarence seems irresistible to the others. I think that, ironically, this may be the very thing that makes me suspicious of him. He has a way about him that brings out the best in this order, and I suppose I should be thankful for his presence, and yet... this niggling doubt just will not subside...

This is a time of great upheaval and transition on the island of Ireland, and these are busy times for us as men of the cloth as we assist local farmers to make the transition from tenant farmers to land owners; it is a heavy responsibility that we bear to ensure that our neighbours are treated fairly and are not cheated, and yet by our very nature as monks we are obliged to fight for fairness and equality. It does concern me somewhat that Brother Clarence seems to be at the helm as we seek to assist the locals at this time, and I can only hope that it is merely a coincidence that Darken Abbey would appear to be benefitting from superfluous supplies and increased attention to maintenance which we have hitherto been unable to afford.

For now, I can only continue to monitor the situation. I have spoken with Brother Eli about my concerns – although a young man, I trust Eli with my very life, and I know that he shares my concerns about Brother Clarence and will keep a discreet eye on him for me."

★ ★ ★

SATURDAY 03rd JULY 1909
DARKEN ABBEY, IRELAND

"Despite the relative normality of my last journal entry observations, strange things – dark things – are most definitely afoot in Darken Abbey, of that I have no doubt.

During the last days and weeks, I have no longer been

able to put these happenings and occurrences down to coincidence. I am entirely convinced that there is more to Brother Clarence than meets the eye, although as yet I do not have definitive evidence with which to approach him. Since his arrival in May, there has been a subtle yet marked change in the attitudes of my fellow monks. With the exception of my trusted Brother Eli, all have an exaggerated levity to their inclination and I have noted an increased vivacity in their approach to every aspect of our daily lives. Of course, this is not a bad thing in itself; indeed, it has done my heart good to see that my brothers have been happy and fulfilled in their calling. But I fear that their focus has shifted from the divine to the mortal, and they look increasingly to Brother Clarence for guidance and instruction. This should not be. Furthermore, Brother Byron and Brother Ernest have become decidedly furtive and cautious, particularly when they are in my presence; this is entirely contrary to their nature, as both young monks have been wholly candid and forthright since joining this order at Darken Abbey over six years ago. I have witnessed them conversing secretively with Brother Clarence, and the trio has been absent from the abbey without what I deem to be good reason. Where they go, as yet I cannot tell, but I do know that when they return it is rarely empty handed. The brothers' often return to Darken Abbey with mysterious sacks which I am led to believe contain money. I have a deep rooted fear in my belly that they are bribing our neighbours, perhaps working alongside wealthy land owners to force farmers to pay over the odds for land. I cannot be sure, but I am distinctly uneasy and can only hope that I am mistaken.

Over and above all these things, however, I am convinced of rumblings in the spiritual realm. I have heard *things*... *felt* things which I cannot explain in mortal terms. I have not shared my concerns with anyone other than Brother Eli as I am unsure who I can go to that has not been subjected to Brother Clarence's persuasions. Besides, I feel that the fewer people I entrust with my suspicions the better; I certainly do not wish Brother Clarence to get wind of my wary notions concerning him.

I fear Clarence will have to be confronted, and soon, although having a greater knowledge of just what he is doing would be most beneficial – forewarned, as they say, is forearmed. I only know that I must be on my guard at all times, and rely fully on the protection of the Atoner."

★ ★ ★

TUESDAY 27ᵗʰ JULY 1909
DARKEN ABBEY, IRELAND

"Things have escalated very rapidly indeed since my last musings in this little journal. Although I am loathe to acknowledge it, it would appear that I have been entirely correct in my assertions about Brother Clarence, but now I am afraid that whatever it is about him that unsettles me so may be much more sinister than I initially believed.

It seems that my fears about Brothers Byron and Ernest were well founded too, and two evenings ago I took it upon myself to follow them as they furtively left Darken Abbey with Brother Clarence. I expected that they would go directly to some homestead and there extort money from some poor undeserving farmer. But I was horrified to find that they went from one door to another and another until several hours had passed and these disgraceful brothers had filled their sacks with coins and bribes and sneaked back into the abbey through a seldom used door at the rear. I have not confronted the misguided brothers yet, as I feel that I must be fully prepared with a plan of action. Besides, I fear that Brother Clarence's corrupting influence may be much more widespread that I initially thought, and I do not wish to spark a revolt. I know that I must put this situation to rights, but I certainly cannot do it alone.

This uncovering of heinous lies and bribery and greed has pained me deeply, and I worry that our reputation at Darken Abbey may have been irreparably tarnished, but in truth this is not my chief concern. I have become convinced that darkness has entered this place of light, and it is my contention that *evil itself* now resides within these walls. I cannot say that my fellow monks share this belief, for none have come forward to me with any such concerns, but I fear that they have been blinkered and have become desensitised to the darkness which they should have sensed weeks ago.

Our order, though small in number, was keenly attuned to the things of the Atoner, and now I fear that small stumbling blocks have given way to greater iniquities, and the end, I fear, can only be calamitous. That is not to say that the brothers have *become* darkness, but they have *tolerated* it in some form or another and thereby have given it a foothold. The result is that we are no longer trusted or respected amongst villagers, and, understandably, local people no longer want us in their midst. There are rumblings in the village, calls for us to depart from the area, and I have no doubt that should we acquiesce and leave Darken Abbey, then the Enemy will waste no time in usurping our position and our influence in this area.

I have one loyal ally in Brother Eli, who I know to be as appalled by these things as I am. We will bide our time, find the root cause, and we will cut off evil at its source. I will not tolerate this forever, and it is my hope that there may yet be time to save Darken Abbey and restore our standing with the local people. It will not be an easy task, but I hold on to the hope that it may yet be achieved."

* * *

TUESDAY 03rd AUGUST 1909
DARKEN ABBEY, IRELAND

"Brother Eli and I have spent many hours watching, waiting, gleaning information, and on Sunday morning past we felt the time had come to confront those involved in what can only be described as the slow demise of our order. I have to admit to being terribly nervous – there was no telling how that meeting would go, but Eli and I were pleasantly surprised to find that almost all of our brothers were *relieved* to be called to task on their actions. There was a widespread sense of remorse and relief, I feel, that someone had finally called a halt to the dubious goings-on in Darken Abbey. We witnessed wide scale repentance, with many of our brothers offering to pay back and return what had been gained through dishonest means. This was a noteworthy gesture – but I fear it may be too late. The rumblings from the village have grown louder, with the locals understandably disquieted and I regret that now they simply want us gone from their midst without explanation or the chance to explain ourselves. In effect, they do not see that *one* rogue monk betrayed them, but instead believe that we – *we* – have stolen from them, *we* have cheated them, *we* have let them down... I cannot blame the vast majority of the brothers – yes, they did wrong, they should have resisted temptation, but I fear that the root of the problem can be traced back to just one individual... One who entered our midst and brought with him corruption, deceit and subtle destruction that spread through our ranks like a plague . . . *Brother Clarence*. To this end, and with a heavy heart, I have begun the process of relocating the brothers, although I realise that this will take several weeks. I feel it will be for the best. I have tried to keep this as quiet as I can, taking brothers away one by one and at short notice, as I fear there may be repercussions from Brother Clarence – I still cannot pinpoint what exactly it is about him that unnerves me so, but I no longer have any doubt that there is *something* more to him than meets the eye.

It still concerns me greatly that Brother Byron and Brother Ernest are not remorseful in the least – in fact, neither showed up for the meeting that Eli and I called. There is trouble afoot with these two, make no mistake. I do not imagine that relocating them will be straightforward, if it is possible at all."

★ ★ ★

TUESDAY 10th AUGUST 1909
DARKEN ABBEY, IRELAND

"I am not a naïve man by any means, but it would seem that there are supernatural happenings afoot that even I cannot comprehend or explain, things which make this journal even more vital to those who will pick up wherever I am forced to leave off – and I fear that this time may not be very far away . . .

Brother Eli and I have been working tirelessly on relocating many of the brothers from Darken Abbey. They have deemed their work *here* defunct, but I do not feel that their mistakes here must necessarily stand in the way of their continued service *elsewhere*. These are good, honourable men who, admittedly, made some questionable choices during the last weeks here at Darken Abbey. But they were led astray with promises of wealth and luxury, I have no doubt of it, and I believe that many were even duped into believing that what they did was in the best interests of Darken Abbey. Nevertheless, there are always consequences regardless of how innocently these brothers allowed themselves to be led astray, and leaving this strange and wonderful place is one such a consequence. It is my sincerest hope that they will be able to carry on their calling elsewhere, but nothing is certain.

Eli and I have had to work carefully and to date we have

been able to relocate nine monks out of Darken Abbey and secure places for them in abbeys throughout the island. I have tried to ensure that their flawed legacy does not travel with them, as they deserve a clean slate, the chance to start over, but I cannot guarantee any of them a warm welcome. I can only wish them well and send my prayers as they leave."

★ ★ ★

THURSDAY 26ᵗʰ AUGUST
DARKEN ABBEY, IRELAND
PRESENT DAY

Phoebe sighed deeply and exhaled loudly, causing a wayward strand of mousy hair to flutter off her forehead. She held tightly to Brother Bennett's decrepit journal, but allowed it and her arm to flop despondently to her side. His words were numerous and she found them stilted and awkward, making the journal difficult to read aloud.

"The information in here is very interesting and all," she remarked. "But there really isn't much that we can take and use to help us find El..."

Unexpected tears sprang again to Phoebe's eyes as she tried to say her friend's name. Poor sweet, kind, unsuspecting Ella. Where on earth was she? What had Malva done with her? Phoebe shuddered and stuffed the negative feelings of impending doom resolutely to the back of her mind. She would *not* give in to panic or fear; she owed it to Ella to be strong and brave so that she could find her friend and bring her home where she belonged.

Phoebe sniffed resignedly. "I mean, so far we have learned from Brother Bennett that this Brother Clarence dude arrived, caused a bit of a stir, had a negative influence on Brother Byron and Brother Ernest, and – long story short – Darken Abbey had to shut its doors as a result. It's unfortunate and

I'm sure it was a very difficult time for all involved. But what I want to know is, did Brother Bennett never catch on that Brother Clarence was in fact Craven? And how did he work out that what he was up against wasn't your every day *human* enemy? And most of all, I want to know how he got past the Behemoth guard dog thing to get at the missing piece of the Key of Esse!"

Phoebe was exasperated by the lack of details available to her and impatient to have all the information she could gather, *right now*. She was aware of the fact that she might be coming across as a petulant child, but at that moment in time she just did not care. She could see that some of the angelic warriors seemed to share her eagerness to act, but Neam voiced what she knew to be the correct course of action for them all.

"Phoebe," Neam spoke in low tones, so that the cold stone walls of the abbey, which seemed so adept in picking up even the most muted of voices, did not even register his voice. "I know that you are eager to move, but to proceed without arming ourselves with all the information we can gather would be folly. Brother Bennett went before you, and although some of us were here when he left this place and can bear witness to all that happened here, the task of winning back Darken Abbey from the forces of darkness has been given to *you and Demetrius*. *We* cannot do it for you. We will assist you in every way possible, but only *you* can complete the mission assigned to you. So, for now, you need to gather all the information and clues and pointers you can, and then go to work. Okay?"

Phoebe knew that the dark skinned, blue eyed warrior was right, and she chided herself for daring to assume that she knew better than he.

"I'm sorry, Neam," she said meekly. "It's just that I'm so afraid that Ella has gone forever, and we'll never find her!"

"You *will* find her, Phoebe," Cosain's voice flowed over Phoebe's jangling nerves like honey, and instantly she felt her taut shoulders relax and her jaw unclench. "And we will be with you every step of the way. But Neam is right, forewarned is forearmed..."

Phoebe knew that her protectors were right, and so with her fractiousness securely in check, she raised Brother Bennett's journal in front of her face once again and read on . . .

CHAPTER 5

"**N**OW, where had I gotten to?" Phoebe queried, flipping with intent through the fine cream pages containing Brother Bennett's neatly hand written musings. "Ah yes, '. . . *the chance to start over* . . .' ".

TUESDAY 10th AUGUST 1909
DARKEN ABBEY, IRELAND

"The brothers who remain in Darken Abbey will, I am sure, prove increasingly difficult to relocate without sounding alarm bells which will be heard by those that we definitely do not want to hear them. For now, it is not unusual for several of the brothers to go for significant amounts of time without seeing each other – a few absences can be explained away in missional trips or devotional times, but once too many brothers leave, the gap will not so easily be covered. We will have to bide our time, make all the necessary arrangements for relocations, then despatch the remaining brothers en masse when the time is right.

I have spoken at length with Brother Eli about what our course of action should be in relation to Brother Byron, Brother Ernest.... and Brother Clarence. Had Byron and Ernest, like their fellow monks, demonstrated the desire to redeem themselves, we would of course have worked with them and aided them in whatever way we could. But I am afraid that their very souls have been stained by treachery, and for now at least, neither brother seems willing – or able – to seek forgiveness. Furthermore, I am certain that they, along with Brother Clarence, continue to make their stealthy and self serving trips out of Darken Abbey, and while they are still cheating and deceiving the local people, then they are still bringing disrepute on our brotherhood and this must be stopped at all costs. It is my opinion – and Brother Eli concurs – that we have no alternative but to hand Brothers Byron, Ernest and Clarence over to the authorities without delay. We are loathe to do this, but at this stage the matter really is out of our hands, and if these men cannot and will not be convinced to amend their ways, then there is nothing else to be done with them. It pains me to pen these words, and I have no doubt that the reality of what we plan to do will be even more gut wrenching, but we must do what is right at all costs."

★ ★ ★

TUESDAY 17th AUGUST 1909
DARKEN ABBEY, IRELAND

"A week has elapsed since my last journal entry, and to say that it has been a most peculiar and unexpected week would be the epitome of understatements. Much has happened of great significance, and I believe to the very core of my being that Darken Abbey is under subtle (for the time being) but sustained attack from dark supernatural powers which would seek to oust us and usurp our position within this community.

Brother Eli and I have been able to relocate eight more monks from our order, and although our ability to remain discreet has been compromised by their absences, I believe this to be of little consequence, because I am convinced that whoever – or **whatever** – wants Darken Abbey has been utilising Brother Clarence as leverage into our midst since he first arrived here some five months ago. I intend to despatch the five remaining monks to their new abbeys within the next few days. For now, however, I must accept that Darken Abbey's role in this community is defunct, and there is no sense at all in endangering any of the brothers. Eli and I will stay to the end to try and uncover the deeper truth behind the demise of the abbey and the dubious dealings which have been carried on from this building. The speed and unexpectedness with which our order fell from grace leads me to believe that there is an altogether bigger – and more sinister – picture to be revealed.

On a practical note, we were obliged to call in the authorities on Sunday evening, and once we had explained to them what has transpired in and around the abbey during the last few months, they sought out Brother Byron and Brother Ernest and took them into custody. Brother Clarence, however, was nowhere to be found. I think that the officers found it difficult to believe what Eli and I were telling them, but we had located some of the brothers' ill-gotten gains and the sight of this loot persuaded them that our sorry tale was accurate. We were at least able to return some of what had been stolen from our friends and neighbours, although I believe that this was a case of too little, too late.

Last night, I paid a visit to the prison where Brother Byron and Brother Ernest are being held, and despite the awful reality of their surroundings, I was encouraged to find both men entirely finally repentant and seeking absolution for their wrongdoing. It was as if, once removed from the presence of Brother Clarence, both men returned immediately to their senses, and were as appalled as I am about their uncharacteristic actions. I was informed that both brothers had willingly revealed the whereabouts of the rest of their stash of stolen goods, and I can only hope and believe that when they have served their time in prison and fully accepted the consequence of their actions, Byron and Ernest will be restored and permitted the opportunity to start afresh.

As for Brother Clarence... well, that is where things become exceedingly unusual. I have not caught sight of Brother Clarence since Sunday morning. It would seem that the moment he realised that his schemes were uncovered and Brother Byron and Brother Ernest were taken into custody, Clarence – or whoever he may actually be – simply disappeared without a trace. I have asked around in the village and beyond, yet not one person can recall seeing the wayward Clarence of late, and no-one has any inkling as to his whereabouts. It is almost as if he was never here... That in itself is peculiar enough, but when combined with the... **goings-on** in Darken Abbey itself then the whole thing is rendered utterly incalculable and inexplicable.

I have been aware of an unease gnawing at my core for quite some time now – noises, sensations, even seeing things that weren't actually there – or so I thought. But during the course of the last week I am convinced that these phantoms have become more than mere imaginings, and I feel that a darkness – granted access, I believe, by Brother Clarence's warped ways – has pervaded Darken Abbey. This darkness is almost tangible and has attached itself to the very fibres of the abbey's walls. Loosening its hold will be no mean feat, particularly when one considers how to rid these hallowed walls of an adversary that, as yet, we cannot actually see.

I have heard eerie noises deep in the substratum of the abbey, mostly at night – not unusual for an old building such as this, but latterly these have become bolder and louder, and now I hear the clattering clearly at all times of the day. I investigated, of course, but could see nothing – until yesterday. On my return from visiting with Brother Byron and Brother Ernest, I could hear the now almost familiar sounds of work underway in the belly of the abbey. I explored throughout the lower levels as I had done before, but last night, in a seldom used corridor, I found a great wooden doorway that I can only assume must lead to some lower level of Darken Abbey which I know nothing about. I have been here many years, and in all my time I was never aware that a lower level even *existed*. Indeed, the lower levels that I explored yesterday were, as far as I was ever aware, all that existed below the main level of the abbey.

The sudden appearance of this doorway was an enigma in itself, but the creature that I uncovered there took my breath away. To my shock and horror, there, standing guard over the doorway was – and I scarcely know how to describe it – a giant creature that was in appearance like a black, overgrown, antagonistic dog with six legs and a head that was easily three times as large as it should have been. Its huge mouth was full of razor-like fangs, and it slobbered like a rabid creature, its black eyes rolling wildly in its head. The creature had a great grey collar around its neck, studded right round with huge metal spikes, each one longer than my hand. There was a hefty chain attached to a metal loop in the abbey wall, but the animal was not, at that time, fastened in any way and was free to roam as it pleased. Perhaps the creature's most terrifying feature was its tail, the tip of which blazed with scorching fire that illuminated the entire chamber yet did not burn the creature or harm it in any way. I did not examine the beast further, opting instead to remain safe and hidden, but in truth little additional examination was necessary to convince me that the creature was not from the realm of the mortal. Needless to say, I made a hasty retreat for I did not like the idea of becoming this monster's lunch! One thing I know for sure, however – there must be a great significance to the doorway that the beast is guarding, and it worries me to acknowledge that I am going to have to get much closer to find out exactly what the hideous creature's purpose is . . ."

CHAPTER 6

"**W**HOA," Phoebe's respect for Brother Bennett was increasing by the minute as she read more of his bravery in the face of pervading darkness. She imagined his frustration as he watched Darken Abbey slip from his grasp and fall slowly but surely into the hands of the Enemy. Phoebe herself empathising with the old monk's outrage as the realisation of just how little he could do to stop it crept over him like a suffocating fog. She wondered too what she would have done had she been in his shoes – gathered up her robes and run for cover, she imagined. But to stay and investigate further, knowing that to do so could place one's life in mortal danger – *that* was the embodiment of courage, and Phoebe had to admire the old man's resolve.

"So Brother Bennett's fears were confirmed," she mused. "There's little you can say to explain away the existence of a giant monster dog, I guess!"

"Precisely," agreed Cosain. "And once Brother Bennett began to put the pieces together, there was no denying that Brother Clarence – or should I say, *Craven* – was very bad news, and the sole source of the decay that had worked its way outward from the very heart of Darken Abbey."

The emergence of new information about the underground doorway in the abbey, and the fearsome creature guarding it had Phoebe entirely intrigued, and she wasted no time in reading on from the worn pages of Brother Bennett's journal.

★ ★ ★

MONDAY 23rd AUGUST 1909
DARKEN ABBEY, IRELAND

"The days which have passed since my discovery of the mysterious door in the underbelly of Darken Abbey have been fraught with the practicalities of relocating the last five monks of our order, but also with the deepening mystery of developments in the unearthly realm. Brother Eli and I are the last remaining occupants of the abbey – that is to say, the last remaining *mortal inhabitants*, for I am certain that we are not alone here.

I have spoken in great depth with Brother Eli about what our immediate course of action must be. All our brothers have been safely despatched to new orders where they may usefully continue in the good work that was established in Darken Abbey. I believe that, if there can any silver lining to these unfortunate events, then it is simply that the brothers will forever be more attuned and watchful for temptation in whatever form it may come. They have learned valuable lessons, although the tragedy in this instance is that the lessons came with a hefty price tag in the form of the cessation of trust and mutual respect between us and our neighbours. I can only hope that in time Darken Abbey will once again be recognised and acknowledged as a place of light and truth and hope. I struggle to grasp the reality that our downfall came so innocently disguised, and feel that it serves only as a warning that vigilance is vital at all times.

Brother Eli and I have dared to venture again into the substratum of the abbey, where I showed him the peculiar door guarded by what he has concluded is a **Behemoth**. I have heard such a creature referred to in literature and folklore, but never did it occur to me that such a beast actually existed. Obviously, this ghastly creature is *not* merely a phantom spoken of in myths, but is a very real threat made of flesh and bone, which has been placed at the doorway to stop us from interfering. Why? I cannot tell as yet, but it is my intention to find out. We believe that the doorway must be the legendary 'Geata Gate', the access route between the mortal world and the unseen realm, and have drawn this conclusion after reading much about the unseen realms of supernatural darkness. I can scarcely believe that this mythical gateway not only *exists* but is actually positioned in Darken Abbey.

On returning to the doorway, we found the great beast Behemoth slumbering, and that fact, simple as it seems, has given me confidence that I will be able to get past it when the time is right. We saw a large metal key protruding from the keyhole in the door; the key was large, maybe a foot in length, and appeared to be made from bronze. It seems to me that if I can secure that key, there may be hope yet for Darken Abbey. Whatever is behind the door could represent either the end of Darken Abbey... or a chance for the regeneration of this unique place. Opening the doorway could spell our salvation – or our doom. But I believe it is something we must do, because inactivity simply is not an option."

★ ★ ★

TUESDAY 24th AUGUST 1909
DARKEN ABBEY, IRELAND

"My hand is still trembling as I pen these words this morning, the encounter of last evening still fresh on my mind. My deepest fears and worst suspicions were confirmed during a most unpleasant encounter just outside the abbey last night as I returned with supplies from the village. Were it not for Brother Eli's quick actions, I believe I may have met my doom last night at the hands of the unearthly beast that identified itself as *Captain Schnither*. From this dark creature, I have learned that evil forces intend to usurp Darken Abbey entirely, and Brother Clarence – the focal point for the malady of greed and dishonesty which has spread like wildfire throughout the brothers – was in fact a devious infiltrator whose origins are not of this world. Clarence – or *Craven*, as his dark captain called him – was deliberately despatched to the very heart of Darken Abbey, and his dastardly work was almost complete before I even had time to realise that anything was amiss. He was – is – a shape-shifter, who appeared to us in affable human form, yet whose soul is malevolence itself. I have no knowledge of Craven's current whereabouts, and this is a source of great concern to me, because who can tell what form he may appear in next? There is every possibility that he may return in an altogether different form and Heaven forbid that I allow him to dupe me a second time! Prudence will be absolutely crucial, I feel. The encounters of the last days have not, I am afraid, left me unshaken, but despite these bizarre circumstances I am resolved to do whatever I can to thwart the plans of Captain Schnither and his dark hordes before I too am forced to desert Darken Abbey.

It is my strongly held belief that the events happening in this building are not merely uncanny in and of themselves, but have an eternal dimension which renders them timeless and relevant. More simply put, it is my conviction that an ethereal battle has commenced here which will rage on throughout the centuries, and there will come a time when One will be chosen to pick up where I am forced leave off... And if such a One is reading these words of mine – I know not when in time – then I urge you to give careful consideration to what I write, and in particular to the journal entries which will follow this one, for I have a feeling that hints and indicators of great significance will be revealed in the days to come. *If you are the Chosen One, Reader, then may the Atoner be with you...*"

* * *

Phoebe looked up from the little leather journal which lay open in her hands. The last few words she had read startled her, and she felt as though Brother Bennett was speaking down through the decades directly to her. Phoebe had become entirely engrossed in the words of the journal, and in the momentary silence it occurred to her that Demetrius and the angelic host were all hanging on every word she read, totally enthralled and waiting for more.

"It sounds..." Phoebe faltered, hesitating before voicing what she was thinking. "Well, it sounds almost as if... as if Brother Bennett is talking directly to *me!*"

"It does," conceded Lasair. "But that is because he *was* speaking directly to you. Of course, Brother Bennett may not have been able to give you a name way back in 1909, but he did not doubt that there would follow after him One who could take his mantel and accept the challenge of restoring the sacred space that Darken Abbey once was. And that One, Phoebe Wren, is you."

"But..." Phoebe was unsure how to put her thoughts into words. "It's all so *huge,*" she said, feeling utterly dwarfed by the enormity of the task at hand. Slight of frame to begin with, Phoebe felt that she had shrunk to miniscule proportions, and if she permitted it to, this tale could swallow her whole until there was nothing left of her person beyond the role she played in this massive chronicle.

Demetrius had always possessed the reassuring ability to read his best friend like the open pages of a book, and despite the extreme circumstances in which they now found themselves, this was no exception.

"Phoebe," he said gently, his voice cutting through her trepidation and speaking directly to the deepest recesses of her being. "You are right, this *is* a big challenge – it's massive, actually. But we must remember everything that we have come through so far, the events which have brought us to this point – if I had asked you a couple of months ago whether you thought you could do something like this, you'd have thought I was crazy! You wouldn't have believed that such an adventure was possible, let alone that you could battle through this far. And this is no different – from here it looks overwhelming, but you've got to take it one step at a time. Cosain and his troops are one hundred per cent on your side. And so am I, Bird."

Phoebe looked up at her friend, so brave and so earnest, and at once she felt a familiar calm flood her soul. Demetrius was right – they had come too far to quit now. And besides, they simply *had* to find Ella. Phoebe nodded, then turned her attention again to Brother Bennett's journal and continued reading his urgent words.

* * *

"I sincerely hope that I will be able to make an impact on this situation before I am either forced to flee or lose my life trying, and I trust that you, Reader, will pay heed to my observations and find the courage to pursue this quest. I have made it my business to spend as much time as I can in Darken Abbey's library, where I read whatever I can find written about the Behemoth. These are writings I have been aware of in the past, but obviously they have taken on a much deeper significance now, and where before I read of a *hypothetical* beast, I now re-read information to learn about the beast which I believe to have taken up residence in this very abbey! It beggars belief, and yet it is glaringly true. The images and drawings available to me in these literary works have been accurately representative of the Behemoth, but only in part, for he is far more ghastly and imposing in the flesh than any pictures could portray him. It is not my intention to alarm you, reader, but it will be better for you to know these things ahead of time – *forewarned is forearmed*.

I have learned too from ancient texts that Behemoth traditionally guards the doorway which connects the earthly realm with the realm of the supernatural, and given the happenings within Darken Abbey of late, I am inclined to believe this to be true. If this is the case, then the door in the abbey's underbelly takes on an enormous significance, and I believe that the only way to thwart Captain Schnither's plans for complete invasion by his hordes is to lock the doorway and remove the key to a place of safekeeping from where the Enemy can never retrieve it.

Reader, I am all too aware that this task may prove too difficult for me, in which case I fear that my writings will be in vain, because if darkness has its way and stakes its claim on Darken Abbey, then neither you nor anyone else will even see this journal. *But*... if I am granted good success and can lock up the mysterious doorway, then the onus will pass on to *you* to despatch the Enemy and his fiends back to where they belong.

I will record as much of relevance as I possibly can until I am forced to stop. I can only hope and pray that this book finds its way into the correct hands... And may the Atoner remain with you, Reader, on your quest."

CHAPTER 7

PHOEBE'S heart was racing as she concluded Brother Bennett's journal entry for Tuesday 24th August 1909. The fact that today's date was 26th August 2009 was not lost on her, and she could not help but assume that there must be some huge significance to the fact that Brother Bennett's journal had come into her possession almost exactly one century after it was written. As yet, Phoebe could not possibly fully appreciate just how significant the timing was, but she would come to discover that what is often marked down to coincidence is in fact the playing out of a deliberately and intricately designed plan. One look at her companions' faces told Phoebe that they were as eager as she was to learn more, and taking a deep breath she read on from where she had left off.

THURSDAY 26th AUGUST 1909
DARKEN ABBEY, IRELAND

"Reader – and I can only hope with every fibre of my being that there *is* a Reader, and that all-consuming darkness has not prevailed – I imagine that you will wonder why Brother Eli and I remain at Darken Abbey when to all intents and purposes our presence here seems futile. I must explain that, for some unknown reason, it would appear that while Eli and I are here, Captain Schnither, Craven and their minions seem to be held at bay and cannot fully exert their dark powers. I am not so naïve as to think that their hesitation will last forever, but for now at least our presence here affords us the time we so desperately need to put in place the things which I hope will thwart them before we too make our escape. Where we will escape to, I know not. I only know that our departure is imminent and now, sadly, inevitable. Darken Abbey has fallen, there is no escaping this horrible reality, but thus far it has not fallen entirely, and it is my dearly held hope that Eli and I will be able to minimise its demise, even though we cannot halt its downward spiral completely.

During the early hours of this morning, Brother Eli and I made our way back down to the clandestine lower levels of the abbey, and were grateful to find the Behemoth had abandoned his station, if only temporarily. The giant beast was slouched just a few feet away, scratching his ear like some surreal version of a household pet, and while Eli kept guard, ready to distract the monster if the need arose, I made my way with great caution to the great doorway where I was able to securely lock the door. I found the key, which I have learned is probably the infamous **Key of Esse**, to be in three parts, and rather than take the entire thing and allow for premature realisation that it had gone, I slid it quietly from the lock, and broke the bottom section off, stowing it securely in a hidden pocket in my habit before returning the bulky key to the lock. The missing section was reinserted into the keyhole, so its disappearance should not be noticed until such times as someone – or something – moves to open the door, by which time I sincerely hope Eli and I will be long gone.

We were successful in locking up the door, thereby preventing any further ghouls from entering Darken Abbey, but I know that Captain Schnither has already brought through numerous dark sentries who he has installed around the place, for I have seen glimpses of their black leathery wings and red eyes, and the presence of trailing yellow vapours belies their presence even when they think they have sneaked by unseen. Staying at Darken Abbey has become all but impossible for Eli and I, and I find myself forced to admit that the time has come to leave. We have done all we can to ensure that the Enemy has not secured full run of this special place, and perhaps one day we will be able to return and route him. If this is not the case, dear Reader, then it may fall to *you* to restore Darken Abbey. I can only imagine how colossal a task this must sound to you, but you should not be afraid – there are celestial warriors armed and ready to defend this cause, and if you are the One to carry on the fight for Darken Abbey, then you will meet the Heavenly Host in time, if you have not done so already. I know without a shadow of doubt that they are nearby and their presence has been the very reason that Eli and I have been able to stay and have not given in to fear and dread.

As I have told you, it is my belief that Brother Eli and I will be obliged to depart from Darken Abbey very soon, and to this end, I will make every effort to point you in the right direction in my least few words. I have decided in my head a secure location for the section of the Key of Esse that I have in my possession, but it successfully reaching this spot will be dependent on many factors, not least of all our ability to escape the abbey unharmed. I plan to draw up a map for you, Reader, which I hope will be of much use to you on your quest. The map will be hidden in a small vault located beneath the floorboards of the living quarters of Brother Eli – it is a tiny space, barely deserving of the title 'vault', designed and hewn out by Eli. He has always been a shrewd, wise man and looking back now I can safely say that I owe a great debt of gratitude to Brother Eli Wren..."

★ ★ ★

'*Brother Eli Wren*'... Of all the prose penned by Brother Bennett, these three simple words leapt off the old worn page and hit Phoebe with a force that was almost tangible. *Eli*

Wren... But that meant... *Could* it mean..? She looked up at Cosain, mouth ajar, the question still unasked, but her eyes begging an answer.

"Yes," said Cosain quietly. "Yes, Brother Eli Wren was your relative, your Great-Great-Grandfather, to be precise."

"But how... I mean, *how* can he be my Great-Great-Grandfather if he was a monk? I thought monks didn't marry? And if he never married, then there was no family..."

"Yes, that was very often the case," continued Cosain. "But Eli was a young man when he and Brother Bennett fled from Darken Abbey – only thirty years of age. Brother Bennett lived out the rest of his days in Nendor Monastery in the north of the island of Ireland, but while preparing to travel north with Brother Bennett, Brother Eli encountered a young lady named Lily and, simply put, she won his heart. Eli took the life-changing decision to leave the monkhood and marry Lily, who would prove to be the love of his life. They decided to make a life together in Arles, settling in what is now your grandparents' home, and they had a son, Benjamin Wren – your Great Grandfather. Benjamin and his wife Eleanor were the parents of Augustus Wren – your Grandfather. Eli may have hung up his robes in favour of a new life with Lily, but he never lost his faith, and guarded the missing piece of the Key of Esse, which was entrusted to him by Brother Bennett, until the day he died. He knew the consequences for the island of Ireland if he allowed the Enemy to regain the key and unlock the doorway to the Mooar Mountain."

Ernan picked up the tale where Cosain had left off. "Augustus and his wife Charlotte became proud parents to your Aunt Stella, and your Father, Jack. So it is no surprise – nor is it a coincidence – that your father and mother have been chosen to set up their Celtic Justice Organisation in the grounds of Darken Abbey. Likewise, it is no coincidence that *you* are the Reader spoken of in Brother Bennett's journal

– the hoped for Chosen One – who will put darkness in its place and return Darken Abbey to its former standing within this area. Despite appearances, goodness never gave up on this place, and so it follows that Brother Eli's descendent would be the One selected to return it to its former glory. Over a hundred years have passed – and now the time is right for light to oust the darkness that has had free rein here for far too long."

"Yes," Phoebe's eyes lit up at the familiar names. "My Papa Augustus and Nanna Lottie! Do they know about any of this? Do you think my Grandfather's grandfather – Brother Eli – told him about the strange happenings in Darken Abbey?"

"We cannot say for sure, Phoebe," advised Cosain. "But there is a very good possibility that your grandparents will prove invaluable to your quest. You can speak with them in good time, but first – you must return to Brother Bennett's writings and establish your next move. Time is of the essence, and Ella needs you."

★ ★ ★

THURSDAY 26th AUGUST 1909
DARKEN ABBEY, IRELAND

"Brother Eli's chamber is located in the west wing of Darken Abbey. This is our residential wing, and Eli's room is the third door on the left of the Serenity Cloister. I cannot guess how many years may have elapsed between my writing this and your reading of my words, and in the event that the abbey's appearance and features may have changed, Brother Eli's room can be distinguished by a small hole in the ceiling in the back left corner, for it was here that Eli made a hanging hook for his robe – he is ever the meticulous and inventive individual! It is vital that you find his room and the location of my map quickly, because I am sure that for you – like us – expediency will be crucial.

Brother Eli gave further instructions that stowed away with his map you will find a small mirror. What this is for I cannot say and Eli never offered any explanation, but it would seem that the value of the mirror must not be underestimated, and so you must ensure that you find it and bring it with you.

Once you have the mirror and the map in your possession, you should waste no time in locating the hidden portion of the Key of Esse. Keep it with you at all times – it will be absolutely vital to the success of your mission – and bring it back as quickly as you can to Darken Abbey. Your task will be to unlock the door in the abbey's substratum, lure the Enemy back through by whatever means necessary, and lock the door behind the vile hordes once and for all. I know that this sounds terrifying, Reader, *preposterous* even, but you must rest assured that good has the ability to triumph over evil... Every time. And you are on the side of goodness, Reader, make no mistake. Your victory, hard won though it may prove to be, is eminently achievable – if you strive for it above all else."

★ ★ ★

Phoebe glanced up momentarily again from Brother Bennett's journal. *"Good has the ability to triumph over evil. Every time."* The words were familiar to her, since the Captain of the Heavenly Host had assured her of the same sentiment. Brother Bennett's reiteration of the words served to reassure her of their universal truth, and she allowed the calming consolation to wash over her troubled soul. Phoebe knew that the journey ahead of her would be difficult and very possibly dangerous, and she imagined that she may be tempted to throw in the towel on more occasions than one, but here in this moment she steeled her resolve for what was to come, and declared quietly to herself that she would see this through to the very end – in whatever form it might come. If this was part of the plan for her – if this was her destiny – then she intended to grab hold of it with both hands and give it her all.

THURSDAY 26th AUGUST 1909
DARKEN ABBEY, IRELAND

"Dear Reader, there are some pieces of information which I think may help you as you set out on your journey. My time here at Darken Abbey has almost come to an end, and it is crucial that I am successful in hiding this journal in the hope that one day you will find it, Reader, but there are several pointers I must still leave you, so I will be brief.

Firstly, you must be on your guard at all times as you move about Darken Abbey. Just because you cannot *see* your Enemy does not mean that he is not there. Captain Schnither and his minions work in stealth, and you should assume that they will be watching you at all times. *You, Reader, are a greater threat to the Enemy than you know...* but make no mistake that *he* knows and fully understands the threat you pose to him, and he will strive to eradicate that threat by whatever means necessary. You should never underestimate his loathing for you, or the lengths to which he will go to stop you.

Secondly, you must be wise about who you trust. The dark minions have the ability to masquerade as angels of light, and their shapeshifting ability renders them difficult enough to ascertain. Things – and people – are not always as they seem. But I believe that you will know the difference, Reader, if you listen to your heart and trust your gut. *You are wiser than you know*.

Thirdly, your Enemy will do anything – and I do mean *anything* – to get back the missing piece of the Key of Esse. *You must not allow this to happen*. The Enemy has been permitted a foothold in this place. Yes, it happened very subtly so that greed and corruption was upon us almost before any of us realised what was happening, but it was just enough to stir up dissent and the rest... well, that is, quite literally for you, history. I can only imagine that the forces of darkness will have been running amok from this day to your day, growing in strength and boldness. The Key of Esse is your one and only means of returning the fiends to the pit from whence they came, and it may be closer at hand than you think. Reader, *You carry more light than you know.*

Fourthly, the powers that will come against you are not of this world. You will encounter principalities and powers which, by their sheer magnitude, will tempt you to feel defeated even before you commence your work. You need to know, Reader, that this mission is your *destiny*, and the Power that is in you is greater than any you may encounter, regardless of appearances. *You are stronger than you know.*

And finally, as I have mentioned, you will have the unbridled assistance of the Host of Heaven; if you have not encountered these ethereal warriors yet, it is only a matter of time... you will. And when you do, you must trust them *implicitly* – trust them with your very life. They will be assigned to you and will protect you at every turn, of this I am certain. *You are more protected than you know.*

Dear Reader, whoever you may be, you have been chosen for such a time as this, and whether you feel equipped or not, you will have at your disposal every weapon and skill required to vanquish the Enemy and restore Darken Abbey. I wish you God speed, bravery – and success... because your future – and the future of the inhabitants of this island – depends on it."

CHAPTER 8

THURSDAY 26th AUGUST
DARKEN ABBEY, IRELAND
PRESENT DAY

PHOEBE turned over the page she was reading in Brother Bennett's journal but found only blank parchment. She flipped forward several more pages, but each leaf was blank and unmarked. The teenager puffed out her cheeks, held her breath a moment, then noisily blew air out through her pursed lips. "So that's it," she said. "That's all Brother Bennett wrote, and that is all he can do to help us. These are our instructions in full. Now we've got to find Eli's map, find the missing piece of the Key of Esse, speak to Papa Augustus and Nanna Lottie, watch out for shape-shifting demons, find Ella – and then persuade some monsters to return to wherever they came from! *Wow...*" She furrowed her brow and frowned at Cosain with unveiled gravity in her expression. Even with the imposing Captain of the Heavenly Guard and his finest warriors standing right next to her, Phoebe had butterflies in her stomach which were fluttering so hard that she wondered if they were actually giant birds, and no matter how hard she willed it, she could not muster up either the courage or the confidence which she felt sure she should be feeling right now. She managed a wry smile at Cosain, and shrugged her shoulders as if to say, '*There's nothing else for it, let's do this thing!*'

Dilis, the youngest of the angelic warriors, whose formidable sword possessed incredible healing powers, looked at his young ward with kindness overflowing from his chestnut hued eyes. "It sounds daunting Phoebe, there is no denying that, but we are with you. *All the way.* We will guard you and Demetrius in everything you do – this is our pledge to you and to the Atoner. All you need to do is follow the natural progression of things, take it one step at a time. And the first step that we must take right now is to locate Brother Eli's map. Finding this document will get the proverbial ball rolling." He smiled kindly at Phoebe, and she felt her angst begin to subside.

"Agreed," said Ernan. "Brothers, we must be battle ready at *all times*. The Enemy will learn soon enough of our presence here, and the dark forces will not hold back, you can be assured of that fact. Keane, Lachlan, Cahir..." Ernan spoke directly to three of his burly brothers. "Station yourselves around the outside of the abbey; be on the lookout for Schnither's troops, don't let any more of them in here. The rest of you, brothers, follow me; we must find the Serenity Cloister and Brother Eli's chamber."

Keane, Lachlan and Cahir saluted their superiors, then extended their mighty wings and shot skywards, disappearing out through the abbey's ceiling as if it were a mere mirage. Ernan and Cosain rounded up the remaining angelic troops and took the lead towards the abbey's west wing with Phoebe and Demetrius following cautiously behind them, as Solas, Dilis, Trean, Neam, Croga, Lasair and Maelis brought up the rear. Phoebe noted that every warrior had drawn his sword and would be ready in an instant to charge headlong into battle should the need arise. She was unsure whether this observation brought her comfort or dread, but resolved to be grateful that the angelic warriors were prepared for any eventuality. She was aware too that the Heavenly Host had cloaked themselves in invisibility, so to any demons who may be looking on, it would appear that she and Demetrius were unaccompanied in the vastness of the abbey. *Sitting ducks. Perfect.* The rogue thought unnerved her, but she banished it from her mind and forced herself to remember that Cosain and his angelic brothers would materialise in the blink of an eye if – *when* – the need arose.

The eclectic group traversed silently through the Great Hall, away from the stone altar at the front, and in the opposite direction to the anteroom. Phoebe and Demetrius had not ventured much beyond the abbey's anteroom and Great Hall, and the unfamiliar territory served to unsettle them further. As they exited the Great Hall through a humble wooden door with an arched top located to the left of the altar, the light afforded by the abbey's great windows began to diminish, and the teenagers had to allow their eyes time to adjust to the dimmed light beyond. Cosain and Ernan led them through the unlocked door, and both Phoebe and Demetrius were shocked at the sprawling extent of Darken Abbey which existed beyond the Great Hall. From the outside, although it had the imposing semblance of grandeur, Darken Abbey did not necessarily have the appearance of being a gargantuan building, but as they stood now in the vast expanse beyond the Great Hall, Phoebe realised the abbey was in fact deceptively large and rambling, and the sheer area to be investigated caused her heart to sink a little. '*Follow the natural progression of things, take it one step at a time...*' Phoebe recalled Dilis's words and forced herself to calm down. She urged herself not to think too far ahead, choosing instead to focus only on what was required of her at this moment.

"If memory serves me well, the Serenity Cloister, which used to house the monks' living quarters, is this way," said Cosain, pointing towards the west side of the abbey. Phoebe had to remind herself that Cosain and several of the other angelic warriors were entirely familiar with this abbey, and had traversed its corridors in centuries past. The thought comforted her and permitted her a sense of security even in these uncertain times.

Phoebe, Demetrius and the still invisible warriors walked on for a few moments until they reached a small vestibule area with several corridors leading off in different directions. Cosain did not hesitate but led the teenagers and their angelic protectors towards the second corridor on the left. "This is it," he said as they proceeded along the old stone corridor. "The Serenity Cloister, along which Brother Bennett and Brother Eli had their living quarters all those years ago. We are looking for the third room on the left. I don't imagine that we will find the rooms as Thadius and Eli left them, but unless there have been major structural changes, the rooms themselves should not have changed much and Eli's map can be secured with relative ease."

Almost before Cosain had finished his sentence, and with a clanging irony that was not lost on Phoebe, a terrible shriek rang out from the direction of the vestibule. Phoebe, Demetrius and the angelic warriors spun around en masse to find two familiar faces hurtling along the narrow stone corridor towards them at a rate of knots. It was Braygor and Graygor, twin demons whose small stature belied their enormous ability to cause trouble and wreak mischief. In and of themselves, the hellish twins did not pose much of a threat in the face of nine lofty angelic warriors, but none of the angels were naïve enough to think that Braygor and Graygor would be unaccompanied. And they were correct in their assumptions.

The angelic warriors made their presence known in the blink of an eye, but far from beating a hasty retreat, Braygor and Graygor swooped and darted amongst the angels' legs, obviously refusing to be intimidated by their opponents' sheer size and strength. Cosain knew all too well that Schnither would never have despatched Braygor and Graygor to challenge the Heavenly Host alone, and his eager eye quickly detected the *real* threat, for following in the twin demons' wake was Krake, a ferocious demon of boundless strength and agility, and Craven, the infamously devious demon who had brought chaos and ruin to Darken Abbey almost a century ago in the guise of Brother Clarence. Both fiends were shape-shifters by nature, but on this occasion their gaits showed no trace whatsoever of their human disguises. Beyond these two formidable foes, Cosain recognised the heinous faces of Bova, Eenu, Jarrda and Yigno – minions despatched by Schnither who were both loyal to their dark master and as physically strong as they were wily.

"Maelis, Lasair – quickly, get Phoebe and Demetrius to safety! Brothers, the rest of you should *take no prisoners*! Do you understand?"

The blunt straightforwardness of Cosain's authoritative shout startled Phoebe, and she realised very quickly that somehow this was different to previous encounters with their dark adversaries. It was obvious that there was no room for compromise or error, and there could be only one outcome – either good would triumph or evil would take the upper hand, there could be no middle ground. The implications of this were not lost on Phoebe and she felt her heart begin to race.

Maelis and Lasair scrambled immediately to either side of Phoebe and Demetrius, their great wings fully extended, forming a protective and practically impenetrable barrier around the frightened teenagers. The angelic guards hurried Phoebe and Demetrius along the Serenity Cloister in the direction of Brother Eli's old room; both had their swords drawn ready for battle and their expressions were fixed and resolute. Behind them, Phoebe could hear from the furore that battle had now commenced in earnest, and she was aware of sparks and flashes as fiery Heavenly swords clashed with dark ghoulish weapons. Maelis and Lasair bundled the teenagers down the corridor a short distance, only breaking formation when they reached the third door along on the left. Lasair put Phoebe and Demetrius behind him and stood firm, sword raised, while Maelis wrangled with the creaky old door that opened into Brother Eli's chamber. As soon as the heavy wooden door groaned open, the angelic warriors shoved Phoebe and Demetrius unceremoniously into the small and sparsely furnished room, then stood shoulder to shoulder just inside the doorway facing out, totally blocking the door – and then some. Lasair and Maelis were poised and ready to send whatever might try to follow them into the Abyss, their faces focused masks of single minded intent. Phoebe looked around the dark and rather dismal little room. The only light afforded to the diminutive chamber came from a small round window in the opposite wall; the window did not have any handle or latch to suggest that it could be opened, besides which it was too small and placed at too great a height to be able to climb out through, so for all intents and purposes the only way out of this room for the four individuals standing in it was via the door they had just come in.

Phoebe swallowed hard and tried not to give the rising sense of nauseating claustrophobia any foothold. She focused instead on the contents of the little room – an ancient wooden bedstead, whose few remaining slats showed grievous signs of decay and wear; a small bedside locker with one cupboard, the door of which hung open and at an obscure angle on its rusted hinges; a tall locker with only one of two narrow doors remaining. There were two rusted hooks on the back of the door, and the sight of these reminded Phoebe that they needed to be sure they were in Brother Eli's old room, and if they were, then she and Demetrius must find the hidden map without delay. Recalling Brother Bennett's writing, she ran her eyes along the ceiling, and there in the top left hand corner, just as the old monk had noted in his journal, was a small hole where Brother Eli had once placed a hook to hang his cloak. This tiny identifying mark would not have been noticeable had Phoebe not been looking specifically for it, but its simple presence in the ceiling assured her that they were indeed in the right room, but more importantly that Brother Bennett's writings were accurate and could be trusted. She marvelled at the detail with which Brother Bennett had written and was immensely grateful that he had taken the time to leave her the tiny clues which, almost a century later, afforded her solace and assurance.

Phoebe turned to Demetrius, who was also surveying his whereabouts, and was about to suggest that they secure Brother Eli's map without further ado, when an almighty crash and a roar cut through the air, and the teenagers spun round to find that Craven had burst into the room with such force that he had knocked Maelis off his feet. Lasair was immediately on Craven's tail, and Maelis wasted no time in jumping back up to his feet and joining his companion in battle against the fearsome fiend. Craven's fury and determination were all too apparent as he rallied against the angelic warriors, but it was very quickly evident that even his great might and skill were no match for the two imposing angels. Maelis and Lasair struggled hard, and the battle was over almost as suddenly as it had begun, with Craven bundled back out through the door of Brother Eli's room, and backwards along the Serenity Cloister at a furious pace. Phoebe blinked in shock and glanced over at Demetrius, who was standing totally still with a look of wide eyed astonishment on his face.

"Come on, Dem," Phoebe shouted. "Let's not hang around!"

"You won't get any argument from me!" Demetrius exclaimed, and together the teenagers dropped to their knees and commenced a hurried search of the floor in Brother Eli's room for the all important map.

CHAPTER 9

ACCORDING to Brother Bennett's journal, Brother Eli had hidden the elusive map in a small vault which he had created in a space underneath the floor in his personal chamber. Phoebe could not help but wonder how they were supposed to dig through the wooden floor boards to get at *anything* that may be hidden below, but she need not have worried because scarcely a minute elapsed before Demetrius called out triumphantly, "*Got it!*"

Phoebe scrambled over to the corner at the foot of Brother Eli's decrepit bedstead where Demetrius had uncovered what appeared to be nothing more than an old rotting floorboard with a gap at one side where a natural knot in the Irish oak had been misplaced. It occurred to her how clever her Great-Great-Grandfather Eli had been to use the wood's naturally occurring knots and quirks to act as leverage, and watched with baited breath as Demetrius hooked two of his fingers through to the underside of the floorboard and pulled gently. The ancient Irish oak floorboard creaked and groaned its complaint at being moved after all this time, but ultimately put up little resistance as it was lifted away, revealing beneath it a small dark cavity which had been dug into the foundations below. There, in the little bespoke cavity was an ancient yellowed document, showing obvious signs of age and neglect, but intact nonetheless.

"*The map*," Phoebe breathed, immediately chastising herself for ever doubting Brother Bennett. "We've got it, Dem. That means we're one step closer to finding Ella!"

"And the mirror," said Demetrius quietly. Phoebe had almost forgotten about Brother Bennett's instruction to bring the mirror with them, and she still had no idea as to why it was so important.

Demetrius silently, almost reverently, lifted the old discoloured map from its hidden catacomb beneath the floor and blew away almost a hundred years of dust and debris. The map had been folded carefully in three, and Demetrius gently undid the folds until the faded document lay open in his hands. He reached down again to retrieve the insignificant looking little mirror. The dulled and spotted glass was intact, and the little looking glass had an unimpressive looking wooden handle. Demetrius imagined the earnest young monk kneeling down to hide the objects almost a century ago, undoubtedly looking over his shoulder in case the fiends who were in pursuit of Phoebe and Demetrius today were coming after him all those years ago.

"Clever chap, Brother Eli," Demetrius whispered almost inaudibly as he and Phoebe surveyed the ancient map. It was an unextraordinary looking document, and nothing in its appearance would have hinted at its magical nature. Demetrius ran his fingers over the soft parchment paper, and almost dropped the map to the floor in shock when the drawings and inscriptions on it suddenly began to glow, almost imperceptibly at first. Within seconds, the place names and images were glowing brightly, the colours assuming a life of their own in vibrant hues. As the startled teenagers looked on, the map continued to come alive, colour and depth spreading across its width until features such as hills and forests took on a three dimensional aspect and looked as though they were real, albeit in miniature form. Phoebe and Demetrius had never seen anything like this before, and they were at once entranced and bewildered as the scenes represented before them came to life and were beamed into the air above Demetrius's slightly trembling hands like some primitive yet effective movie projector.

"Dem! Look..." Phoebe pointed to a spot at the right hand side of the map. "It's Darken Abbey." As the teenagers looked closer, they saw that the section of the map to which Phoebe referred had begun to undulate and move, and as the abbey took on a three dimensional appearance, they could see light beaming out from its impressive stained glass windows, all of which were gloriously intact. Suddenly, the entire scene was beamed into the air, taking on the semblance of reality, if only in the realm of light and space. Phoebe and Demetrius watched as the tiny replicas of the abbey's huge main doors burst open and out raced two miniature figures clad in the unmistakable monastic garb of long brown robes and leather sandals. The effect of the projection in front of them reminded Phoebe of an old silent movie, and she was entirely mesmerised by the peculiar sight that was unravelling in front of her eyes. She ran her hand gently through the scene, mesmerised as the images bled and colours ran through each other like paint in water before floating back to their original condition.

"That must be Brother Thadius Bennett," said Demetrius, who was equally incredulous at what was unfolding before his eyes. "And that..." he said, pointing at the second figure. "Must be Brother Eli Wren – your Great-Great-Grandfather, Bird." He continued to watch the living map as the two tiny figures raced away from Darken Abbey and towards the village at the foot of the hill. Behind them, the abbey seemed to pulsate and strain as if under enormous pressure until several of the tall stained glass windows exploded outward in a flurry of colour and light and flying glass, as several dark shadowy figures shot off the map and vanished, followed by numerous illuminated figures, whose light, even in miniature form, was so bright that Phoebe and Demetrius drew their heads back and squinted their eyes.

"No way!" exclaimed Phoebe. "It can't be..." But there before her eyes, playing back from decades past, were the same angelic warriors who had saved her life only moments before. Phoebe and Demetrius were able to identify Cosain by his extraordinary height – at eight feet tall, he stood head and shoulders above his companions, despite their own enormous size, and even in greatly reduced proportions Cosain's presence was still impressive. The teenagers could make out Lasair by his fiery red locks, Lachlan by his unruly tresses and beard, and Cahir by his lack of hair, but the others were too small and moving too quickly to identify with any real degree of certainty. Regardless of the fact that Phoebe and Demetrius were watching history played back in miniature, it was easy to see that the Heavenly Host had facilitated the successful escape of Brothers Bennett and Eli, and had in effect ensured that it would be possible for Phoebe and Demetrius to be here now, fulfilling the destinies to which they had been called. As the movie-like playback began to fade, Phoebe could see that several shadowy figures remained inside Darken Abbey and could only assume that Captain Schnither, Craven and the rest of the dark fiends had claimed their stake on the abbey when the last remaining monks had finally fled.

As the map gradually faded back to its original two dimensional state, Phoebe and Demetrius looked at each other, stunned into silence by what they had just witnessed. Demetrius quickly but carefully folded the map along its original creases, and as the sounds of a fading battle brought them back to reality, they clambered to their feet and headed for the door of Brother Eli's chamber. Demetrius was about to peep round the door to ensure that the coast was clear, when a thin trail of yellow vapour coiled its way along the Serenity Cloister, alerting the teenagers to the approach of something dark and supernaturally malicious. Quickly, Demetrius pushed Phoebe along the wall to the right of the doorway, and they stood, pressed against the cold stone, not daring to breathe, until the telltale yellow vapour and raspy breaths stopped right outside the open door to Brother Eli's chamber. Phoebe closed her eyes and willed her frantic heart to beat more quietly; Demetrius gently slid the map into the right hip pocket of his dusty jeans and looked around to see if there was anything he could use as a weapon should the beast outside the door decide to enter. There was nothing readily available, so Demetrius clenched his fists, ready to fight for his and Phoebe's lives, although he was simultaneously aware of just how puny this resistance would be. Suddenly, with a flash of brilliant light, Maelis swooped along the corridor, catching the approaching dark fiend unawares, and sending him squealing and cursing to the Abyss with one deft swipe of his deadly sword in an explosion of angry orange smoke. The angelic warrior didn't pause for breath as he alighted in Brother Eli's chamber, grabbed Phoebe by the hand and shouted over his shoulder for Demetrius to follow as he swept out of the room and back along the corridor towards the vestibule, where it became apparent that the recently fought battle had been a victory for the Heavenly Host. Cosain, Ernan and the other warriors had regrouped and although the furore was over for now, they were very obviously on high alert and eager to depart from Darken Abbey as soon as possible.

The group of young mortals and warrior angels who had arrived in the vestibule a short time ago now retraced their steps at a much greater pace back into the Great Hall towards the anteroom and out the side door of the abbey. There was urgency in their movements, and the angelic bodyguards never broke their defensive formation. Once outside, they were quickly joined by Keane, Lachlan and Cahir, and Phoebe wondered what they had encountered.

"Captain," said Cahir. "There were no new dark arrivals out here, but we witnessed several demonic fiends who exited the abbey to scout around before returning from whence they came."

"Good work," replied Cosain. "And good news, for there are certainly enough creatures within the abbey without further adding to their ranks." He turned to Phoebe and Demetrius; "Did you find Brother Eli's map? And the mirror?"

"Yes, we got them both," replied Demetrius, protectively patting the hip pocket of his jeans which contained the old document and the little mirror. "The mirror doesn't seem to do much of anything in particular, but I guess we had better bring it along, seeing as Brother Bennett was very particular about it. But you didn't tell us that the map is an all-singing, all-dancing map though!" the teenager exclaimed, his surprise at the map's unique qualities still very evident.

Cosain allowed himself a bemused smile. "Yes," he said. "It is a *very* special map, easier to read and understand than most. And I imagine that the mirror will reveal its use to you in time. Brother Bennett probably had this in mind when he warned you in his journal that '*things are not always as they seem*'. Keep the map safe at all times, Demetrius, it will lead you to the Key of Esse, which will be the pivot on which your entire assignment rests. And do not be surprised if the map reveals more of its... *unusual* qualities to you, I think you will find it versatile to say the least. Now Phoebe, you and Demetrius must come with Solas and me; the others will meet us at our destination."

"Our destination?" queried Demetrius. "Shouldn't we follow the map?"

"Yes, Demetrius, that is precisely what we will do," answered Cosain, and as he spoke a radiating vortex of bright and warming light opened up before Phoebe and Demetrius, and they stepped instinctively into its reassuring glow with Cosain and Solas. The portal snapped shut as the rest of the Heavenly Host took to the skies en masse, and the ethereal glow which had pervaded Darken Abbey receded leaving the old building basking in the gentle earthly light of the weakening August sun.

CHAPTER 10

R ECENT experience had taught Phoebe that where the
vortex of light was concerned, a journey of a thousand
miles could be over in a few seconds, and this time was no
exception. The whirlwind journey seemed to end almost
before it had begun, and Phoebe and Demetrius found
themselves suddenly standing in very familiar territory.

"Cosain," said Phoebe with hesitancy in her voice,
reluctant to voice what was abundantly apparent. "We're...
we're *home*." She knew she was stating the obvious, but could
think of no apparent reason why the portal had transported
them from Darken Abbey to her own home when they should
be following the route laid out by Brother Eli's map.

"Yes," said Cosain. "You are home. Because this is where
it all started."

Phoebe looked up at the great warrior, the bewilderment
she felt clearly showing on her earnest young face. She raised
both hands with her palms turned upward and shook her
head in an *'I'm lost'* manner.

"Check the map, Demetrius," Cosain instructed, as
Demetrius pulled the old map from his pocket and spread it
out on the stone wall at the front of the Wrens' home. "You
will find that the map will instruct you very clearly as to
where you need to be and what you should be looking for.

See?" Cosain nodded in the direction of the opened map.

Phoebe and Demetrius turned their attention to Brother Eli's map which lay dull and one dimensional on the wall. Suddenly, the old parchment began to glow as radiant colour spread across it from one side to the other, imbuing the document with life and colour before one section lifted off the flat surface and was projected into the air.

"Whoa," exclaimed Demetrius with a huge grin. "I don't think that'll ever get old!"

But it was not the map's magical qualities that impressed Phoebe so much as the familiar location which had appeared from it. Phoebe gasped as she stared in wonder.

"It's Papa Augustus and Nanna Lottie's house! Dem, look!"

The teenagers watched in awe as Phoebe's grandparents' old house materialised in holographic form before them. The house looked fresher and a lot less lived in than it did now, but it was unmistakable as the same dwelling nonetheless. They could make out nearby Darken Abbey as it remained flat and lifeless on the map, and as they looked on, the two tiny figures they had seen exiting the abbey came into view, running down the gravel road towards the house, long brown monastic robes flowing wildly out behind them.

"Brother Bennett and Brother Eli," said Demetrius, somewhat unnecessarily because Phoebe was in no doubt about whom it was. She continued to watch as the projected images of the fleeing monks approached the house, seeking refuge from the beasts they had left behind in Darken Abbey. The door of the house opened and a young woman beckoned Brothers Bennett and Eli inside, closing the heavy wooden door behind them with a reassuring thud.

"*That*," said Cosain, in answer to Phoebe's unasked

question, "That was Lily – your Great-Great-Grandmother, and the woman who won Brother Eli's heart. Unlike most of the villagers way back then, Lily still held the monks in high regard, and was not quick to forget how kind and helpful they had been to her village. Had Thadius and Eli run to any other house, the welcome may not have been so warm, but Lily – like both of you – was in the right place at the right time, and so the fleeing monks found refuge. They did not stay long, however – just long enough to formulate a plan and rest a little. But it was long enough for Eli to know that his future did not lie in the monastic realms but with this young woman who had saved his life in more ways than one."

Cosain smiled at Phoebe, who was hanging on his every word. "I never knew any if this," she admitted. "I guess I never really asked about it, I just assumed that my ancestors led ordinary lives, like me... at least, like mine *used* to be!"

"There really is no such thing as an *ordinary* life, Phoebe – every life holds the potential to be extraordinary. After all, the great adventure of life is by its very definition *extraordinary*." Cosain smiled as he continued with his explanation of events. "Thadius and Eli knew that they could not afford to become complacent, and remaining in the village too long would put many lives in danger, so they waited until night fell, then left Lily's house and travelled north, crossing the border into the North of Ireland the next day. Brother Bennett remained devoted to monastic life, and found his place in Nendor Abbey, where he lived out the rest of his days in a life of simplicity and servitude. But Brother Eli found that he could not join his mentor, and after a few weeks and much soul searching, he began the journey back to Arles, and more importantly, to Lily. The pair were married soon afterwards and built a happy life together, with Eli remaining watchful of events at Darken Abbey every day, and they lived out their days in the house that your grandparents live in to this day. It is there that we must start our quest."

"*Wow,*" breathed Phoebe, startled by the unexpected turn of events. "All this time we were only a short walk from what might prove to be the biggest clue we need to defeat Schnither and his minions and find Ella."

"Yes," replied Ernan. "Brother Bennett told us in his journal that the answers '*may be closer at hand than you think*'. He and Eli had to ensure that the Enemy never found the missing piece of the Key of Esse, but they also needed for you to be able to locate it."

"Crazy," murmured Phoebe. "We owe them a debt of gratitude for their foresight and cleverness."

"That's for sure," agreed Demetrius. "They risked their necks so we could do what we need to do today. That's so very brave!"

"Agreed," said Cosain. "So let's not let them down. I think you know where we need to go."

Without further prompting, Phoebe took the lead and set off with Demetrius and the angelic warriors in the direction of a place she knew well – Papa Augustus and Nanna Lottie's house.

CHAPTER 11

PHOEBE'S grandparents' house was just a short walk from the Wrens' homestead. It was a large whitewashed two storey house with a beautiful garden out front that was bursting with colour from azaleas, bluebells, poppies and a myriad of other flowers and shrubs. The old building was the idyll of quaint countryside living, and regularly drew admiring glances from passers-by. In just a little over five minutes Phoebe and Demetrius were standing on the old familiar porch of her grandparents' home. Cosain, Ernan and the other warriors remained a short but discreet distance away; they knew that this was a meeting which would have to take place without them, but they remained alert for any sign of the Enemy. They would not be lulled into a false sense of security by the picturesque surroundings and were all too aware that Captain Schnither and his hordes were no respecters of location.

"I hope they're home," Phoebe remarked largely to herself as she tried the black wrought iron door handle on her grandparents' front door. Despite the wonderful comforting memories that this old house evoked, Phoebe still felt a flutter of nerves in her belly, and it was to her great relief that the handle turned and the big red front door swung open. Phoebe and Demetrius stepped inside and were at once met with the welcoming smell of fresh scones baking in Nanna Lottie's oven.

"*Papa! Nanna!*" Phoebe called from the hallway of the big old house. For a house that was almost one hundred and fifty years old, it had a cosy, homely feel about it. Phoebe's grandfather Augustus Wren – the only child of Benjamin and Eleanor Wren – had been born here, and he and Charlotte had moved back into the regal old house when his parents passed away. Augustus and Charlotte had redecorated the house, building an extension at the back to give them two extra bedrooms upstairs, and a lounge and a huge family kitchen downstairs, but they had retained many of the building's original features, and even as a young child Phoebe had always loved the high ceilings, decorative architraves and wonderful marble fireplaces. Besides the steady '*tick tock*' of the old mahogany grandfather clock which stood in pride of place in the hallway next to the living room door, the house was quiet, and Phoebe began to wonder whether anyone was at home. She need not have worried.

"Ah . . . Phoebe, Demetrius; hello sweethearts!" Nanna Charlotte walked out into the hallway from the kitchen, rubbing her floury hands on her flowery apron as her face wrinkled into a beaming smile. "What a lovely surprise! Come through my dears, you're just in time for a cuppa and a freshly baked scone – they're cherry you know, your favourite Phoebe." Charlotte winked at her granddaughter and smiled a smile that seemed to illuminate her entire visage.

Nanna Lottie was a glorious lady, with a welcoming demeanour and a huge heart which she always wore unabashedly on her sleeve. She had a wonderful way of making everyone feel like family, and had welcomed Demetrius like one of her own from their very first meeting. She had greeted him on that first encounter with a huge embrace and told him she loved him, and Demetrius had never once doubted her infectious sincerity. Phoebe had always adored both of her grandparents, but she shared a special bond with Charlotte – or Nanna Lottie as she was affectionately known to her beloved family. Charlotte was a devoted wife, mother and grandmother, and had a youthful demeanour which belied her sixty five years. Her emerald green eyes had a perpetual sparkle which hinted at a mischievous streak that was only ever just below the surface, and she and Phoebe had often enjoyed little giggles shared only between them.

"Thanks Nanna," smiled Phoebe, as she was gratefully engulfed in Charlotte's warm embrace. "Is Papa at home?"

"Yes Dear," smiled Charlotte. "He's out in the back yard tinkering at something or other." Her eyes twinkled playfully as her kind face wrinkled into a knowing smile. "You know your Papa, he always has a project that needs his urgent attention! Why don't you and Demetrius go on out back and see him, and I'll bring us all out some afternoon tea?"

"Okay Nanna, thank you," Phoebe gave her grandmother a quick kiss on the cheek then she and Demetrius made their way out through the large family kitchen and utility room to the back yard.

"Hey Papa," called Phoebe as she spotted her grandfather, clad in blue overalls, spanner in hand, working in the little summerhouse at the bottom of the beautifully kept garden. Augustus looked up from whatever it was that he was working on now, and waved the spanner at his granddaughter. This simple little exchange washed over Phoebe with a warm familiarity that made her feel safe and secure in the midst of the tumultuous journey on which she found herself, and she was grateful in this moment to just feel grounded and at home.

"Hello Phoebe sweetheart, hi Demetrius," Augustus called, downing tools and wiping his forehead on the sleeve of his red checked shirt. "Sure is warm for August, eh?" Although he was only five years older than his wife, Augustus somehow looked every one of his seventy years, while Charlotte could have passed for a woman ten years younger than she actually was. Grandpa Augustus was a kind, gentle man, with a generous and humble nature, but where Charlotte had a sense of frivolity and fun, Augustus was more reserved and decorous, although his earnest love for his family was very evident. He was the kind of man who never did anything by half, and actively sought out random acts of kindness that he could bestow on those around him.

"Yeah Papa, it sure is," replied Phoebe, desperately wanting to sit her grandfather down and ask him a million tumbling questions, but realising too that this was not something that she could just launch into cold. She would have to work up to the big pressing questions, and had resigned herself to the necessity for some small talk. "What are you working on today, Papa?" she asked, working hard at sounding nonchalant and desperately resisting the urge to blab out all of her rambling thoughts.

Augustus met Phoebe and Demetrius halfway down the garden, and embraced them both in greeting. He smiled at the teenagers standing in front of him, and replied, "Oh, I'm just tapping away at the old lawn mower. It's giving me a little bit of bother, but I'm sure it's not serious – nothing me and my spanner can't sort out anyway!" Augustus studied his granddaughter and her friend for a few seconds in thoughtful silence before his eyes grew earnest and his face assumed a more serious expression. "Something tells me this isn't just a social visit my dears..." he said as his forehead furrowed, making him look older and somehow wiser. Augustus's quiet demeanour disguised the depth of his thoughts and insight, and it was true that the old man could sense and understand more about people than he ever let on.

Phoebe's eyes widened, and for a split second she considered pretending that she didn't know what her grandfather meant by his insightful comment. But as she held his gaze, she knew that Augustus could read her like an open book, and slowly she nodded her head. Phoebe was surprised at how quickly he had seen through her apparently motiveless visit, but knew instinctively that she could trust him with everything and anything.

"You're right Papa, this isn't just a social visit," Phoebe said quietly. "We really need to talk to you." She glanced at Demetrius whose eyes were fixed on Papa Augustus with an undiluted expectancy and urgency that mirrored Phoebe's own.

"I knew that this day would come eventually," continued Augustus with just a hint of resigned apprehension and a muted sigh in his gentle voice. "I did wonder if maybe your father would be the One, Phoebe, but when life led him away to Africa to devote his time and talents to being a surgeon, I knew that his destiny lay in other directions. But when you all came back to Ireland, and I got to spend some more time with you my dear... Well, it didn't take me long to figure out that *you* are the One, that it is *your* destiny to put right what went wrong all those years ago up at the abbey."

Phoebe found herself entirely lost for words, her mind racing to find a suitable response. Or *any* response, for that matter.

"*What?*" She eventually blurted out the most basic of questions as though its answer might contain the very meaning of life. "But Papa, how do you know about... about the abbey, or my destiny, or what Dem and I need to talk to you about?"

There were just so many questions, so much that she wanted – *needed* – to know, but for this moment in time she could barely string a sentence together. Obviously, Augustus was entirely au fait with events from a century ago, and Phoebe could scarcely wait for him to share his secrets. Her head was swimming with anticipation mingled inextricably with nervousness, and she felt relief wash over her when she heard her Grandmother's voice.

"Tea's ready!" Charlotte's sweet voice broke the momentarily stunned silence, and Phoebe realised that her jaw was hanging slack and she was staring at her Grandfather who held her gaze with ageing blue eyes that silently reassured her, "*It's okay Little One, I can help you, I have all the information you will need.*"

"Oh . . ."

Charlotte glanced from her stunned granddaughter's pretty face to her husband's ageing and ruggedly handsome visage. Augustus caught the expression on his wife's face, and slowly nodded his head. The simple gesture was all it took for Charlotte to realise what was transpiring and she stopped in her tracks as she surveyed the beloved little gathering standing in her back garden. She set down the painted wooden tray bearing four mugs of hot tea and a plate of still steaming and thickly buttered cherry scones and beckoned Phoebe, Demetrius and Augustus to the little wooden picnic table located on the paved patio area just outside the back door.

"Come my dears," Charlotte invited. "Sit. Let's talk, shall we?" Obviously, Nanna Lottie was privy to whatever information Papa Augustus had, but her gently smiling expression countered the tension in his furrowed brow and somehow made everyone relax, secure in the knowledge that everything would – one way or another – be okay.

Augustus took Phoebe's small soft hand in his big weathered hand, and laid a strong arm gently along Demetrius's shoulders as the three made their way to where Charlotte had taken a seat at the picnic table. They sat together in silence for a moment while Charlotte added milk and sugar to the four cups of tea and layered jam and cream on the freshly baked scones. She distributed the welcome snack between the four of them, then breathed in deeply and exhaled with something akin to a sigh, but without any trace of angst or anxiety. Charlotte reached across the table and lovingly took hold of her husband's hand. She smiled kindly at the old man, whose blue eyes were full of concern despite his best efforts to appear relaxed. Phoebe could see his woes subside as his wife of almost fifty years reassured him with nothing more than a tender look that said more than a thousand words ever could. It was only a fleeting moment, but Phoebe felt that they had been frozen in time as she watched the voiceless exchange between her beloved grandparents.

"It's okay my Love," Charlotte soothed eventually with a smile, patting Augustus's hand in a kindly manner. "If Phoebe is the One to finish the task that Eli started all those years ago, then she will be equipped with everything she needs. She will not be alone. We know that. And we must believe it."

Augustus smiled at his wife, obviously comforted by her wise words, and it occurred to Phoebe that her parents shared a similar bond, which closely mirrored Augustus and Charlotte's.

"You are right my Dear, of course," smiled Augustus, patting her hand gently, then he turned his attention to Phoebe and Demetrius who were waiting with baited breath to glean whatever they could from this upright old couple. Augustus smiled a weak smile of resignation then spoke directly to his granddaughter and her friend: "Now, where to begin exactly? Phoebe, Demetrius – perhaps you should tell me what *you* know, and then I can fill you in with *my* experiences. That way we will have the advantage of each other's knowledge, and I feel you will be best equipped for whatever it is that you will need to do next, eh?"

Phoebe and Demetrius nodded quickly in agreement, then Phoebe sucked in a deep breath and began to relay her incredible story to the grandparents she adored and trusted implicitly.

CHAPTER 12

"**A**ND so," Phoebe concluded, "After all that madness, here we are! It has been the *craziest* few weeks; sometimes if I think about it all too much, I barely know what's real and what I have just imagined!" She leaned her elbows on the top of the picnic table and rested her chin on her clasped hands, scanning the faces of Augustus and Charlotte to try and gauge their reaction.

It had taken a little over an hour for Phoebe to relay her incredible tale to her attentive grandparents, with Demetrius chipping in now and again whenever Phoebe needed to catch her breath. She had started from the very beginning, explaining how she, Jack and Eva had been involved in the aeroplane crash en route home to Ireland, how she had attended her parents' funerals and had been living with Ella and the Quill family. Phoebe told them how she had encountered Cosain and the angelic warriors who had accompanied her and Demetrius on the breathtaking second journey from Africa back to Ireland, with all the encounters and adventures along the way. Phoebe told her grandparents about Brother Bennett's journal, and Brother Eli's map and the little mirror, and expounded her shock at learning that Eli was in fact her Great-Great-Grandfather. Even as she listened to her own voice recounting such extraordinary events, Phoebe found her own words difficult to digest, and as she finished her account of events, she shook her head in wonderment and incredulity, as if the motion might untangle her thoughts and somehow force them to make sense.

"Wow," Phoebe sighed. "Listening to that all playing back was too weird! Did that *really* all just happen to *me?*"

Augustus smiled kindly at his granddaughter, and nodded his head authoritatively. "Yes, it does sound too fantastical for comprehension, but we believe you, Dear. We believe every word – just the way we believed every word when my grandfather, Eli Wren, told me about Cosain and Schnither and the eternal battle in which *he* found himself all those years ago. Eli was all too attuned to the perpetual battle which rages between light and darkness – it is a battle which few people witness in the temporal, but it is real nevertheless. He knew that to be true, just as we know – and now you know too. I cannot say why some of us see what others do not see... perhaps there is something in our nature that makes us more sensitive to the things eternal, I'm not sure, but I do know that we have a part to play in this great battle."

The thought seemed to play on Augustus's mind, and for a moment he was lost in his own musings before continuing with his explanation. He was not a man of copious words, and Phoebe wondered exactly what her Grandfather had witnessed that made him so certain of the existence of warring forces of good and evil in the unseen realms.

"Eli Wren was, as you know, my grandfather. He was a monk in Darken Abbey until the abbey finally succumbed to dark forces in 1909, and the reputation of the monastic order was sullied by greed, bribery and corruption. When evil Captain Schnither and his henchmen finally succeeded in forcing the monks out of the abbey, the old building lost its light and a deep darkness set in. This darkness spread like an advancing disease across the island – it was as if the removal of the monks caused a snuffing out of goodness and light, and the positive influence they once had was replaced by an oppressive heaviness and hopelessness that no-one could quite explain, but no-one could deny. Looking back, it is clear that Captain Schnither's dark minions had executed their duties with great skill, and local people who once lived in harmony with their neighbours began to quarrel over land and religion and belongings. Of course, they could not know that their disquiet had been deliberately caused by dark supernatural forces, but the harmony which once existed amongst locals was disrupted, and goodness was swallowed up by greed and self-serving ambitions."

"So," Phoebe said tentatively, "You're saying that Darken Abbey was more than just an abbey, and Eli and his brothers were more than just monks... They were actually stemming the flow of evil in this area?"

"*Exactly*," confirmed Augustus. "And once Thadius Bennett and Eli Wren were forced out of the picture, Captain Schnither met with little or no resistance from the locals who, by and large, were ignorant to his corruption and scheming ways, and he has been wreaking havoc ever since. Of course, not everyone can be manipulated by Schnither and his hordes, but he has had free rein long enough and it would seem that it has fallen to you and Demetrius to send him packing from Darken Abbey once and for all."

Demetrius had been listening intently, absorbing all the information that Augustus could make available to him, and now he gathered his thoughts and spoke. "Can you give us any guidance, Augustus? I think we both feel more than just a little overwhelmed by the mission assigned to us. I mean, who are *we* to be assigned such a huge task? How can we possibly take on these dark forces and evict them from Darken Abbey? It just seems like *such* a huge request..."

Augustus smiled at the earnest sixteen year old sitting across the table from him. Demetrius was wise beyond his years and possessed a calm assurance that Augustus had found only rarely in all his seventy years. The old man was thankful for Demetrius's steadying influence in his granddaughter's life, and delighted in time spent with the fearless youngsters. He paused a moment, apparently searching for just the right words with which to respond. "Demetrius," he said finally, "You must remember the words that Brother Bennett penned in his journal – '*You are a greater threat to the Enemy than you know... You are wiser than you know... You carry more light than you know... You are stronger than you know... You are more protected than you know...*' I understand that is a lot to take on board and may be difficult for you to believe right now, but as you venture on in this great escapade, you will learn that these are eternal truths, and that the role you both play has greater significance than you could comprehend at this time. Your destinies are inextricably bound to the eternal realm – what you are about to do will have implications not only in this mortal realm, not only in our world, but will reverberate in the very Heavenlies. But – and this is something you must never forget – if you are not *for* the Light, then you are *against* it. You both are carriers of the Light, and as such you will have at your disposal all the forces of Heaven to assist you in your task."

Phoebe and Demetrius looked at each other – there was so much for them to wrap their thoughts around, but suddenly they both felt somehow ready for whatever would be thrown at them. The truths and affirmations spoken over them by Augustus and Charlotte permeated to the very core of their beings, and the teenagers felt inexplicably empowered and battle ready. They knew that whatever lay ahead was bigger than both of them, but they felt an assurance that they would be equipped for whatever they were to be tasked with.

"Okay," Demetrius concurred. "Then we are ready for this... Agreed, Bird?"

Phoebe smiled at her brave friend and nodded her head slowly. "Yes," she said. "I guess I'm as ready as I'll ever be."

"In that case..." continued Augustus, "There are a few things you need to know – and a few items you will need to carry with you at all times. Follow me."

The gentle old man arose from his bench and moved slowly towards the house. Phoebe, Demetrius and Charlotte followed him through the kitchen and back out into the hallway. Augustus stopped next to the old mahogany grandfather clock, and beckoned for Phoebe and Demetrius to draw alongside. The teenagers' eyes were riveted to the clock as Augustus opened the glass door on the front and gently stopped the pendulum in its rhythmic tracks. Phoebe's eyes widened in surprise – this old clock had kept time in her grandparents' home for as long as she could recall. She remembered being mesmerised by its impressive size and beauty as a very young child, when she would stand in front of it, watching the ever swinging pendulum and wondering why it never stopped or missed a beat. Augustus held the weight at the end of the great pendulum in one hand, and with the other he began to slowly and carefully unscrew the rod that held the pendulum. He worked at the long metal rod for a few moments before stepping back from the Grandfather clock with a small and insignificant looking section of the pendulum clasped in his weathered hand.

"Papa!" gasped Phoebe as a slow realisation dawned on her. "Is that..?"

"The missing piece of the Key of Esse," Charlotte smiled a little nostalgically as she confirmed what Phoebe suspected. "Yes, Eli was a wise man and hid it in plain sight. Make no mistake that this little piece of metal will be absolutely crucial to your quest. Without it, you can never open – or more importantly, *close* – the doorway to the Mooar Mountain... the Geata Gate. Legend has it – although we know from experience that there is plenty of substance to the legend – that this doorway is the entry point between this earthly realm and the unseen dark spiritual realm. It makes sense that Darken Abbey was chosen as the location for the Geata Gate because the abbey has always been a thin place, a place closely attuned to the supernatural realm. Unfortunately, the dark demonic beings realised this too and made it their mission to steal Darken Abbey for their own malevolent purposes."

"May I?" Phoebe asked, nodding towards the dull and insignificant looking piece of metal held so reverently in her Grandfather's big hand.

"Of course," replied Augustus, and Phoebe scarcely dared to breathe as she gently lifted the section of the Key of Esse in her hands. She turned it over, examined both sides, and upended it to look along its length. From this angle, Phoebe could see that the metal had been sculpted so that there were five grooves running the length of it, all equidistant from each other. When examined length on, the cross section of the metal resembled a rounded five-point star with small protruding pins at one end where the section slotted into the rest of the Key of Esse. There was nothing overly ornate or striking that would set this piece of metal apart, and yet as Phoebe felt its weight in her hands, she was overcome with the importance of this key and the task that was hers. She sighed, and her grandfather instinctively recognised how overwhelmed she was feeling.

"Don't worry Little One," he said gently as he placed a protective arm around her shoulders. The term of endearment had also been used several times by Cosain and reminded her that she had the unwavering support of the mighty Heavenly warriors. "Keep the section of the key safe until such times as you have the chance to reunite it with the other two pieces – as a whole, the Key of Esse will be the most powerful tool available to whoever possesses it, so you need to make sure that it is in *your* possession once it becomes a whole. And I have a couple of items which will help you do that." He motioned for them to return to the picnic table in the back garden, and Phoebe was glad. It was a beautiful late summer afternoon, and somehow being outside, surrounded by nature in all its beauty, soothed her nervous soul.

Augustus reached again into the pocket of his overalls, and pulled out a small and intricately designed gold pocket watch. His blue eyes shone as he surveyed the little time piece, which dangled on the end of a gold chain dulled by age, and he smiled as if pondering a secret known only to him. The watch was lacklustre and tarnished, but its cover still bore the beautiful engravings from a time long since passed. The delicate swirling patterns appeared at first glance to have no particular ordered pattern, but as she surveyed it with growing curiosity Phoebe realised that the etchings formed the shape of two wings, feathery and reminiscent of the mighty wings of the Heavenly Host.

"That's a very pretty watch Papa," said Phoebe, "But I don't see how it's going to help us . . . ?"

"Ah," smiled Augustus. "Remember that *things are not always as they seem*, my Dear. This little watch can help you out in ways that are not immediately obvious. It belonged once to my grandfather, Eli Wren, who passed it along to his son, Benjamin, my father, who gave it to me. No-one knows exactly where it originated but one thing is for sure – this is definitely more than just a pocket watch..."

Phoebe and Demetrius were intrigued, and hung on Augustus's every word, eager to learn what was so special about the relatively humble looking little watch. Given the journey on which she found herself, Phoebe did not imagine that there could be anything too fantastical for her to believe, and she was eager to learn just what powers or qualities the pocket watch might possess.

"Should you find yourselves in great peril," Augustus continued, "You must use this pocket watch. When faced with impending danger, simply open the front cover, thus..." The old man's eyes twinkled with an excitable expectation as he watched and waited for the teenagers' responses.

Phoebe and Demetrius watched with baited breath as Augustus slowly, almost reverently, opened the front cover of the old gold pocket watch. For a moment, it looked as though nothing had changed and Phoebe felt disappointment creep over her shoulders, until Demetrius gasped softly and nudged Phoebe with his elbow.

"Look Phoebs, look at the birds..."

As Phoebe lifted her eyes from the pocket watch to survey the scenery around her, she realised that birds were bizarrely suspended mid-flight and motionless; the wind no longer rustled the leaves of the trees, and the distant rumbling of infrequent vehicles on the country road had been silenced. Augustus smiled at his granddaughter and spoke his confirmation; "Yes, this is more than *just* a pocket watch. When used by those who see beyond the natural, it has the power to stop time itself. Use it whenever you feel threatened and time will stand still for everyone and everything but you and Demetrius. It can buy you valuable time and get you out of tight spots, make no mistake about that. But you must be careful Phoebe – the watch is powerful, but its power is not without limit. It will have little or no effect on certain enemy forces – including the Behemoth."

The teenagers were clearly impressed by Papa Augustus's magical pocket watch, although the warning that its power would not be effective on every dark being troubled Phoebe somewhat. She decided not to give voice to her concerns and looked on silently as the old man handed the pocket watch over to Demetrius who set it gently on the table next to the missing piece of the Key of Esse.

"What else Papa?" asked Phoebe, eager to find out what

else she and Demetrius would have in their arsenal.

"I have these for you, Phoebe," replied Augustus, removing a pair of metal rimmed eye glasses from his overall pocket. The small round glasses looked even less significant than the pocket watch, with their thin bendy legs and fragile frames. "When you put these on, you will have the ability to see the unseen. And by that I mean that you will see Schnither's minions even when they are in hiding. Furthermore, you will be able to discern Shapeshifters, even when they appear in human form. This will be an invaluable advantage to you, because as Brother Bennett learned to his cost, sometimes people are not all they appear. These glasses will confirm for you what your soul suspects."

"Wow Papa," said Phoebe, genuinely impressed by the hidden qualities of these everyday objects. "Who knew anything like this existed outside of books and movies!"

"I know my Dear, but when it comes to the ethereal realm, *anything* is possible – and you will need all the help you can get. One last thing you should know," Augustus hesitated and Phoebe sensed that what he was about to say next would be even more incredible than what she had heard up to this point. "The map which you have in your possession will in itself be a weapon against your enemy. By now you will have witnessed some of its properties, but you need to know that if you come under attack from any of Captain Schnither's dark hordes, the map can provide you with a blanket of invisibility if you open it out and wrap it around yourselves. You must be aware that this will be only a temporary invisibility, it will wear off after a few minutes, but if it buys you just a little extra time then it just might provide the cover that could mean the difference between success and...." The old man's voice trailed off, but there was no doubt in anyone's mind that the alternative to success was not even an option.

Phoebe and Demetrius were silent for a moment as they

tried to take in everything they had just heard. The teenagers and their grandparents finished their tea, and it was Charlotte who eventually broke the pensive silence.

"Be careful my Dears," she said, and for the first time there was concern etched across her kindly face. "We knew that this day would come, and it is a great thing you do, with far-reaching implications... But, oh my! I did hope the One would be someone... well, someone *else*, just not you my sweet granddaughter!"

Charlotte's eyes flooded momentarily and she blinked furiously to stop the tears from spilling onto her cheeks. She regained her composure and smiled a warm and tender smile at Phoebe. "Still," she said, "This is your time, and it is your destiny, and I know that you and Demetrius will be equipped with everything you will need for the journey ahead. Now, you had best be on your way my loves, don't keep poor Ella waiting..!"

"Just one more thing before you go, Phoebe..."

Phoebe had risen to her feet, and now she stopped to look at her grandfather as he uttered the words. When he spoke again, his query was not directed at his granddaughter.

"I would really love to meet you in person Captain Cosain... Would that be okay?"

Augustus's request took Phoebe entirely by surprise. "How..." she stammered. "How could you know that he was here?" she asked, stunned to learn that her grandfather was aware of the presence of the Captain of the Host, despite the fact that Cosain had kept himself concealed from human eyes.

"I have suspected for many years that Cosain was keeping an eye on Charlotte and me. My grandfather spoke often of the Captain of the Heavenly Army who battled the enemy to allow him and Brother Bennett to escape Darken Abbey, and I have always believed that Cosain was mindful of us through the years as we awaited the arrival of the One whose destiny it would be to restore Darken Abbey."

"You were correct, Augustus, I have been here; we all have."

Cosain's gentle but authoritative voice spoke from out of the blue, and as Augustus and Charlotte looked on, he and the rest of his angelic troop materialised and stood on the back lawn next to Phoebe and Demetrius. The sheer size and immensity of the ethereal warriors took Augustus's breath away, and the old man sank down once more onto the wooden bench from whence he had just arisen.

"You have done well to guard the Key of Esse, Augustus" Cosain continued. "Eli deemed it best to hide it in plain sight, and it would seem that his logic proved accurate. Thank you for your faithful stewardship of this crucial object." Cosain bowed his head respectfully towards the old man, and Phoebe realised that despite their unearthly power and influence, the angelic warriors regarded people like her Grandfather with the highest of esteem. "Rest assured that we will travel with Phoebe and Demetrius every step of the way," Cosain continued, "And the objects you have given them will undoubtedly prove invaluable to their quest. Thank you for keeping your faith and believing that good would one day be restored. That day has arrived, and although it cannot be fully realised without a fight, we will do everything in our power to ensure that Phoebe and Demetrius fulfil their destinies as Light Bringers."

"Thank you Captain," said Augustus humbly. "Charlotte and I always sensed you were near. It has been an honour to finally meet you." The great angelic warrior lowered his head humbly; "The honour has been mine, Mr. Wren," he said, smiling at the brave mortal before him.

Augustus and Charlotte embraced Phoebe and Demetrius. "God speed my dear ones," said Charlotte. "Remember, we're here if you need us."

Phoebe smiled and nodded her thanks, and with that, a bright vortex of swirling, warming light sprang up in Augustus and Charlotte Wren's back garden as they looked on in awe. Phoebe, Demetrius and the angelic warriors stepped immediately into the centre of the brilliant light, and the vortex snapped shut behind the exiting group, leaving Augustus and Charlotte with only their thoughts and a blue Willow pattern plate of half eaten cherry scones.

CHAPTER 13

A S the light from the vortex faded, Phoebe and Demetrius felt themselves come to a standstill at the foot of a high and bleak looking mountain. This destination was very different from all previous vortex journeys, and Phoebe could not tell whether she shuddered because of the cold air or the foreboding scene in front of them. They looked around to try and establish their whereabouts, but the rugged and imposing landscape was entirely unfamiliar to the slightly bewildered teenagers. Cosain, Ernan and the other warriors stood next to them, swords drawn, and looking decidedly edgy.

"Where are we, Cosain?" asked Phoebe. "This really doesn't look like Ireland any more..." She knew that she was stating the obvious, for the terrain around her was in stark contrast to the gently rolling hills and lush greenery of Ireland, but she needed an answer.

"You are correct, Phoebe," replied Cosain. "We are not in Ireland. Indeed, we are quite some way away from Ireland. This is Mooar Mountain," he hesitated and an alarm bell sounded somewhere in the back of Phoebe's head. "This is the desolate abode of Abaddon the Defiler, Captain Schnither and their malevolent army."

Phoebe felt fear rising in her throat, and she battled hard to force herself to stay calm. "But what are we doing here? Shouldn't we get out of here before anyone realises we have arrived?" Phoebe's eyes darted over the barren and forbidding landscape which was largely devoid of any features other than a few dead trees, rocks and thorny briar bushes. It occurred to her that rarely had she ever seen so many shades of grey all in the one place.

"Ordinarily, we would never come here, but on this occasion it is unavoidable," explained Cosain as Phoebe regarded him with confusion dancing in her green eyes. "This is where Malva will have taken Ella – into the Mooar Mountain. Right now she is somewhere inside this mountain, undoubtedly under close guard. Schnither will be expecting us to come for Ella so we must keep our wits about us at all times. Demetrius, will you check the map please? We need to be as well prepared as we can possibly be."

Phoebe felt frightened tears welling up in her eyes, and blinked hard to stop them from spilling unchecked on to her cheeks. "Poor Ella!" she exclaimed. "She must be so frightened in there..."

"Do not worry, Ella will be safe for now," Ernan assured the teenagers. "Schnither will not allow any harm to befall her because he knows that while he has *Ella*, he has *us* in the palm of his hand. Schnither will assume that we will find the Key of Esse and then come to rescue Ella. It is not her that he ultimately wants – it is the key. But we cannot let him have it; we must protect it at all costs. For the Enemy to secure the final piece of the Key of Esse would mean unrivalled access to and from the earthly realm for the powers of darkness via the Geata Gate in Darken Abbey."

"So what are we waiting for?" Demetrius had been quietly taking in his surroundings, but now he was ready to move and was already looking for an access route into the Mooar Mountain. "Let's go get Ella and see to it that that hellish doorway is locked shut once and for all!"

"Not so fast, Demetrius," cautioned Cosain, placing a steadying hand on the eager young man's shoulder. "If we invade the mountain unprepared, Schnither and his minions will easily gain the upper hand; they will think nothing of stealing the key and killing us all, make no mistake about that. We will be outnumbered in there, *but* we can outsmart them, so it is vital that we know exactly what we are going to do."

The fearsome Captain of the Heavenly army beckoned the other warriors around him. "Croga, Cahir – I need you both to remain on the outside of the mountain. Schnither will have his sentries posted along its perimeter, so you will need to distract them – and engage them if necessary – but please ensure that the watchmen do not have the opportunity to raise the alarm or alert Schnither of our arrival. The element of surprise will be crucial to us."

"Yes Captain," replied Croga unquestioningly as he pulled his twin swords from across his back, and he and Cahir set off up side of the inhospitable mountain.

"Ernan, Solas, Dilis, Trean, Neam, Lasair, Maelis, Keane, Lachlan..." Each warrior stood to attention and saluted his Captain as Cosain called their name. "The rest of you will accompany me and the children..." Cosain corrected himself after catching a withering look from Phoebe. "Sorry...You will all accompany me and the *teenagers* into Mooar Mountain. We will need the map to guide us since the mountain is a maze of dark paths and dismal corridors – getting lost would be disastrous to our mission, but it could be easily done..."

"You mean," said Demetrius incredulously, "That you have actually been *inside* the Mooar Mountain before?"

"I have," Cosain's voice was sombre as he responded to Demetrius's question. "I followed Craven here in 1909 after he had wreaked havoc in Darken Abbey. But I acted in haste, and it almost cost me my life. I knew better than to journey into the Mooar Mountain alone, but I was angered by what Craven had done in the guise of Brother Clarence, and I was bent on revenge... But I learned my lesson, and we will not make the same mistakes again. Now, Demetrius, the map please, let's see what needs to be done and get to it."

As Demetrius pulled Brother Eli's map from his back pocket and unfolded it, the old parchment began to glow with life and muted hues of grey and black as the Mooar Mountain rose to life and was projected into the air. The three dimensional image began to rotate slowly and one side of the image peeled away, revealing a maze of corridors and chambers within the mountain. Neither Phoebe nor Demetrius had noticed the inclusion of the Mooar Mountain on the map before but Cosain assured them that they would always see what they needed to see, whenever they needed to see it.

"My Great-Great-Grandfather Eli must have known of this mountain," whispered Phoebe. "Otherwise how could he have known to include it on the map? But why on earth would he know anything about its layout or interior? Cosain, did Eli come here?" Phoebe could scarcely bear to find out, but desperately needed to know just how her Great-Great-Grandfather had come to enter the Mooar Mountain.

"Yes, Phoebe, he was here," replied Cosain. "Eli could not save Darken Abbey, but he never gave up on his quest for vengeance. He sought out Brother Clarence – Craven – every day of his life, and although he was never successful in finding him again, Eli's search caused him somehow to stumble upon the Mooar Mountain. Very few mortals have ever found this place, and those who do find it for a reason. It was here that Eli found the pocket watch and glasses that your Grandfather Augustus gave you. I have no doubt that the Enemy must have intended to use them for his own dark purposes. Eli realised their power and potential and removed them from the Mooar

Mountain, hoping that some day they would make it into the hands of the One who would complete his quest, and would prove vital in defeating Schnither and his dark hordes. Eli was never sure how he found the mountain, and he was never able to find it again. He was fortunate to escape its walls with his life, and he never made a return journey. Yes, Phoebe, the task that was Eli Wren's to commence has become your destiny to see through to completion. Now we must prepare to enter realm of the mountain and take back Ella."

As the angelic warriors examined the mountain's layout, Phoebe and Demetrius could only guess at what horrors might lie ahead of them. It was one thing to encounter Captain Schnither and his gnarly demons in the familiar earthly realm where the teenagers felt at ease in their surroundings, but the prospect of taking on the Enemy in his own sphere was a daunting one to say the least, and would require all the courage the teenagers could muster.

After a few moments of pondering and whispered planning, of which Phoebe and Demetrius had no part, Cosain and his troops stood up from their huddle and addressed the waiting teenagers. The angels' temporary rebuff had caused Phoebe to feel slightly sulky, but she reminded herself that she could not afford to appear childish or immature, especially at this crucial part of her journey, so she chided herself and shook off any remaining petulance before giving Cosain her full attention.

"Phoebe, Demetrius – I believe it will be best for us to split into two groups to enter the mountain. Phoebe, you will come with me, and Solas, Dilis, Trean and Neam will accompany us. Demetrius, you will go with Ernan, Lasair, Maelis, Keane and Lachlan. We will enter the mountain by different routes – my troop will enter via a hidden door halfway up the side; Ernan, your group should proceed to the top of the mountain and gain access from there. It is my contention that Ella is probably being held in a small anteroom just off Abaddon's chamber – this will be the most difficult room in Mooar Mountain to access, and will be heavily guarded. Demetrius, you should bring with you the map and Augustus's glasses, and Phoebe will bring the pocket watch. Remember that you have these at your disposal – use them well, they could be the difference between success and failure for us all." The Heavenly Captain's face was sullen, reminding Phoebe – if any reminder was necessary – of the gravity of the journey on which they were about to embark. Cosain turned his attention to his second in command. "Ernan, God speed my brother. Be as quiet as a dove – but as shrewd as a snake. And remember our oath to guard these mortals' every step."

"Understood, Captain," said Ernan soberly, as he respectfully saluted his commander-in-chief, then gathered up the warriors assigned to his command.

The thought of being separated from Demetrius terrified Phoebe; somehow, she always knew that everything would be alright as long as she was with him, and now they were being despatched in different directions. But as frightened as she was, Phoebe trusted Cosain implicitly, and so with a quick hug and a reassuring smile, Phoebe and Demetrius parted ways and set off with their respective guardians to seek entry into the foreboding mountain.

CHAPTER 14

IN the hazy half-light, it took only a matter of seconds before Demetrius, Ernan and the other angels vanished from Phoebe's sight as if the rolling fog coming down the sides of the mountain had swallowed them whole. Phoebe forced her eyes forward in the direction that Cosain was moving, and made a concerted effort to focus on the Captain of the angelic army rather than her uncanny surroundings. Cosain had never let her down so far – why should she doubt his ability to see her safely through now? Somehow though, as Phoebe scrabbled along the stony path that twisted and wound up the side of the Mooar Mountain, the landscape and eerie light made confidence and calm assurance much more difficult to secure, and being apart from Demetrius only served to unsettle her all the more. She thought of how he and the angel warriors had been entirely enveloped by the gaping jaws of the ghostly mist and shuddered despite her best intentions to remain calm and focused.

Phoebe and her angelic guards moved fairly quickly but entirely furtively further and further up the side of Mooar Mountain, all the while maintaining a careful watch for dark sentries who would seek to foil their stealthy approach. The narrow pathway was overgrown and stony, making the ascent particularly treacherous for Phoebe who stumbled frequently and had to be aided by her diligent protectors.

"Not much further now," Cosain assured Phoebe, who was beginning to flag a little from the steep and difficult climb. "The doorway to Mooar Mountain is well hidden, but if memory serves me well I should be able to locate it without too much..."

Cosain did not finish his sentence, but stopped suddenly in his tracks. He raised a clenched fist and beckoned for Phoebe and the other angels to stop, as he set the forefinger of his left hand over his lips, signalling for the now motionless group to remain still and quiet. Phoebe strained her eyes to see through the haze whatever it was that had set Cosain on edge, but her weak mortal eyes could distinguish very little through the foggy blur. Suddenly, and without any warning, the gluey mist which seemed to perpetually enrobe the Mooar Mountain cleared a little, and there only a few feet in front of the halted group stood four enemy sentries, who breached the foggy atmosphere like a ray of strange and unnatural sunshine through cloud. Phoebe gasped in horror as the fog shifted further and the four watchmen became fully visible – they were huge, each one at least nine feet tall, so that even Cosain appeared dwarfed by their gargantuan frames. Phoebe stood entirely motionless, barely even daring to breathe; it suddenly and surreally occurred to her that her demise may now be inevitable, faced with these unearthly and monstrous creatures. They had stumbled upon these enemy guards, and Phoebe was sure that they would prove formidable foes. As she steadied herself after the initial shock of coming across the giants, Phoebe slowly realised that they were standing totally still, not moving a muscle. As she looked closer, squinting her eyes for clarity, she realised that the giant watchmen's eyes were wide open and their great chests rose and fell with breathing, yet each appeared to be in some sort of trance and had obviously not seen Phoebe or any of the angels approaching.

"Anakite watchmen," breathed Cosain in hushed tones

by way of clarification, although the explanation itself meant little to Phoebe. Realising that his young ward had not understood the implications of his description of the giant guards, Cosain continued with his hushed explanation; "The Anakites are a mutated semi-human race of giants descended from angelic beings. Their kind was created when a rogue faction of our angelic brothers broke away from the rule of The Atoner and intermarried with mortal women, resulting in these giant crossbreeds you see before you. When awakened, the Anakite giants pose a very real threat – they are strong and tenacious, highly skilled in battle and utterly determined. But they remain in the dormant state you see before you until such times as they are roused from their slumber by intrusion or threat. Obviously, it will be in our best interests to ensure that we pass by them without awakening them, but they are positioned directly around and over the doorway into the Mooar Mountain, and finding the opening may unavoidably result in wakening the Anakite sentries."

Phoebe merely nodded her understanding, since Cosain's sombre warning had rendered her temporarily mute. She had read of the giants of ancient times, and was bewildered and bemused in equal parts to find herself actually standing in front of these imposing mutants. Even in their comatose state, the Anakites struck icy daggers of fear into Phoebe's heart and she was reluctant to take another step in case by so doing she would inadvertently rouse them from the watchmen slumber. Each colossus held a huge and fearful sword as tall as Phoebe, and their weapon rested squarely in front of them with the point of the blade digging into the earth while its dormant owner held tightly to the hilt with both vice-like hands. The Anakite guards' garments closely resembled those of the angelic warriors, and Phoebe was certain that she could distinguish what she assumed was some sort of family likeness in their fearsome yet strangely noble facial features.

"Follow my lead, and stick tight," Cosain whispered to Phoebe, who still had not dared take a step in any direction. "Brothers, be vigilant."

The Captain of the angel armies motioned towards a clump of thick and thorny briars with a nod of his head. "The doorway is behind that," he whispered, and Phoebe nodded her understanding back at him. Slowly, the warriors edged forward towards the doorway. Each had his eyes fixed on the slumbering Anakites and proceeded cautiously for fear of awakening them. The angelic warriors stopped just in front of the briars where Cosain had indicated that the doorway was hidden, and Phoebe realised that they were now hemmed in by the Anakite watchmen who were towering over them like high-rise buildings. She hardly dared to breathe as Cosain gingerly pushed aside the thorny bushes and felt his way along the side of the unyielding rock until his hand found the ancient lever which opened the doorway into the Mooar Mountain. Cosain pushed down on the lever and for a moment nothing happened. Phoebe stood watching, scarcely daring to breathe, until quite suddenly a large slab of damp grey rock slid angrily into the mountain, and a puff of offensive gases was emitted from the opening which now lay exposed. Whether it was the groan of the stone doorway or the stench of the noxious gas Phoebe could not be sure, but what she did know was that something had triggered the reflexes of the giant Anakite watchmen and in a split second all four had progressed from slumbering to wide awake, enormous swords raised and ready to attack.

"Anakite brothers!" roared the first giant, his veins straining and bulging in his thick neck, "Do not let these intruders invade the mountain! Stop them!"

And with that rallying cry the four sentries burst into life and became whirling thrashing menaces obviously intent on eliminating the threat posed by Cosain and the other angelic warriors.

"Neam!" yelled Cosain, who had taken to the air and was frantically parrying the blows being rained on him by the Anakite guards. "Get Phoebe inside! Hurry! Solas, Dilis, Trean and I will deal with these four!"

Before she knew what was happening, Phoebe found herself half carried, half pushed through the doorway and into the dank gloom of the Mooar Mountain. Instantly, she felt the damp chill in the air cling to her form like a close fitting garment, and she stood rigidly still, willing her eyes to adjust faster to the gloom inside. Neam wasted no time in activating a lever located just inside the mountain, and with more groaning protests, the great stone door slid shut, leaving Cosain, Solas, Dilis and Trean locked outside in a ferocious battle with the Anakite watchmen. Phoebe looked round at Neam, who was breathing rapidly, blue eyes wide and alert.

"What now, Neam?" she gasped, panic-stricken. "What about Cosain and the others? We must help them, we can't just leave them out there!"

"No," responded Neam, the tone of his voice telling Phoebe that this was not open for discussion. "We cannot risk venturing back out there until Cosain lets us know that the coast is clear. And we cannot venture further into the Mooar Mountain alone. So for now, we wait." Neam looked at the frightened girl before him, and his face softened as he was reminded of her mortality and inexperience. "It's okay Phoebe," he soothed in a much gentler voice. "Cosain knows what he is doing; we just need to be patient."

Phoebe nodded at Neam with uncertainty flashing wildly in her eyes, and involuntarily took a couple of steps closer to her angelic guardian, who placed a protective hand on her shoulder. Outside, she could hear the scuffle and fracas of battle, and decided that the best she could do for now was to offer up a silent plea for help to the Atoner.

CHAPTER 15

O N the other side of the Mooar Mountain, Demetrius was
making his way ever closer to the summit, accompanied
by Ernan, Lasair, Maelis, Keane and Lachlan. Unlike their
Anakite-battling friends, Demetrius's group had thus far
managed to avoid all enemy sentries, and Demetrius could
only assume that Croga and Cahir's scouting expedition
had been successful in removing any potentially problematic
fiendish watchmen prior to the arrival of the small cluster of
angels and their young charge.

It was a tough climb up the side of the Mooar Mountain,
and Demetrius found the air becoming noticeably thinner as
the group neared the top, so it was with conflicting feelings
of relief and trepidation that he saw the craggy summit of
the mountain coming into view. Ernan, Lasair, Maelis, Keane
and Lachlan all wielded their formidable swords, obviously
well prepared for any potential surprise attack, and the grip
which all five maintained on their deadly weapons served
to unnerve Demetrius somewhat, although the teenager
resolved to show them his most manly face at all times.

"Look, just up ahead," Ernan spoke, and as Demetrius
followed the direction in which the mighty warrior pointed, he
could see a rocky plateau which appeared to be the summit of
Mooar Mountain. "Our way in," said Ernan, as he clambered
over the final ledge of their climb and stood on the top of the

mountain. Demetrius gladly accepted a strong hand up from Lachlan, and he stood side by side with the angelic warriors, surveying the mountain with its grey and dismal landscape, although misty conditions prevented him from seeing very far. "This is how we gain entry, Demetrius," continued Ernan, pointing to what appeared to be nothing more than a small pile of insignificant boulders. Ernan read the confusion on Demetrius's face and continued, "Remember that things are not always as they seem my friend. It's going to be a little bumpy, so best prepare yourself for a rough ride."

Demetrius wondered how he could possibly prepare himself for a bumpy ride when he did not know what that ride entailed, but he watched closely nonetheless as Keane approached the mound of rocks and slid them en masse to one side as if they were made of nothing more than cotton wool. As the stony gateway moved aside, a large opening with what looked like a roughly hewn water slide was exposed. The chute apparently led down into the heart of the Mooar Mountain, and Demetrius began to understand why Ernan had warned him to brace for a bumpy ride.

"Oh okay, I see now what you meant about a rough ride," said Demetrius as he surveyed the shaft which had been hacked out of the rock and looked to be anything but smooth.

Ernan smiled at his young ward then beckoned for Lasair, Maelis, Keane and Lachlan to follow his lead as he sat on the edge of the opening with his mighty legs hanging down the inside. "Come on, we should get inside before we are spotted," he urged, as Demetrius sat next to the angelic warrior and tried to ignore the jitters in his belly. "You will need to go with the flow here, Demetrius. If sliding feels right, then slide as far as you can and save your energy. But if you need to crawl – then crawl, or scramble or tumble, whatever it takes to get down here. This chute leads directly into the Cardinal Hall and we most definitely do not want to linger there any longer than we have to. The Cardinal Hall is the meeting room used by Abaddon the Defiler when he needs to address his demons – we can only pray that he has not convened a meeting at present, because landing into the middle of *that* would definitely not be advantageous!"

"*Understatement of the year*," muttered Demetrius under his breath, although Ernan's raised eyebrow told him that he had been overheard and he gave his guardian the lopsided smile that he had called upon many times in the past to get him out of trouble. Ernan gave Demetrius's shoulder a reassuring squeeze before he launched his great body into the opening and commenced his dive, feet first, into the darkness below. Lasair and Maelis followed immediately, but it took a little nudge from Keane before Demetrius followed in their wake, closely pursued by Keane and Lachlan who brought up the rear. For the first few seconds, Demetrius felt as if he was in free fall, and had to consciously stop himself from flailing his arms and legs about in terror. He was aware that he had warrior angels in front of him and behind him, and as the plunge into the darkness slowed to something of a downward scrabble, Demetrius was able to compose himself sufficiently to take note of his surroundings. It took several seconds of downward travel for Demetrius's eyes to adjust to the gloom, but when they did he could see that he was descending through a mass of corridors and passageways built into the side of the Mooar Mountain. For how long or to what depth he had descended, Demetrius could not tell, but soon he could see a dim glow rising up through the gloom towards him. His warrior guardians had the advantage of having their mighty wings to steady their descent and Ernan, Maelis and Lasair had already landed gracefully in the Cardinal Hall when Demetrius half rolled, half tumbled out of the end of the rocky thoroughfare and landed unceremoniously in a tangled heap at their feet. Keane and Lachlan arrived only a couple of seconds after Demetrius, as Lachlan offered the teenager his powerful arm and pulled him to his feet. Demetrius stood and twisted his body to the right and then to the left as if checking that nothing had been broken, then he rubbed a bruise on his right elbow and furrowed his brow.

"You did well, Demetrius," whispered Lachlan with a wink. "That was not an easy descent for an angel let alone a mortal!" Demetrius was not so sure, and his throbbing elbow suggested different, but he appreciated the great warrior's attempt to make him feel better about his efforts.

"Brothers, Demetrius, follow me; we cannot afford to stop here any longer than is absolutely necessary. We have been fortunate to find no dark meeting convened, but who knows when the demon army might converge on this hall,"

Ernan's instructions left Demetrius in no doubt about the need to keep moving as the group set off along one of the five dank corridors which led out of the Cardinal Hall. Demetrius pondered the stark warning that the great hall in which they had landed was the main gathering place for the demonic hordes. It was empty now, but he did not want to even imagine what would happen if Schnither summoned his minions to congregate right here and now. The thought of the five adjacent corridors flooding with screeching angry demons all headed his way made Demetrius feel dizzy, and an overwhelming need to get out of the great hall overcame him. Demetrius shuddered, and stepped up his pace to ensure that he kept up with Ernan, not wanting to get left behind in this awful place. He was flanked in front and behind by imposing ethereal warriors of light, and yet Demetrius felt chilled to his core by the evil which almost seemed to seep from the walls of this forsaken place and permeate the air around him. He wondered how Phoebe was getting on – had she made it successfully into the heart of the Mooar Mountain? Had she encountered much opposition? Maybe she had even found Ella already? No, that was expecting too much too soon. The thoughts made Demetrius's pulse quicken and anxiety rise in his throat, so he forced himself to focus instead on the task at hand. "*One step at a time, Dem,*" he chided himself.

The corridor down which Ernan was leading the little group was dark and cold, so cold in fact that the walls felt damp to the touch, and the only light afforded to Demetrius and the angelic warriors came from dully glowing oil torches which were lit in irregular intervals along the wall, furious little splashes of colour protesting angrily against the all encompassing darkness. It occurred to Demetrius that far from being welcoming, this peculiar light served only to throw eerie shadows along the corridor, making him wonder which shadowy shapes were mere silhouettes, and which were hiding a hideous monster lurking under the stealthy cover of darkness. He swallowed hard and forced his feet to carry him along after his protectors, anxious that he should not become separated from them at any time. Losing his way and becoming detached from the angelic warriors just did not bear thinking about in this dank and ominous otherworldly underbelly.

They traversed along the apparently endless corridors, twisting this way and winding that way, and passed several large wooden doors, all of which were tightly closed. The oppressive walls of rock on either side were making Demetrius claustrophobic, and he was beginning to wonder when this journey might end when Ernan signalled for the eclectic group of adventurers to halt. He pointed ahead to where the gloomy corridor rounded a corner to a dimly lit vestibule, and the shadows flickering along the walls of this open area told Ernan that someone – or *something* – was stationed up ahead.

"This is it," whispered Ernan with a severity in his voice that Demetrius had never heard before. "Around this corner are the private quarters of Abaddon the Defiler; it is always the most heavily guarded area in the Mooar Mountain, and I believe that this is where Malva will have stashed Ella. If we are fortunate, Abaddon may not be in residence here – he is very partial to roaming the realms of man on the lookout for

mortals to accuse and belittle and devour, but if he *is* here...
then let's just say that we will have a battle on our hands."

"Lieutenant," said Maelis in hushed tones, his sharp
green eyes sparking with fervency. "Should we not wait for
Cosain and our other brothers? Surely adding them to our
ranks would greatly improve the odds?"

"I agree, Maelis," answered Ernan. "Ideally, we should
hold off until Cosain and the others join us – but we cannot
be sure of their whereabouts or how long it will be before
they can get here, and we really cannot delay."

"Understood," acknowledged Maelis with a curt nod of
his head that caused his jet black braided hair to fall forward.
"Then you have our absolute best at all times, Sir."

"Thank you, Maelis," said Ernan, the deep respect for
his fellow warriors evident in his visage. "I never doubt the
loyalty and best efforts of any of my brothers."

Ernan turned his attention to Demetrius, who was
working hard to stop his wobbly legs from giving up on him
completely. "Demetrius, the challenge around this corner
will be your most difficult to date. Lasair, Maelis, Keane,
Lachlan and I will assume invisibility, and you must use the
map for similar results. Wrap it around your shoulders and
you will become invisible, although be aware that the effect is
temporary and will wear off relatively quickly. You should also
be aware that while our – and your – invisibility is absolute in
the earthly realm, it is diluted in the ethereal kingdom."

"Diluted?" repeated Demetrius "You mean..." The
teenager did not finish his sentence because he was reluctant
to have affirmed what he suspected.

"Yes," Ernan concurred. "You cannot be *seen* by the
enemy – but it is very probable that the demons will be able
to *sense* you, and us. They are dark and vile in nature, but

they stem from the ethereal realm, as we do, and so their senses will be attuned to our movements. We must proceed with great care – all of us."

Ernan looked around his small but committed troop of angelic warriors, and each nodded their understanding to their noble leader.

"We will use stealth to round this corner and size up our opponents. We will need to get past them in order to enter Abaddon's chamber and find Ella, but in opening the door we will inevitably alert them to our presence, therefore our invisibility will buy us time and nothing more. A battle *will* ensue – we must be prepared to fight... even to the death."

Ernan's stark words made Demetrius's blood run cold, but he reminded himself of Neam's words – *"Good will triumph over evil. Every time."* – and took courage from the assurance that this was his destiny, he was on the side of goodness and light, and he was accompanied by the mighty warriors of the Atoner who were focused on ensuring that he fulfilled his calling.

Ernan's loyal angelic brothers nodded their acceptance of their leader's instructions, as Demetrius reached into the back pocket of his jeans and pulled out the mysterious old map. He was desperate to know how exactly such a small piece of parchment could possibly grant him all-encompassing invisibility, but had learned enough to know to expect the unexpected. Demetrius unfolded the ancient map with great reverence. Part of him fully anticipated the revelation of more of the map's qualities, while another part of him almost expected nothing to happen. He tried to listen to the trusting part of himself and silence the doubter, but in the end he knew that all would be revealed in the next few moments. Demetrius surveyed the unfolded map as it lay open in his hands and held his breath as he gently lifted it to wrap the weathered old chart around his shoulders. As he began to drape the map around his shoulders, perhaps hoping rather than believing that it would work, he was astonished to find that the insignificant looking piece of parchment had expanded so that it fit around his shoulders and hung to the floor, entirely covering his body. It was as if the map had been designed with him in mind, and its edges met around him like a custom made garment. Neither Demetrius nor Phoebe had had a chance to test the map's invisibility qualities to see if it worked, so it was with great relief that Demetrius saw Ernan's nod of approval and realised that he was now invisible to the outside world. It was a very peculiar feeling, since to Demetrius the world around him looked entirely unchanged, and he had to assure himself repeatedly of his invisibility. He watched as Ernan and the angelic warriors disappeared from sight, but found that with the enchanted map around his frame he could still see their silhouettes, and was therefore able to stick closely by their sides as the invisible entourage made its way around the corridor to face whatever lay ahead.

CHAPTER 16

PHOEBE huddled closer to Neam in the oppressive gloom inside Mooar Mountain where the pair had been waiting for several minutes now. The noise of the clash outside had raged around their heads, assaulting their ears, as Cosain, Solas, Dilis and Trean battled hard against the four gargantuan Anakites, until the furore began to subside and fade, and Phoebe had to strain her ears to hear.

"Cosain must have beaten those awful giants... *right?*" whispered Phoebe, looking up at Neam with tentatively hopeful eyes. What she saw in Neam's expression made her heart sink. Where she expected to find an answering hope that matched her own, Phoebe saw instead thinly veiled concern. "What is it Neam? What are you thinking? Tell me – please."

Neam hesitated, apparently choosing his words carefully before he spoke. "It's quiet out there, Phoebe – it's *too* quiet. And if Cosain had routed those fiends he would have joined us here without delay. I'm afraid..." The warrior's blue eyes glanced at his young ward, and he seemed to swallow the words he had intended to say, not wishing to instil any more fear in her.

"You're afraid of *what*, Neam?" begged Phoebe. "Please don't keep me in the dark. I can handle it – whatever it is."

"Well, it's just that I'm concerned that the Anakite

watchmen may have somehow overpowered the others..."
Neam's voice trailed off and he paused before he spoke again.
"There can be no denying that they are worthy adversaries, so
it is just possible... I must get out there and help my brothers,
but I cannot endanger you Phoebe. You must stay here while
I assess the situation."

"*Neam!*"

There was an urgency in Phoebe's voice that cut straight
through the angel's train of thought and caused him to focus
all of his attention on her. "The pocket watch," she exclaimed.
"How could I have forgotten? If the giants *have* gotten the
upper hand, then maybe we can use it to help Cosain and
the others."

"Of course, Phoebe, that's it! If Cosain and the others
have been taken captive, you can use the watch to buy me the
time I will need to release them! But you must stay behind
me at *all times* – promise me, Phoebe?" The look on Neam's
face left Phoebe in no doubt that he would not tolerate
disobedience in the matter.

Phoebe quickly nodded her agreement as Neam pressed
down on the lever that opened the doorway into the Mooar
Mountain. There was no way to open the great stone door
quietly, and its creaking and groaning announced Neam and
Phoebe's arrival before they could even step out into the
half light. For a moment, Phoebe's view was blocked by the
enormous warrior exiting the mountain in front of her, but
as Neam stepped aside she surveyed the scene into which
they had arrived, and the horror and nausea rising in her
throat made her gasp. Just ahead, hauling Cosain, Solas, Dilis
and Trean along the side of the Mooar Mountain were the
four Anakite watchmen, all bloodied and bruised from battle
but nonetheless victorious as they dragged their exhausted
captives behind them. Cosain and the other warriors were
tightly bound with ropes around their wrists and ankles,

which were fastened to their waists, preventing them from moving at any speed. The strange ropes looked like molten steel as they glowed red and pulsated and seemed to burn the angels' skin. The great warriors' bodies were stooped and battered, and Trean in particular appeared to be having great difficulty in walking.

In a fraction of a second, the Anakite guards had been alerted to Neam and Phoebe's presence, and spun around roaring obscenities in their direction. Two of the monsters relinquished hold of their angelic captives to the remaining two giants, and started to run at great speed towards the terrified girl and her guardian. The Anakites' long legs sprang over the side of the Mooar Mountain as if the terrain were flat and level, and they would have been upon Neam and Phoebe had Neam not yelled out in a ferocious voice, "Now, Phoebe! *Now!*"

In a split second, Phoebe flexed her left hand around the little pocket watch, and her right hand shot up instinctively to the cover. Her fingers were trembling violently, and Phoebe willed them to be still as she flipped up the cover with her thumb and held her breath, hoping and praying that the pocket watch would work its magic, and quickly. In the blink of an eye, the two invading Anakites froze mid-bound, and looking past them over their broad shoulders Phoebe could see that their terrible allies were frozen solid too, their faces contorted in ghoulish masks of rage as their burly arms threw threatening but unmoving fists in Neam and Phoebe's direction.

"Neam," gasped Phoebe. "It worked. *It worked!*" She was so delighted that she felt she might burst, but knew that there was no time to waste on victory dances – they may have won this battle, but there was a whole war ahead of them which might not prove so easily achievable. Neam was at his stricken Captain's side in a heartbeat, his deadly sword slicing through the Anakites' enchanted ropes with ease. The ropes the monstrous watchmen had used were like no earthly ropes Phoebe had ever seen. They were not solid matter but seemed to flow and undulate, and were strong enough to subdue even the might of Cosain and his fellow warriors. Neam's sword, however, sliced through the cords as if they were cotton thread, and Phoebe was encouraged in her soul that even the strongest binds of darkness were no match for the strength of the light.

"Captain," exclaimed Neam. "Are you hurt? What happened?"

Cosain nodded as he rubbed the welts on his wrists where the molten ropes had been, and placed a strong hand on Neam's shoulder, perhaps in gratitude or perhaps to steady his great form after the trauma of what he and the other angelic warriors had just endured. Before he could respond to Neam's question, Trean spoke.

"It was my fault," murmured Trean, who had collapsed onto a flat rock where he sat, piercing blue eyes clouded with sorrow and his almost-white hair hanging mournfully around his drooped head. "I was not watchful enough, one of the Anakite watchmen caught me unaware, and I fell... I *fell*, *Neam!* Cosain and the others were trapped because they were trying to help me... I was so clumsy and so foolish..."

Phoebe's heart ached for the gentle giant who sat before her, so crestfallen and despondent; she wanted to rush over beside him and throw her arms around him and tell him that he was an incredible warrior and guardian, but sensed that it would not be appropriate right now, and she held back. Instead, Cosain, Solas, Dilis and Neam gathered around their dejected brother and assured with gentle but firm words of truth that he had not failed, and that the foe who had overcome him on this occasion was a fearsome force to be reckoned with.

"Besides," interjected Dilis. "Neam and Phoebe were able to turn this situation around, and it matters not who played which role in a victory – when one of us is victorious, we are *all* victorious, brother."

The tender vulnerability of which the imposing angelic warriors were capable brought tears to Phoebe's eyes, and she marvelled at the way in which they supported and preferred each other at all times.

"Brother," said Solas, looking at Trean with concern. "You are injured."

"It's nothing serious," said Trean, who was obviously putting on a brave face as he flinched when Solas tentatively examined a substantial wound on Trean's left leg. "I can continue on with you, it will not hold me back." The contrite warrior had taken great solace from his brothers' words of affirmation, and Phoebe noted that his head and shoulders had lifted so that he now more closely resembled his former noble self. The other angels genuinely felt no anger or resentment towards Trean, and Phoebe was impressed and deeply touched by their obvious respect for each other.

"Perhaps it will not," smiled Solas. "But Dilis can see to your wound before we venture into the Mooar Mountain. There is no need for you to soldier on wounded when we can rectify it here and now."

Trean smiled and nodded his agreement as Dilis came alongside him and drew his sword. As he placed it gently along Trean's wound, the injured warrior winced in pain, but as the sword's healing powers began to penetrate the wound, the blade glowed and radiated until the gash that had been sliced in Trean's leg began to knit back together. Phoebe marvelled as the angel's flesh healed and mended, and the wound was sealed up until there was nothing left of its existence.

"Better?" asked Dilis with a kind smile.

"Much better," replied Trean. "Thank you my brother."

Dilis offered Trean a strong hand and helped pull the great warrior up on to his feet. Trean put his full weight on the leg which just moments before could not have supported him, and gave out a whoop as he punched the air with his fist. "I'm ready to roll!" he exclaimed, smiling at his Captain and comrades. "Let's teach Captain Schnither and his ghouls a lesson they won't forget in a hurry!"

The other angels had all sustained minor wounds, inflicted largely by the cruel ropes which had bound them, but as Phoebe watched and marvelled their unblemished skin began to heal and regenerate until not a single tell-tale mark remained. She thought of the gnarly demons she had encountered, and recalled how every battle scar they had ever sustained remained on their leathery skin for all to see, and could only assume that goodness had a way of removing forever that which did not belong on ethereal bodies.

"Now brothers," said Cosain, aware of the need to keep moving. "We must get inside Mooar Mountain and find Ella; that is our priority. The Anakite guards will not remain frozen indefinitely; the effects of the pocket watch will wear off, albeit slowly, but our enemies are by no means out of the picture. Phoebe, Demetrius and Ella have many tasks ahead of them, the epitome of which will be sending Captain Schnither and his hordes back here where they belong through the Geata Gate in Darken Abbey. But we cannot do that until we have ensured the safety of Ella..." Cosain spoke directly to the angelic warriors assembled in front of him, "Remember, we made an oath to the Atoner that we would protect the chosen mortals at all costs, and while Ella remains in Malva's clutches, they *all* remain in danger."

Solas, Dilis, Trean and Neam nodded their understanding, then the angelic warriors and Phoebe made their way through the still open doorway into Mooar Mountain. As the great stone entryway slammed shut behind them Phoebe felt a familiar chill run through her body. With the closing of the door, all natural light was snuffed out like the extinguishing of a candle, and she found herself thrust back into the dank and gloomy underworld of the mountain. She involuntarily squeezed her fingers a little tighter around the small gold pocket watch in her hand and was very grateful for the comfort and reassurance it afforded her. She resolved never to let Cosain or the other angels out of her sight and was thankful for the just perceptible ethereal glow that radiated from their towering physiques as she followed them deeper into Mooar Mountain. The corridors were dark and claustrophobic, and the only light in the cavernous dungeon came from dimly glowing oil lamps scattered here and there along the maze of hallways. Phoebe wondered where Demetrius, Ernan and the other angels were. Had they traversed these bleak corridors before her? Maybe they were close by? Or maybe they hadn't even made it into the belly of the mountain... She found that all this conjecture served only to unsettle her, so Phoebe resolved to focus on the task at hand, and find Ella. She owed her that.

CHAPTER 17

DEMETRIUS'S heart was thudding so hard in his chest that he was certain anyone in close proximity to him *must* be able to hear it. He was following Ernan, Lasair, Maelis, Keane and Lachlan nervously along the last little stretch of musty corridor before they would round the final corner and encounter whatever ogres were awaiting them. Despite his best efforts to hold his nerve, Demetrius could not persuade his gasping breath to settle, and the more he tried to regulate his breathing, the more erratic it became. The thoughts that assailed his mind horrified him – what if the map didn't work and the demons saw him? Or what if it *did* work, and he really *was* invisible, but he *dropped* the map and was revealed in all his frailty in front of a hideous and powerful enemy with nowhere to run and nowhere to hide? *"Oh what if, what if,"* Demetrius chastised himself. *"Just stop trying to figure this all out and let it happen."*

Demetrius did his best to shrug off the gnawing negative thoughts and had to hurry to keep up with Ernan and the others. In the dim light he found it difficult to be sure that their concealed silhouettes were still in front of him. Conditions for the teenager were problematic at best, but he was convinced of the importance of the task at hand and even more certain that this was his and Phoebe's destiny, so he steeled himself and continued to move forward with a stubborn resolve that would not be dictated to by doubt or fear.

Lieutenant Ernan did not hold back as he led the angelic warriors along the corridor. Had they been visible, the little band, although small in number, would have made for a formidable sight with fiery swords drawn and celestial features set like flint. As they arrived unobserved in the small vestibule, Demetrius's heart began to thud with renewed vigour as he surveyed the scene laid out before him. Two large and intricately carved wooden doors had been set into one of the rocky walls of the vestibule. They looked to be ancient and Demetrius could only guess at how long they had been there. Millennia, he imagined. Despite his gnawing fear, it occurred to Demetrius to marvel at the beauty of these great doors – their carvings were complex and elaborate, and somehow they looked out of place in this dark cesspit that was the unholy headquarters of Abaddon the Defiler and his heinous minions. There was a large round doorknob made from burnished copper on each door, and Demetrius hoped that one of the angelic warriors would open one of the doors before he had to attempt it as he was unsure that he would even be able to fit his small human hands around the sizeable handle. Two dimly glowing oil lamps were lit, one on either side of the great doors, and they cast ghostly shadows along the craggy walls. But it was the creatures standing guard in front of the door that really took Demetrius's breath away. Four hideously huge beings, obviously not of human descent, were perched in the vestibule, guarding the doors. Each held a dull spear approximately six feet in length, but Demetrius was sure that despite appearances there was nothing dull whatsoever about the business end of these cruel weapons. The guards were hulking great monsters, who loosely resembled the form of a man in that each had two great arms, two burly legs, and a head, but they were far from human. It occurred to Demetrius that they were almost crocodilian in appearance, with a green serpentine tongue and pointed teeth that looked as though they might be able to cut through metal... or bone for that matter. For all their brawn, they did not appear to be overly intelligent, an impression that was reinforced when one randomly allowed his spear to slip from his gnarly grasp, striking his colleague on the head as it fell before clattering to the ground.

"Hey, watch it you great oaf!" growled the injured guard, rubbing his head with a scowl while the offender scrambled to retrieve his wayward spear. He was obviously petrified in case the clamour had disturbed his dark master on the other side of the great door, and watched for movement with baited breath until he was sure that Abaddon was not going to come out and punish him – or worse. As the great beast resumed his position to the right of the doorway, he heaved a heavy sigh of relief, and gripped his spear visibly tighter.

Demetrius had remained motionless as he watched the darkly comical scene unfold, and now he gulped back a lump in his throat as he and the angels prepared to move towards the great door and gain entry into Abaddon's chamber. Suddenly, one of the hideous sentries stood to attention and hissed at his fellow guards, "What was that?"

"What are you on about Grod? What was *what* you halfwit?"

"I heard something, Droch!" insisted Grod, then added with a snarl, "And don't call me a halfwit if you value your teeth!"

"Are you threatening me, *halfwit?*" jeered Droch, repeating the insult and squinting his eyes as he moved threateningly towards Grod.

"Why you great oaf..." Grod snarled at Droch, his lip curling upward at one side in a furious sneer. But just as he was about to show the mocking guard who was boss, Demetrius displaced a tiny pebble with the toe of his shoe and Grod stopped dead in his tracks, his eyes and ears straining.

"Grod's right," snarled the third guard, Gorach, who was also straining his ears and peering into the gloom for any sign of an intruder. "There *is* something out there. Listen."

Demetrius stood motionless and barely breathing. Just ahead of him Ernan and the other warriors had halted and were waiting, poised for battle but hoping that the guards would not investigate too extensively.

All four monstrous guards now stood deadly still, squinting around the gloomy vestibule and sniffing the air for any hint of an intruder. "There is definitely *something* out there," said Olc, the beastly fourth guard. "I feel it in my bones."

"*You feel it in your bones?*" jeered Gorach. "Why? Have you got magical bones? Can your *bones* tell me what I'm thinking right now?"

Grod and Droch snorted with laughter as Gorach poked fun at an infuriated Olc, who looked as if he wanted to end their mirth permanently. "I'll wipe those smirks off your ugly faces!" he threatened, shaking a chubby clenched fist at his belligerent colleagues, but his warning only served to make his fellow sentries guffaw all the more. As the four monstrous guards engaged in their ghoulishly comical stand-off, considering whether or not to start a proper fight, Ernan seized his chance and signalled for Lasair, Maelis, Keane, Lachlan and Demetrius to make their move. The angelic troops did not need to be told twice and they moved silently and unseen towards the great double doors to Abaddon's chamber. Lachlan reached the doors first and as Ernan nodded his consent, the great Viking-esque angel grasped the copper handle on the door on the right in his great hand, and turned it with a gentleness that belied his size, moving it as slowly as he possibly could in order to prevent alerting the warring guards. Demetrius and his angelic guardians knew collectively that it would be practically impossible to secure entry to Abaddon's chamber without notifying the guards to their presence, but they had agreed that they should get as far as possible before drawing any attention to themselves, and it seemed now that *this* was as far as they would be able to go unseen. Lachlan had turned the door handle as far as it would move and now he stood, holding it in position, awaiting Ernan's command to move forward. Ernan looked each of the angelic warriors squarely in the eye so that each was aware that this was the moment of truth, then he nodded to Lachlan, who put his shoulder to the heavy wooden door and heaved so that it swung slowly inward. The doors' old hinges creaked and groaned, and Demetrius held his breath as he awaited the inevitable wrath of the four monstrous guards. When their assault did not come, Demetrius glanced over his shoulder as he entered Abaddon's chamber and realised that the idiotic guards had been so busy squabbling noisily amongst themselves that they had failed to notice the intruders stealing into the forbidden room. Ernan and the other warriors were safely inside the gargantuan room when Olc looked up and realised that the great door had been opened.

"*Intruders!*" he roared, grabbing the spear which he had set aside during the squabble and lurching furiously towards Abaddon's chamber. "I *knew* it you fools! I *told* you! They must have arrived cloaked in invisibility! How could you have missed it? This is all your fault, you ridiculous excuses for watchmen!" The beast's angry words tumbled awkwardly from his mouth as he ran, mirroring his clumsy gallop towards the door.

The other gruesome guards quit their petty bickering instantaneously as if each had been jolted back to reality by some unseen electrical charge. They realised in unison that they had been duped, and reeled together in the direction of the open door like four great loose cannons. Inside Abaddon's clandestine chamber, Lachlan wasted no time in slamming the ancient door shut and locked it by slotting a huge wooden bar into the metal fittings half way up the door. Demetrius heaved an audible sigh of relief which was followed immediately by the realisation that although the angelic search party had been successful in locking the ghoulish guards *out*, they, by default, were also locked *in*. He looked anxiously around the enormous room and was well aware that their presence could not remain a secret for very long, as the enraged guards continued to hammer and pound on the wooden door, roaring their fury at the intruders. Demetrius glanced around the imposing room in which he and the angels found themselves, but could see very little through the smoky gloom. The room, like the rest of the Mooar Mountain, was dimly lit, and a bluish grey smog-like vapour rolled eerily across the floor, further diminishing Demetrius's ability to see very far in front of him. Demetrius realised that his and the angels' arrival here was no longer unheralded, and since Augustus had told him that the map's invisible qualities were only temporary, he unwrapped the map from around his shoulders, and folded it carefully before returning it securely to his hip pocket. Demetrius paused for a moment, awaiting the reappearance of Ernan, Lasair, Maelis, Keane and Lachlan when they too shed their invisibility. As the seconds ticked past concern grew in Demetrius's chest, and eventually he called out in a hushed whisper, "Ernan? Lachlan? *Anybody?*" Demetrius held his breath and waited for an answering whisper that never came, and the stark realisation that he had become separated from his angelic protectors caused a rush of blood to Demetrius's head so that he felt quite faint and had to put a hand to the damp stone wall to steady himself.

"*Okay, Dem,*" Demetrius counselled himself. "*There's no need to panic. Ernan and the others are in this room... somewhere. It's only a room... right? How big can it be? Definitely no need to panic...*"

He forced his racing thoughts to slow down to allow him

to formulate a plan, but nothing he could think of seemed to have any real substance. Ideas teased and danced through his mind, but very few of them made any logical sense. After what seemed like a lifetime, Demetrius made the decision to search out the Heavenly warriors. If they could not come to him, then he would go to them. He hoped that by now they would have shed their invisibility and he would find them without too much difficulty... although something told him that this may not be as straightforward as it sounded. He began to edge his way cautiously around the smoggy room, sticking as close to the walls as he could – at least with the solid stone wall at his back he could be fairly sure that no-one could launch a surprise attack from behind. Demetrius's heart was racing, and he wondered whether Abaddon and his dark hordes might possess a shark-like ability which would draw them irresistibly to the electric impulses he felt sure he must be giving off. He swallowed hard and continued to feel his way along the unyielding stone wall, calling out to Ernan and the other angels as loudly as he dared every now and then.

Just as Demetrius was beginning to wonder whether he was in fact alone in this great chamber, something caused the gaseous vapours to stir just off to his left. He froze, pinned somewhere between waning hope and waxing terror, and pressed his body as tightly as he could to the cold stone wall in the desperate hope that perhaps the gloom would afford him some camouflage. Demetrius waited; he was afraid to look in the direction of the movement, and yet he could not stop himself from peering into the darkness, desperate to establish who – or *what* – was here with him. The rolling mist in the room rose and fell again, as if the whole chamber was breathing, and Demetrius was now in no doubt that someone was approaching. He twisted up his face and narrowed his eyes, desperately longing for the fog to part and Ernan's broad form to appear. But Ernan did not appear. Nor did Lachlan, or any of the other angelic warriors. Much to Demetrius's surprise and confusion, a tall, noble figure glided silently into view. Far from a hideous beast exuding evil, an immaculately groomed figure in the form of a man seemed to float towards Demetrius with a sophistication and grace that mesmerised the teenager. The man was elegantly dressed, his pristine purple pin striped suit almost ostentatious in its perfection, and his shoulder length jet black hair shone, even in the dull light afforded by this gloomy chamber. As the stranger drew closer, something in his unblemished features struck a chord with Demetrius, and it occurred to him that this individual was almost... well, *angelic*. In the oppressive darkness, a gold ring set with a huge ruby sparkled on the forefinger of the man's left hand, and as Demetrius studied the jewel, mesmerised by its opulent beauty, the stranger spoke.

"Demetrius, I assume," the stranger said with a warm voice that flowed like honey. "I have been wondering when you would arrive. It was inevitable really... I mean, did you honestly expect to just creep in here and take *her?*" There was a sinister flash in the stranger's eyes as he spoke the words which unnerved Demetrius and made the skin on his arms crawl. "And as for those piffling buffoons..."

Demetrius wasn't sure who this striking stranger was, or exactly to whom he was referring, but the words from Brother Bennett's journal suddenly and inexplicably resounded in his head – '*...you must be wise about who you trust. The dark minions have the ability to masquerade as angels of light, and their shapeshifting ability renders them difficult enough to ascertain. Things – and people – are not always as they seem. But I believe that you will know the difference, Reader, if you listen to your heart and trust your gut. You are wiser than you know...*' Demetrius could not be sure which oppositional entity he was dealing with here in this claustrophobic chamber, but his gut told him not to trust the well presented stranger in front of him, and he decided to take heed.

The tall stranger had glided effortlessly ever closer to

Demetrius, and was now only inches from his face as he continued; "Did you really think that you could trus-s-st those bumbling *angels-s-s?*" The words slithered and hissed from the stranger's lips, and for the first time Demetrius caught sight of his eyes which were grey and devoid of emotion, and showed no sign of light behind them. "As soon as they got you here, they des-s-serted you! They are of no use to you, *Demetrius-s-s*. All this time you have been fooled by them... But it's not too late, Demetrius... *I* would forgive your foolishness-s-s and you would be welcomed here as *my friend...*" Demetrius could feel the stranger's icy breath on his face, and the outrageously rancid odour confirmed that this peculiar individual could not be human.

In an instant, Demetrius remembered the little pair of metal rimmed glasses in his pocket. Before the stranger in front of him could protest, Demetrius had pulled the glasses out and placed them squarely over his eyes, with the narrow bridge resting on his nose. As Demetrius examined the stranger through Augustus's glasses, he gasped in horror as the creature's true appearance became apparent. There before him towered a fearsome and imposing being, some nine feet tall with four huge black wings extended behind him, and blood red lips which were now screeching at him in unbridled fury. The soothing voice had been replaced by a harsh and hacking roar, and Demetrius could only assume from the creature's astounding awfulness that this must be Abaddon the Defiler, Dark Prince and ruler of the Mooar Mountain. He turned his head away as if by so doing he could lessen the horror that was raining down on him incessantly and closed his eyes tight, awaiting the inevitable.

"Why do you cower and avert your eyes-s-s, mortal?" hissed Abaddon, who had realised that his cover as a mysterious stranger had been blown and had reverted back to his fearsome true self. "Do you dare ignore me? Do you not know who I am?" His terrible voice had risen to a tumultuous roar, and Demetrius felt that his hammering heart might burst out of his chest. Summoning all his strength and courage, he opened his eyes slowly and turned to look Abaddon square in the face.

"Yes, I know who you are," whispered Demetrius. "Are Abaddon the Defiler..."

"*S-s-s-o*," jeered Abaddon, leaning threateningly close to the trembling boy. "You are not so s-s-stupid after all. Your knowledge is quite impressive... for a pathetic human..."

"I hadn't finished my sentence," said Demetrius with just a hint of trembling in his voice. He stood fully upright now, shoulders squared, his eyes never averting their gaze from Abaddon's. "You are Abaddon the Defiler, this is your dark and seedy realm... and I have come here to rescue my friend and see to it that you and your army are banished from Darken Abbey and the island on which I live... forever!"

Abaddon had obviously not been expecting such bravery – or foolishness – from one so young and so *mortal*, and his cackling laughter reverberated around his dismal chamber long after his mirth at Demetrius's audacity had subsided.

CHAPTER 18

A S Phoebe and her angelic protectors ventured deeper
into Mooar Mountain, Phoebe was perpetually aware
that their path led them ever downwards. Their descent was
gentle, not sudden, but every step led them further away
from the outdoors and made any possible escape route
longer and more arduous. Phoebe struggled with a growing
sense of claustrophobia, and it pained her to think that poor
Ella had been held here, alone in this darkness, for so long.
She determinedly clamped her teeth together and resolutely
followed Cosain and the other warriors along the seemingly
endless maze of dark, damp corridors, using both hands to
guide and steady her uncertain descent.

After a few minutes Cosain, who was heading up the little
search party, raised his hand and motioned for the others to
stop. "Listen," he whispered, "Up ahead..." Phoebe strained
her ears to ascertain what it was that Cosain had heard. They
had paused just before the end of the corridor, and she could
see up ahead that it opened out on to a wider passageway
which ran adjacent to the one she and the angels were in.
Suddenly, the distant sound of running feet and swishing
leathery wings crescendoed to a nearby roar and Phoebe
watched aghast as a flurry of black creatures raced along the
main corridor, apparently all headed for the same destination.

"Ernan and the others must have infiltrated Abaddon's

chamber," Cosain said with a sense of urgency in his voice. "But the guards must have rumbled them. Quickly, they need our help, we've got to get to them!"

Phoebe instinctively squeezed the little gold pocket watch in her hand. For all its apparent insignificant if offered her welcome reassurance and Phoebe was sure that it would prove its worth again in the not too distant future. As she jogged along to keep pace with Cosain and the other warriors, she found herself feeling almost excited by the prospect of finding Ella, and somehow knew deep within herself that however treacherous things might become in these next minutes, she was a Light Bringer, and ultimately she was on the winning side.

At the end of the twisty passageway, the rescue group paused again as Cosain checked around the corner in the direction of the stampeding demons. The coast was clear now, so Cosain led Phoebe and the other angels stealthily along the hallway until they came to a final bend in the path, around which was the vestibule where the protesting demons had now congregated, jostling and squabbling just outside Abaddon's mysterious personal quarters. Cosain looked on as the four sentries stationed at the great doors argued and protested in loud voices, vigorously deflecting any culpability away from themselves and pointing instead at each other, blaming the recent angelic infiltration on everything from Grod's butter fingers in dropping his spear, to Droch's deafness in failing to hear the intruders approaching.

There were far too many demons hustling and jostling in the vestibule for Cosain to even consider his warriors taking them on. Yes, there was a chance that the Heavenly combatants could overpower them, but at what cost? Cosain would not risk having any of his brothers – let alone his young mortal ward – captured or wounded, and in the time it would take them to overpower the rioting demons, Malva could have seized his chance and moved Ella away from where he was holding her. Instead, Cosain turned towards Phoebe, ready to issues instructions, but she already knew instinctively what it was that she needed to do. Before Cosain could speak, Phoebe nodded intuitively at the great warrior, and waved the golden pocket watch at him. Cosain smiled despite the gravity of the situation and nodded at the girl – despite her frail humanity, Phoebe was growing in wisdom and bravery, and he felt honoured to be able to assist her in fulfilling her destiny.

Without further instruction, Phoebe took a few paces forward, around the corner and into the demon-laden vestibule. She could scarcely believe what she was doing, and wondered whether this was maybe just a dream from which she would soon awaken. For a few seconds, the squabbling horde did not even notice her presence, so she put her forefinger and her thumb between her lips and blew, sending out a shrill whistle that caused several hideous beasts to throw their gnarly hands up to cover their ears while their misshapen faces contorted in discomfort. There was a brief moment of stunned silence, as if Phoebe's whistle had startled the evil minions into inactivity for a nanosecond. On turning their confused attention to Phoebe they were apparently unsure of what they were seeing and a hundred pairs of evil eyes surveyed the young mortal with confusion and contempt. The little oasis of calm was brief and fleeting and as suddenly as the demons had been silenced, they began to protest and screech again, lumbering noisily en masse towards the side of the vestibule where Phoebe stood, resolute and unflinching. The approaching ogres were so transfixed on Phoebe that they were taken entirely by surprise when Cosain, Solas, Dilis, Trean and Neam stepped around the corner, and in the split second that it took for them to register the presence of the Atoner's angelic warriors, Phoebe had flipped open the front cover of the pocket watch, and watched as the dark advancing enemies froze solid before her, several of them wearing stunned expressions which were almost laughable. Demons of all sizes and shapes froze mid-stride, some with ferocious weapons flailing mid-air, some with their jaws gaping open in silenced rage, and still others whose clenched fists now hung suspended in space as though weightless. It was a bizarre and motionless scene that Phoebe now surveyed through wide and wondering eyes.

"Well done, Little One," said Cosain, laying a mighty hand gently on Phoebe's shoulder. "You are growing all the time in courage and ferocity, and the awareness of who you are as a Light Bringer of the Atoner is becoming ingrained in your make up... I can see it, Phoebe."

Phoebe smiled up at the fearsome warrior. She knew in her soul that he was right, and although she did not fully understand the changes in herself, she knew that she was where she was meant to be.

"Come brothers, we must not become complacent. We have taken care of this mob, but there are myriads more in the recesses of Mooar Mountain and we don't want to be standing here when *they* arrive!"

Cosain led the way across the vestibule, weaving around numerous demons whose bodies had been frozen in time, but who watched his every move with furious eyes. '*If looks could kill...*' Phoebe thought as she followed quickly after Cosain, with Solas, Dilis, Trean and Neam bringing up the rear. They did not hesitate at the door of Abaddon's chamber, but pushed open one of the two great doors then moved silently across the threshold and into Abaddon's impressive private quarters. Phoebe gasped at the cavernous size of the gloomy room, and was aware that the rolling vapours meant that she probably wasn't even seeing half of it. Cosain beckoned Phoebe and the other angels closer.

"Stick together," he whispered. "There is something amiss here, something is not quite right. We gained entry too easily... It is just *too quiet*."

Cosain led his troop and Phoebe further into Abaddon's chamber; they moved as quickly as they dared but with the greatest of care, for Cosain fully expected the room to be rife with snares and perils. Suddenly, a crashing, deafening boom caused the angelic warriors to spin around in the direction of the doorway, and Phoebe was horrified to find that the door through which they had just entered had been slammed shut, and a great wooden beam dropped in place across two metal latches so that the doors were locked and they were, in effect, trapped. This fact had barely registered with Phoebe when the dark swirling mists that filled the room were ripped apart, and four hideous beasts came crashing towards the angelic rescuers. Phoebe recognised the contorted faces of their assailants from Darken Abbey – Bova, Eenu, Jarrda and Yigno. She recalled Cosain's instructions to his troop back in the abbey – '*take no prisoners*' – but judging by the fact that the four gnarly demons were very obviously alive and well, she deduced that they had somehow wriggled free of the angels' grasp and had returned here to their mountainous headquarters.

In the murky dinginess of the room, Phoebe imagined that engaging the tricky ghouls would be a difficult task, but Cosain and the other warriors wasted no time in locking horns with their assailants and in mere seconds sparks were flying as fiery angelic swords clashed violently with dark demonic blades. Neam had pushed Phoebe gently but firmly out of the way and she waited now, hunkered down close to the cold walls, doing her best not to draw any unnecessary attention to herself. The skirmish which ensued was ferocious, and although the dark beasts were outnumbered four to five, they were proving to be worthy adversaries, and Cosain and his troops were forced to employ all their skill and swordsmanship.

For several long minutes, mighty angel swords clashed with heinous demon weapons, and in truth the battle could have gone either way at any moment. Phoebe was beginning to wonder whether Cosain and the other ethereal warriors might actually be overcome, when the shadowy mists surrounding the battling opponents were lit up with an unearthly light of purest white as Ernan, Lasair, Maelis, Keane and Lachlan exploded forward through the smog and joined their Heavenly brothers as they rallied together against the powers of darkness. With these new additions to the mêlée, the end result instantaneously became a foregone conclusion, and Bova, Eenu, Jarrda and Yigno realised immediately that they no longer stood a chance of gaining the upper hand. The gnarly creatures threw down their swords like petulant children and reluctantly raised their twisted arms in furious defeat. They were wheezing and panting from the enormous effort they had made in battle, and strange hissing noises were emanating from Eenu who was clearly incensed at having to admit defeat. As the ten angelic warriors encircled the four conquered demons, Ernan addressed his captain.

"What shall we do with them, Cosain? Should we send them straight to the Abyss? Surely that is exactly what they deserve!"

Cosain, breathing heavily from the exertion of his encounter with the four angry beasts, hesitated, weighing up his options before he spoke. "No," he said very definitely. "We may need them. They may be privy to information which can help us. Tie them up for now."

"*Pah!*" spat Eenu, his emerald green eyes sparking with rage and hate as he surveyed the Captain of the Heavenly army. "If you think any one of us will ever help *you...*" He squinted his eyes as he sneered at his captors. "...then you're even *stupider* than I thought!" Inspired by their ring leader's bravado, Bova, Jarrda and Yigno joined in with his jeering. "Yeah," sneered Jarrda. "*Stupid angels!* How do you think you and that puny girl are ever going to get out of here? This is *Abaddon's* chamber – you don't get out of here unless *he* says so!"

"You should have stuck to playing your harp, *Captain!*" jeered Bova, whose quip obviously struck a chord with his fellow demons and the four of them cackled and guffawed with laughter until Yigno had to hold his sides.

The angelic warriors had maintained a dignified silence whilst the dark rascals taunted and jeered, binding them with triple stranded silver rope that each warrior carried on the leather belt around his waist. But now Solas stepped forward as his comrades continued to bind their captives. "You will learn, minions, that we have no need for harps, and the weapons that we do carry are much less amusing than you seem to think." The great warrior looked taller than his seven foot height as he towered over the captive demons, who had suddenly sobered up and stopped their raucous laughter. "You *will* remember the Atoner and Who it is you defy..." said Solas, as he drew his glowing sword from its sheath. Bova, Eenu, Jarrda and Yigno recoiled in fear as the imposing angelic being brought his sword close to their cowering bodies, then roared in pain as he branded each one with the tip of his blade, leaving a smouldering imprint that resembled a shield with the crest of the Atoner in its centre.

"*No-o-o!*" screeched Yigno as he recoiled in pain and horror at the brand that had been indelibly tattooed on his leathery skin. "We cannot remain here in Mooar Mountain with the crest of the Atoner on our skin! *What have you done?* We will be exiled – for all eternity! Where will we go? There will be no place for us in all of the galaxies, you have condemned us to wander displaced and shunned for all time!"

"That is as it may be, but you *will* remember the authority of the Atoner," said Cosain, as he secured the final knot in the silver ropes which now bound his enemies hand and foot. The angelic troops turned to remove their captives from the room, when Phoebe spoke up.

"*Demetrius...*" she said, panic rising in her voice despite her best efforts to contain it. "Ernan, *where's Dem?*"

Phoebe had assumed that Ernan and the others had left Demetrius in a safe place while they assisted Cosain, Solas, Dilis, Trean and Neam, but now that the skirmish had abated and Demetrius still had not emerged from his hiding place, grave concern engulfed Phoebe like a cold fog rolling unhindered over a hill.

Lieutenant Ernan exhaled a long and troubled breath and furrowed his brow as he turned towards Phoebe. "Demetrius..." he paused, looking back at Cosain. "We... Well... we lost him."

Phoebe felt her head reel and her stomach lurch as Ernan's stark words hit her like rocks. She placed a hand on the stone wall to steady herself, and focused hard on not being sick. "You... You *lost* him..? But how?" she squeaked, the voice she heard barely reminiscent of her own. "When?"

"We gained entry to this room using invisibility," said Ernan, explaining to Phoebe and those of her guardians who did not already know how they had entered the chamber together but somehow Demetrius had been separated from them soon afterwards. "We really have searched every inch of this room, Cosain," concluded Ernan, his dark eyes mournful. "The boy just is not here..."

"Not *every inch...* "

The unfamiliar faceless voice that cut through the semi-darkness was smooth and sweet, almost lyrical, and Phoebe knew that it did not belong to any of the angelic warriors standing in front of her. She strained her eyes into the misty air and blinked in stunned silence as the fog rolled back like vaporous waves and a striking form emerged from its depths.

"Abaddon..." said Cosain with something almost reminiscent of reverence in his voice. He straightened to his full height and placed his right hand securely on the formidable sword that hung in its scabbard by his side.

"Ah, nothing gets past you *Cos-s-sain*, does it?" Abaddon's voice oozed sarcasm and his lopsided grin made him look insane. "Who were you expecting to see in here, eh? Father *Chris-s-s-tmas?*"

As Abaddon the Defiler emerged further from the swirling mists it became clear that he was not alone. Trailing in his wake was a downcast Demetrius, hands bound with the same molten steel ropes which the Anakite watchmen had used to bind Cosain, Solas, Dilis and Trean outside the mountain. The sight of her best friend bound and shackled by Abaddon made anger bubble up unbridled in Phoebe's heart, and she sprang forward as if to tackle Abaddon single handedly. In an instant, Cosain had blocked her path. "Phoebe," he said in whispered tones, although his voice carried an authority that she did not dare contradict. "You can no more take on the might of Abaddon the Defiler than an ant could hold back the tide. *Trust me*, Little One..."

The Captain of the Heavenly army turned back to his dark nemesis. "What do you want, Abaddon? Don't play games with me. Tell me your terms for I have no doubt that you have them worked out in great detail."

A scornful smile spread slowly across Abaddon's dreadful face. "*Hmmm...*" he growled in low soft tones. "That is the ques-s-stion. *What do I want..?*" And he drummed the four bony fingers of his right hand slowly and deliberately on his angular chin. "You know precis-s-sely what I want, *Cos-s-sain*... And I am sure that you will remember Malva's request, little Miss Wren – we want what I know you have... I must have the Key of Esse." Abaddon paused as his eyes searched first Phoebe's face, then Cosain's. "But perhaps..." he drooled slowly, "Perhaps the real question here ought to be what do *you* want, Cos-s-sain? Obviously, I know *who* you want – although *why* you would want these puny mortals is beyond my comprehension. So tell me, *Captain*," Abaddon grinned at Cosain with scarcely veiled malice in his flint grey eyes. "Why is it that you would risk life and limb to come into *my* abode to rescue these insignificant children of men, *hmmm?* Surely if you're so fond of the little mortals, there are millions-s-s more where these came from? If it is a pet you want, can you not just *take your pick?*" Abaddon spat the words as he formed them as if the mere mention of mortals – the pinnacle of the Atoner's creation – offended him.

Cosain looked his nemesis unflinchingly in the eyes. "It is Demetrius and Ella that I seek, Abaddon. Obviously, I can see that you have Demetrius in your... *care,* and I imagine that you can tell me the whereabouts of Ella. Why don't you save us both some time and energy and just hand them over, then we'll all be out of your hair, Abaddon. Like you say, they're just mortals – hardly of any use to you."

"Ah, *Cos-s-sain*, you do ins-s-sult me! The mortal children are of no use to me, you are correct – but for you to come here to Mooar Mountain, and bring your *big brave band of brothers-s-s* with you..." Abaddon paused for effect as he smirked at the angelic warriors whose eyes were all fixed on him. "Well, that tells me that these particular mortals-s-s are not insignificant at all... Obviously, the Atoner has lofty plans-s-s for them – and I'll bet my life that those plans won't benefit *me* in any way!"

The mere mention of the Atoner seemed to agitate Abaddon immensely, causing him to twitch and wriggle as if he was being attacked by some unseen stinging bee.

"What are these mortals-s-s, Cosain? *Who* are they? Surely they can't possibly be..."

Abaddon paused abruptly and squinted his steely eyes, then opened them wide in realisation as he glared first at Demetrius and then at Phoebe.

"*Aha!*" he shouted, his tone almost gleeful. "These pathetic little creatures-s-s are *Light Bringers!* I'm right, aren't I *Cos-s-sain?* The Atoner has selected *three teenage mortals* to be Light Bringers to Darken Abbey! What an *ins-s-sult!* Does He think my forces are *that* easily abated? Surely He could have selected opponents worthy of me?"

Abaddon's dulcet tones had dropped to a dull roar and the fury that he felt had been translated into his voice which now boomed and reverberated off the cold stone walls of his chamber making it seem to Phoebe that he had them entirely surrounded. His guttural voice sounded from every side as he continued: "Well, the Atoner will s-s-see just how mis-s-sguided He has been! Darken Abbey is *mine,* and I will do with it what I pleas-s-se! *He* won't stop me; *you* won't stop me; *Jack and Eva Wren* won't stop me – and you can be *s-s-sure* that *mere mortal children* won't s-s-stop me! I *will* have the Key of Esse and it shall be mine to use as I pleas-s-se for all eternity! I will take the missing piece – and what is more, I will *keep* the children! They will belong to me as will Darken Abbey – you cannot have it, and the Atoner will not have it!"

Before Cosain or any of the others could react, Abaddon vanished back into the undulating grey fog, hauling Demetrius unceremoniously along after him and in the blink of an eye the two were gone, encased once more by the putrid vapours.

"*Dem!*" Phoebe screamed as she lunged at the space where just seconds before Abaddon the Defiler and Demetrius had stood. But she was too late. The Dark Master and his helpless captive were gone, with no physical sign that either had ever been there, and Phoebe had no idea whether she would ever see her best friends again. As Cosain moved to comfort the frantic teenager she could do nothing more than clench her fists, bury her face in her protector's side and weep hot relentless tears of frustration and fear.

CHAPTER 19

FOR a few moments, Phoebe was utterly inconsolable. It was as if all the adventure and trauma and utter craziness of the last few weeks had suddenly become too much for her to bear and she sobbed until Cosain's garment was damp with her agonised tears. The other angels stood motionless, heads bowed and swords sheathed. Seeing Phoebe so distraught was difficult for them to bear, and yet each knew that in this moment there was nothing any of them could do to console her. Dilis in particular found Phoebe's angst difficult to watch, and the youngest of the warriors had to turn his head away as his own eyes filled with sympathetic tears which threatened to overflow down his noble face.

Eventually, Phoebe's sobs began to subside and she straightened and wiped her eyes with the back of her hand. She worked hard to regain her composure then turned and looked up at Cosain through embarrassed, lowered eyes.

"It's.. I.."

Phoebe struggled to get the words out through the racked breaths that escaped her throat despite her best attempts to keep them in.

"I could have saved him, Cosain... I could have saved Demetrius! I should have used the watch. *Why* did I not use the watch? Then Dem would be here with us and we'd be on our way to find Ella and get out of here. But I didn't *think!* I just froze, Cosain... Or that cursed key, why didn't I just give Abaddon what he wanted, maybe he would have given Ella and Dem back... This is all my fault!"

There was kindness but also an unmistakable firmness in Cosain's voice as he responded to his young ward: "No Phoebe, this is *not* your fault, you must never believe that. Abaddon has the ability to implant lies and half-truths in your mind, and here in Mooar Mountain his powers and abilities are at their strongest. He *wants* you to think that you failed somehow, that you let Demetrius down – but know this Phoebe... *You have not failed anyone in any way.* You have a destiny to fulfil, set out for you by the Atoner himself, and you are exactly where you are meant to be. Besides," Cosain relaxed his shoulders and unfurrowed his brow. "The little pocket watch would not have worked against Abaddon. Even if you had tried to use it, he is just too powerful; it would have had no more effect on him than a bucket of water could quench the sun. And had you given Abaddon the missing piece of the key – well, he would simply have taken it from you, and kept Demetrius and Ella regardless. No, you were right to hold on to the key, it will give us leverage. Do not fret, Little One – we may have conceded a battle, but victory in this war will ultimately be ours."

Phoebe sniffed and kicked awkwardly at a small stone with the toe of her shoe. She looked up at her angelic protectors sheepishly, embarrassed by her recent emotional outburst, but found only concern and fondness on each ethereal face. Their understanding settled her, and she chided herself for worrying that they would think anything but the best of her. She loved that about Cosain and the others – they never criticised or scorned her for being a frail mortal, but always supported and encouraged her with the purest of intentions.

"Thanks guys," Phoebe said quietly, chewing nervously on her lower lip. "You've been very patient with me - again."

Keane smiled kindly at the young girl before him. "We've all been on the receiving end of patience at some point or another, Phoebe, don't ever think otherwise. And we're totally committed to helping you – the Atoner has entrusted you to us, we won't fail you... or Him."

Encouraged and uplifted by Cosain's and Keane's truth-filled words, Phoebe sucked in a deep breath and readied herself again for the off. She smiled weakly at Cosain, telling him without words that she was okay and ready for whatever the next step was. Cosain nodded his understanding before rounding up his troops.

"Abaddon knows that Demetrius is important to us," he said thoughtfully. "This means that wherever that fiendish trickster has taken him, Demetrius is at least safe for now – of that much I am sure. Abaddon won't risk injuring Demetrius when he knows he can potentially use him as leverage. For now, I suggest we move to find Ella." Cosain paused and looked directly at Phoebe. "She was here, in this chamber..."

"How can you be sure she was in this room, Captain?" asked Neam, his bright blue eyes curious but trusting as he voiced the question that was on Phoebe's mind.

Cosain raised his left hand, which was rolled into a loose fist. As he uncurled his fingers, a small red object glittered in the dull light of the room. Phoebe gasped. "Ella's hair clip! She *was* here!"

Cosain nodded and continued, "Yes, she was here. Malva must have moved her when you arrived, Ernan. But that means that she cannot be far away, and we are definitely on the right track. We must locate and secure Ella, then find Demetrius and get out of Mooar Mountain. We have lost the advantage of the demons being oblivious to our presence – this may make our task more difficult, but it is definitely still achievable."

As he spoke, Cosain moved towards the great doors of Abaddon's chambers, and pried up the beams which had been closed over the doors and heaved them both open. In the vestibule beyond, the beastly guards and dark creatures were still frozen solid, their frustration and rage glaring out through their unblinking eyes. Maelis exited Abaddon's chamber hauling Bova, Eenu, Jarrda and Yigno behind him. The fuming gargoyles had writhed and struggled against their bonds, and were now visibly exhausted by their futile efforts. Their heads hung low in shame and frustration, and each hideous face was a mask of furious resignation. Their newly branded shoulders were still raw with the crest of the Atoner and it was clear that this holy mark was causing the monstrous creatures more pain than any war wound ever had. Maelis found a clear spot in the packed vestibule where he deposited the four raging creatures.

"Now, Phoebe," he said with a raised eyebrow. "Let's get this little gang out of harm's way, shall we?"

Phoebe lifted the gold pocket watch in her right hand, and pointed it in the direction of Bova, Eenu, Jarrda and Yigno as she opened its front cover. Despite their renewed screeching and thrashing, the four demons were helpless against the watch's mysterious powers and they each froze solid with curses and obscenities still rolling from their purple lips.

"That'll teach you to mess with my friends, you *goons!*" Phoebe exclaimed with more bravado than she may have shown had the monsters not been immobilised, then she turned curtly on her heel and followed Cosain and the others out of the vestibule and along another corridor which seemed to lead deeper still into the forsaken mountain.

It was eerily quiet as the rescue team made its way further into Mooar Mountain and the silence unnerved Phoebe somewhat despite her best efforts to remain calm and focused. She wished desperately that she had the advantage of having Brother Eli's map in their possession, but persuaded herself that having Cosain lead the way was better than a faded old piece of paper anyway. Cosain and his troops were battle ready, with their swords drawn and their eyes peeled. Obviously they weren't taking any chances.

After what seemed like a winding descent of many miles – but was in fact probably no more than a few hundred metres – Cosain signalled for the group to halt as he beckoned Lieutenant Ernan to his side. The pair conversed in hushed tones for a few seconds before Cosain addressed the group: "Phoebe; brothers... Up ahead lies the Croi Chamber, the nerve centre of Mooar Mountain. This will be the most heavily guarded area in the entire Mountain, and Ernan and I agree that it is the most likely holding place for Demetrius, and possibly even Ella as well." Cosain paused for an instant and his jaw jerked almost imperceptibly before he continued. "We have located the Croi Chamber – that is progress, and you will all agree that we have come too far to stop now. However, it is here that our task becomes... well, *tricky*. Abaddon knows that we are here, he knows that we will not leave without Demetrius and Ella, and he will have assumed that I would bring you to this point. In other words, he will be ready for us... He will be *more* than ready." Cosain's golden eyes took on an intensity which Phoebe had never seen before and she noticed that his already fierce grip on his sword tightened involuntarily. "Brothers, this will be the fight of our lives. Abaddon knows that there is more at stake here than just the lives of three young mortals. He knows that if we can retrieve Demetrius and Ella and return to Darken Abbey, then his reign of darkness in the area will be jeopardised. But we have sworn to assist and protect these young Light Bringers, and we must fulfil our oath to the Atoner. Are you with me brothers?"

One by one, Solas, Dilis, Trean, Neam, Lasair, Maelis, Keane, Lachlan and Ernan all placed their right arms silently across their mighty chests so that their clenched fists lay over their hearts. As one, the imposing warriors nodded their loyalty to their noble Captain and to the Atoner. Cosain turned then to Phoebe, who suddenly felt very small and puny in the spotlight of his gaze. "And what about you, Phoebe Wren?" the Captain of the Heavenly army asked softly. "Are you with me now, at this most challenging of times? Do not feel afraid or ashamed if you are not. I will understand if you want to turn back. No-one will think you any less brave."

Phoebe stood in silence for a moment. Although she could scarcely imagine what might lie ahead of her, she knew that the battle which would ensue would probably make every demon and every furore she had encountered to date pale into insignificance. The enormity of it all made her stomach churn and her knees wobble. But she turned her thoughts to her friends; dear sweet Ella and brave, kind Demetrius, and then her decision was made. Without further hesitation, the teenager turned to Cosain and declared, "Yes, Cosain. Yes, I'm with you. And I'm sticking with you until we see this thing through!"

The Captain of the Heavenly Guard smiled his approval before turning back to his fellow warriors. "Then let us agree our strategy, for there is not one moment to lose."

CHAPTER 20

IT did not take long for Cosain and Ernan to agree their plan of action with the rest of the angelic warriors. Cosain's intentions were crystal clear and unmistakably straightforward – infiltrate the Croi Chamber, neutralise the inevitable dark resistance, retrieve Demetrius and Ella, and retreat out of the Mooar Mountain as quickly as possible. It all sounded relatively simple, yet Phoebe knew that executing the plan would be anything but easy.

The angelic bodyguards were edgy and on high alert as they moved silently towards the elusive Croi Chamber. Phoebe had been placed firmly at the back of the approaching group, with Neam as the only rearguard. Cosain had not offered her any alternative, but now as she crept along behind her protectors she was very glad of the dense wall of defence they afforded her. Phoebe wondered why the angels did not employ invisibility in an effort to buy them some extra time, and concluded that the situation must have escalated to the point where a few additional minutes really would not make any difference to the outcome. She wondered what might be in store for them in the mysterious Croi Chamber, and could only imagine what they might find there. But she did not have to wonder for very long.

Cosain did not hesitate or slow his pace as he approached the Croi Chamber, but as he and his troops resolutely rounded a bend in the path, swords raised, defiant battle cry on their lips, and expecting to be met with the fury of a thousand demon warriors, they were met instead with absolute darkness and a silence so thick and deafening that Cosain could hear his own heartbeat. As Phoebe and the others caught up on their Captain, they realised that he had stopped in his tracks, obviously caught off guard by the pitch black and the silence that had met him where he had expected an explosion of sulphur and screeching and flashing red eyes. The smell of smoke from very recently snuffed out wall lamps hung in the stale air, and little plumes of undulating grey vapours were just visible against the blackness.

"Captain?" enquired Ernan in hushed tones, although in the obsidian blackness he could not be entirely sure to whom his question was addressed. Cosain was not far away however, and on hearing his lieutenant's voice he immediately issued the order, "*Retreat! It's an ambush. Move back – now.*" But before Ernan or any of the other warriors could take even a single step back towards the relative light of the gloomy passageway there was an explosion of flame and a loud crack as an unseen creature relit one of the extinguished wall lamps, initiating a chain reaction along the damp stone walls which saw eight other wall lamps blaze back to life in quick succession. The hallway exploded into blood red light as what looked like an infinite number of gnarly monsters sprang to life from the shadows and dark recesses outside the Croi Chamber, and lurched en masse towards Cosain and his warriors. Phoebe gasped as the eerie light revealed the full horror of the monsters which had been hiding in the darkness awaiting the arrival of the angels. There were creatures of every shape and size; some she had seen before, most she had not, and many she hoped she would never have to see again. The evil beings had succeeded in catching Cosain off guard, and the simultaneous glee glinting from a thousand red eyes was unmistakable.

In a heartbeat, Cosain, Solas, Dilis, Trean, Neam, Lasair, Maelis, Keane, Lachlan and Ernan had gathered themselves and rushed headlong into the furore, their celestial blades burning fiery white as they cut and swooped. In the upheaval of the unexpected, Phoebe found herself jostled and pushed, bumping between strong angelic bodies, cold stone walls and leathery demon wings. This was the first time she had ever seen Cosain anything other than in complete control, and the chaotic commotion around her was confusing and frightening. In the midst of the mêlée as the angelic guardians struggled to regain the upper hand, Neam rushed forward to assist his captain and Phoebe was knocked to her knees. She instinctively stretched out her hands to steady herself as she fell and to her horror the little gold pocket watch tumbled from her fingers as they made violent contact with the damp stone floor. The watch bounced its way across the uneven floor, somehow avoiding being crushed beneath stampeding demon feet, with Phoebe clutching desperately at it as it rolled further from her grasp. She kept her head low and crawled forward between dozens of burly legs, winding a path through ever jostling angels and demons in pursuit of the little pocket watch. Her knees and the palms of her hands were grazed and sore, and she knew that crawling further into the midst of the battle was not a wise thing to do, but the need to reclaim the magical watch far outweighed her fear of being trampled.

The dull red light in the heart of the Mooar Mountain did not make Phoebe's quest to retrieve the pocket watch any easier, but after a few moments of dodging demons and avoiding angels she spotted the small golden object lying where it had come to rest in a small crack between the floor and the stone walls. Her heart made a little somersault of gladness at this tiny victory, and she reached forward to secure the watch. Phoebe knew that once the little timepiece was back in her possession, she could open it and freeze the enemy demons in time, and given what she could see of the battle, it seemed that Cosain and his brothers could use the help. Her fingers had barely made contact with the watch's gold casing when she felt an enormous hand grab her roughly by her left ankle. Phoebe did not have time to turn around to see who had grabbed her, but she knew from the talon-like claws digging into her skin that it was not one of her angel guards who had found her. Despite the pain caused by the vice-like grip, Phoebe made one last desperate attempt to grab the time-stopping pocket watch. She was so close now, so close... Retrieving the watch could change everything, but before she could secure it Phoebe found herself hauled off the ground and swung unceremoniously through the air until she came face to upside-down face with her assailant – it was the maimed but dreadful Captain Schnither. As Phoebe swung helplessly back and forth in front of her jubilant one-armed captor, she tried desperately not to cry out or show her fear. Being elevated upside-down by this great brute was making her feel nauseous and it took every ounce of strength she possessed not to pass out, but she resolved nonetheless not to give him the satisfaction of seeing her fear.

Schnither tilted his one-eared head to one side and squinted his red eyes as a sinister smile of sheer glee snaked across his hideous face. He surveyed his captive prey and was obviously delighted with his own achievement. Phoebe could see three rows of spiky teeth rotting behind his hacked lips as the demon captain allowed himself a moment to gloat. Yellow vapour oozed from his mouth and nostrils, its pungent and now familiar stench making Phoebe gag. At over seven feet tall, Captain Schnither was already an imposing sight, but as Phoebe hung suspended by her aching ankle he might as well have been seventy feet tall, and she felt sure that if he dropped her... well, it would not be pleasant. Despite the battle between good and evil raging all around them, Phoebe felt as if she and Schnither were trapped in a moment where neither time nor surroundings existed. She forced herself to settle and surveyed her vile captor with a newfound courage which made no sense to her but was entirely undeniable.

"Please," Phoebe barely recognised her own voice as she hesitatingly addressed her captor. "Please Captain Schnither, just put me down, let me go. It..." She hesitated, unsure of the wisdom of uttering the bold words that she was thinking, but decided to give them voice regardless. "It would be better for you if you did..."

Schnither seemed confused by the young mortal's words; he was at once amused by her audacity, impressed by her bravery and vexed by her impudence. Why was she not terrified and pleading for mercy? The contradictions in this human child irritated him.

"*Ooohh...*" Schnither jeered, "Is that so? Had I better put you down, little girl? Tell me, why would that be, Phoebe Wren? Are your puny little human friends going to beat on me?" Schnither's face was a hideous mask of mockery and he was obviously enjoying torturing Phoebe. "Ooohh please, no! Those big *scary* mortals..! Or perhaps you think Cosain and his bumbling band of brothers might wade in and rescue you and teach me a lesson? Hmmm... Let's see..." Schnither turned in the direction of the thunderous fracas, twisting Phoebe around so that she too could see events unfolding. Although the angelic warriors were battling valiantly against wave after wave of demon onslaught, Phoebe could not help herself and gasped as she surveyed the scene. Despite their best efforts, Cosain and the others were slowly but surely being beaten back, and there could be no denying this horrible truth. They rallied tirelessly against myriads of twisty demons, sending countless monsters squealing to the abyss, but the onslaught seemed to be never ending and for every defeated fiend a dozen more battle-ready beasts sprang up from nowhere to take its place.

"So you see, *little mortal,*" continued Schnither, his sheer joy now scarcely contained, "I don't think that it *would* be better for me to let you go at all. In fact, I think it would be better for those stupid angels to admit defeat right now. I'm in a good mood so who knows..." His smile was more of a sneer, revealing ferocious looking denticles. "I may even spare their pathetic lives... *if* they agree to swear allegiance to me." Schnither could contain his rapture no longer, and erupted into peals of unnatural laughter. The sound was so alien to the suffocating gloom in Mooar Mountain that several battling demons paused to see what had caused their dark captain such amusement. Cosain too was distracted by Schnither's hooting laughter and looked up just long enough to see his sworn enemy dangling a powerless Phoebe in front of him. As she swung helplessly back and forth, the shuddering caused by Schnither's sniggers caused her to wobble precariously until something jangled loose from her pocket and clattered on to the rough stone floor. To Phoebe's horror, she realised that it was the missing piece of the Key of Esse. The Captain of the Angelic Host reeled in horror at the sight and at that exact moment Schnither glanced across the packed vestibule and caught his opponent's eye. Schnither followed Cosain's gaze to where the Key of Esse now lay unguarded, and his sheer delight at finding the key abandoned on the floor could not be concealed. The Dark Captain reached down with his one remaining arm and scrabbled about with his gnarly digits until he secured the section of the key, unceremoniously clanging Phoebe off the unforgiving stone floor as he did so. Schnither straightened and for a fleeting moment Cosain and his dark nemesis held their stare above the furore of battle, a look of unmistakable jubilation plastered across Schnither's heinous face.

As Cosain moved to annihilate the latest dark fiend that had attacked him and go after Phoebe, Schnither flung his helpless prey over his left shoulder and grabbed one of the wall lamps with his now empty hand, pulling down sharply so that a door of solid rock projected from the damp stone wall. Schnither stepped on to a rotating platform which immediately spun round closing him and Phoebe away in a secret chamber behind three feet of solid rock, leaving Cosain staring helplessly at the empty space where they had been. The whole awful episode had taken only seconds, and as he looked on an unfamiliar sense of loss and defeat hit Cosain like a tidal wave.

CHAPTER 21

PHOEBE kicked and punched as hard as she could, but even her fiercest blows had little effect on Schnither as he carried her through the secret rotating doorway away from her allies and into a small dark anteroom. The area in which she now found herself was on the other side of the hallway from the Croi Chamber, and Phoebe felt despair close in around her like a heavy shroud as she thought of Demetrius and Ella – so near and yet so very far away. Drained from the relentless onslaught of fear and emotion, and physically exhausted from struggling, Phoebe reluctantly resigned herself to the fact that, for now, there was very little she could do to change things and began to focus instead on her surroundings. The room into which Schnither had carried her was small and bleak. There were no obvious distinguishing features, and a solitary oil lamp offered little by way of light. Phoebe could not make out any trace of the secret doorway through which she and Schnither had just passed, but ahead of them on the other side of the little anteroom she could see two enormous wooden doors. The doors resembled those of Abaddon's chamber but were easily twice the size, and the stunning beauty of the intricate carvings that had been meticulously etched into each door looked out of place here in this darkest of recesses. Their beauty and intricacy sneered at the ugliness of the Mooar Mountain, and the irony of their majestic presence here in this awful place was not lost on Phoebe.

The silence inside this secret place was almost deafening, and was a stark contrast to the uproar that had surrounded Phoebe just moments before. There was no denying the sense of foreboding which was quickly building to a crescendo in Phoebe's soul, although she made every effort to settle herself and think clearly. The eerie stillness contrasted sharply with the battle which raged on unabated on the other side of the great stone wall, and it slowly dawned on Phoebe that whatever lay beyond the great wooden doors in front of her must be a place of the utmost significance. There were no guards on duty that she could see, and she realised that the reason for this peculiar absence was that nobody else even *knew* about the existence of this room – after all, why would Abaddon station guards outside a room which, to all extents and purposes, did not exist? Phoebe swallowed hard as fear rolled upward from her heart to her head and the seriousness of the situation hit her like a train. There was absolutely no point in struggling any more; Phoebe was clearly no match for the might of Captain Schnither, and she felt sure that she ought to conserve any strength she had left... she was certain that she would need it, and soon.

Schnither tentatively approached the enormous doors with a subdued Phoebe still slung over his muscular shoulder. His breathing was rapid and erratic and Phoebe could not tell whether the Dark Captain was elated or terrified. *Probably both,* she concluded. Schnither paused just before the elaborate wooden doors and hoisted Phoebe further up on to his shoulder as if he was afraid that she might slip off and run away. He seemed to straighten and gather his thoughts before inhaling deeply and exhaling noisily three times, then he hunched up his shoulder and tilted his head so that Phoebe was wedged in between his body and his angular chin, and released his grip on her just long enough for him to grab hold of an impressive door knocker made of glittering gold and strike it twice against one of the wooden doors. Schnither set his hand back across Phoebe holding her firmly in place; he obviously did not want to lose his prize. The unlikely pair waited, apparently equally anxious to see what would transpire next. After a few agonising moments, Schnither propped Phoebe back in the crook of his powerful neck and reluctantly struck the great door again. The stark noise reverberated through the little anteroom and seemed to be amplified by the dense stone walls. Another few seconds passed and just as Phoebe was beginning to wonder whether Schnither had messed up and brought her to the wrong place, one of the huge gold door handles moved slowly and one of the two wooden doors was suddenly and inexplicably ajar. Schnither clenched his jaw so tightly that Phoebe could hear his teeth grating as he moved forward into the gloomy unknown. Knowing that her gnarly captor was afraid did nothing to allay Phoebe's concerns, and she felt her own jaw clench involuntarily, mirroring Schnither's, as they progressed into an opulent and sprawling room. There was no sense of triumphant jubilation as Captain Schnither stood tentatively on the threshold of the cavernous room; indeed, he somehow seemed to diminish in stature and Phoebe could tell that he was nervous and very unsure.

"Come forward, Captain Schnither," said a slow faceless voice from out of the gloom, and Phoebe's blood ran cold as she immediately recognised the dulcet tones. It was Abaddon the Defiler, without a doubt. So *this* was his domain, his secret lair which was hidden to all but an elect few. Schnither shuddered and tightened his grip on his young captive before inching cautiously away from the relative safety of the doorway and towards the centre of the sprawling room. The enormous door through which the captor and his prey had just stepped slammed shut as if by magic, but Phoebe knew that Abaddon had most probably secured it with just the slightest twitch of his fingers. His power intimidated her and she knew that Abaddon the Defiler should never be underestimated, but Phoebe forced herself to remember Neam's assertion that, *'good will triumph over evil... every time'* and found some solace in this truth. She *had* to believe it despite her current circumstances otherwise she might as well just admit defeat now – and that was definitely not an option for the plucky teenager.

"*Ah,*" came the same honeyed voice again, "I see you have *finally* brought me the little mortal who for *s-s-so long* proved *jus-s-st too tricky* for you to pin down." Sarcasm and disdain dripped unmistakably from Abaddon's words and even though she could not see his face from her upside down and back to front vantage point, Phoebe knew that Captain Schnither would be incensed to be so belittled.

"Yes my Liege..." Schnither's voice sounded puny and small, a far cry from the arrogant and boastful tones which Phoebe had become accustomed to hearing from the Dark Captain. He bowed his awful head low and did not dare to look Abaddon in the eye. "Yes, I have brought you Phoebe Wren, the Atoner's chosen Light Bringer. So now you have all three mortal children – what are your plans for them, Sire?"

In an instant, like lightning bursting through a storm cloud, the ghostly mists which had been gently swirling around the great room were ripped apart as Abaddon lunged forward in the direction of a cowering Schnither, his ordinarily emotionless grey eyes now flashing with indignation.

"And what makes you think that *you* have any right to question *my* plans-s-s, *Captain S-s-schnither?* Do you think yourself an equal with *me?* Should I cons-s-sult you on this or *any* matter? What business is it of yours what I choos-s-se to do with the mortals?"

The building fury in Abaddon's voice thundered throughout the vast room, and Phoebe was suddenly very thankful that she was upside down and back to front and could not see anything of Abaddon's hideous form.

"Oh... no... uh... no Abaddon, my Liege, most definitely

not Sire! You do not need to consult with me – or anyone – on anything... *ever!*" stuttered Schnither who obviously feared for his life. "It was not my intention for one moment to suggest that you need any assistance with your decision making my Liege, oh wisest of masters..." The Dark Captain appeared to think better of blabbing out anything more and fell silent until he suddenly remembered that he had an ace up his belligerent sleeve.

"Abaddon, Sire, I almost forgot..."

Schnither inched as close to the Dark Master as he dared, but was careful to keep outside of his punching range. The quivering monster ensured that Phoebe was securely wedged between his bulging shoulder and his jowls before slowly opening his knobbly hands to reveal the missing section of the Key of Esse lying meekly on his sweaty palm.

Schnither was unashamedly crawling now, trying desperately to appease his enraged master, and Phoebe was sure that she could feel his bulking body trembling. This turn of events almost amused Phoebe, despite her situation, and she allowed the tiniest of smirks to crawl across her face. '*Serves this idiotic gargoyle right!*' she thought with more than just a hint of satisfaction at the tongue lashing that Schnither was receiving.

Captain Schnither set the key gingerly into Abaddon's outstretched hand then backed slowly away, obviously desperate to put some space between himself and the Dark Master, but not wanting to make any abrupt movements. As her captor inched further away Phoebe was afforded a view of what had caused Captain Schnither such terror and trembling. Abaddon the Defiler was so close that Phoebe could have reached out and touched him, had she been so inclined. He was standing to the full extent of his impressive height and towered massively above Schnither, making the Dark Captain look insignificant in comparison. Abaddon's four black wings were fully extended behind him, blocking out what little light there was in the room, and all at once Phoebe understood why Schnither was trembling with fear and dread; this was a fearful and nightmare inducing sight that made her stomach lurch and her head reel.

"Ah, the elusive missing piece of Key of Esse... *Good...*" Abaddon uttered the single word through curled lips, and it bore much by way of threat and implied warning. "And you do well not to question me again Captain Schnither... *ever.*" Abaddon regarded the insignificant looking piece of metal in his possession before striding purposefully to an elegant writing desk situated along a wall in the great room where he snapped open a small drawer and tossed the key inside. His fury seemed to have subsided for now, and now he turned his attention instead to Phoebe. He pointed a bony finger at the youngster slung over Schnither's shoulder, regarding her with something close to contempt. "*That,*" he commented, nodding towards Phoebe, "hardly seems worth the bother. Nevertheless, you have s-s-succeeded in your task Schnither... *eventually.* Now, bring her here."

Schnither followed Abaddon into the centre of the room where a huge wooden chair had been placed. Abaddon motioned to Schnither to set Phoebe on the chair, and as he tipped her right side up blood rushed away from Phoebe's head and for a moment she felt that she may pass out. She sat motionless in the oversized chair and tried to steady herself by slowly blinking her eyes and gently shaking her head, and when she felt sure that her balance had been restored she looked around her and realised that Schnither had secured her to the wooden chair using the same molten steel ropes that Phoebe had seen the Anakite guards use on the angelic warriors outside Mooar Mountain. She felt a familiar sense of panic surge through her but knew that any form of resistance was futile, and instead forced herself to suppress her fear and show Abaddon and Schnither that she would not be intimidated by them.

Phoebe's eyes darted back and forth as she tried to take in her surroundings, but given the enormity of the room and the misty gloom it was difficult to see much. What was glaringly obvious however, even in the limited light, was the sumptuous and lavish excessiveness of this room. Thus far, everything she had witnessed of the Mooar Mountain and its deep dark rooms had been characterised by gloom and austerity and misery. But here in Abaddon's clandestine quarters lavish opulence oozed from every part. Gold and silver were in abundance, and jewels of every size and hue glinted quietly even in the dim light. What Phoebe could make out of the furnishings in the muted light were rich and luxurious, and she imagined that this room would not look out of place in the wealthiest of earthly palaces. She noticed a small hatch in the ceiling above her head and the little doorway captured her imagination, immediately drawing her in and making her regal surroundings pale into insignificance. She wondered whether there could be any potential for escape through the ceiling hatch, but did not have to wonder for very long as Abaddon made a downward motion with his hand and the hatch swung open bringing with it a strong shaft of daylight which flooded over Phoebe in its simple brilliance. This unexpected link to the outside world had an instantaneous soothing effect on Phoebe's soul and she turned her face skyward, squinting into the light in an effort to see something – anything – familiar in the midst of this bleak and unnatural location.

As suddenly as the hatch in the ceiling swung open, natural light was bounced off a number of huge mirrors hung around the walls of the cavernous room, instantaneously throwing light into even the darkest recesses of the great chamber. Phoebe was momentarily caught up in the delight of seeing daylight flood the room as she gazed around it in awe. The bright yellow light of day revealed more of the room's luxury and lavish excesses, but it was not the furs or furniture or finery that caught Phoebe's attention. Her eyes came suddenly to rest on a sight which stole her breath away and flooded her with renewed horror.

There, on the opposite side of the huge and lavish chamber hung two large oval mirrors which stood out from an ordered row of similar mirrors. Each was gilded in glittering gold and more ornate than anything that Phoebe had even seen before. But it was not their beauty which held her horrified stare, for there encapsulated somehow behind the glass of two of the mirrors, were Demetrius and Ella.

CHAPTER 22

FOR one terrible moment that seemed frozen in time, Phoebe gawped at the image that assailed her senses, unable to take in or process what she was seeing. She blinked and shook her head rapidly, then closed her eyes tight for a few seconds in the hope that when she opened them she would realise that she had merely imagined what she thought she saw. But this was not the case. As Phoebe slowly turned her gaze once more in the direction of the two great mirrors, she baulked anew at the sight of Demetrius and Ella, encapsulated behind the glass like unfortunate bugs suspended between specimen plates. Neither one moved a muscle, although their eyes were wide open and pleading silently for her to help them.

"Are they..." Phoebe could not bring herself to say the word.

"Are they *alive..?*" sneered Abaddon the Defiler as he lowered his chin and peered at Phoebe through menacing squinted eyes. "Look clos-s-ser, *little bird...*"

Phoebe felt herself flinch as Abaddon referred to her using the nickname that Demetrius had given her. Somehow his use of that simple term of endearment offended and wounded her more than any venom the Dark Master could direct at her. This had obviously been Abaddon's intention, and he turned away so Phoebe could not see his face then smirked cruelly as his blatant disrespect found its mark.

"I am wounded – *wounded* – that you would even *think* that I had harmed your little friends-s-s, Miss Wren," continued Abaddon, his scornful and mocking voice thinly disguised by apparent sincerity. "What do you take me for? A *mons-s-ster..?*" He turned again and looked at Phoebe with a bogus sadness in his eyes that Phoebe found repulsive.

Phoebe lowered her gaze and defiantly refused to rise to Abaddon's provocation. Instead, she looked past him and peered intently at the mirrors hanging on the far wall of the chamber, looking and longing for any sign of life from her friends, however small or apparently insignificant it may be. Phoebe scarcely dared to breathe as she focused on the faces of her encapsulated friends and when at last the faintest misting of the inside of the mirror assured her that Demetrius and Ella were in fact breathing, she emitted an audible gasp of relief and joy.

"S-s-see?" said Abaddon with a smirk. "I told you they were still in one piece – and would I lie to you?"

If there was one thing Phoebe knew for sure, it was that Abaddon most definitely *would* lie to her, and it would not even cost him a thought. Cosain had already alerted her to the fact that the Dark Master rarely spoke in truths, and she knew that here in his own realm his lies were potent and flowed with ease, and she could so quickly be tempted to believe what he wanted her to. Phoebe clamped her teeth together and refused to rise to the Dark Master's goading – if Abaddon's words could not be trusted, then she would not dignify his lies with a response. She was aware that in all probability she resembled a petulant and childish princess from a fairy tale, pouting there on her outlandish throne, but she did not care and resolutely refused to respond to Abaddon.

"Ahh," jeered the Dark Master, "The little bird has taken offence. How *s-s-sweet...*" Abaddon had crossed the plush carpeted floor and was standing just a couple of feet away from Phoebe, leaning in towards her so that his face was threateningly close to hers. Phoebe could feel his breath hot on her cheek and every sinew of her being begged her to turn her face away, but she stubbornly resisted the urge to gag and look away, and chose instead to stare straight into the Dark Master's imposing grey eyes. To her great surprise, at this proximity Phoebe found Abaddon's visage to be anything but hideous. Yes, his physical form shot a bolt of terror straight into the very soul of the beholder, but here in its nearness his form seemed softened and his fearsome features took on a kind of... What? Could that be *beauty* in the Dark Master's form? Phoebe worked hard on keeping her thoughts to herself and her reactions to a minimum, but the revelation of Abaddon's apparent other side stunned her to such an extent that she simply could not veil her reactions completely, and as she continued to stare Abaddon down she knew that he had seen her doubts and misgivings.

"Do you s-s-see it, Phoebe Wren? You do, don't you? Don't you realise that I have s-s-suffered *terribly* from all the bad press and the malicious *s-s-spin* about me?" soothed Abaddon as he leaned back from Phoebe's incredulous gaze. "You really shouldn't believe all the hype and the horror stories about me you know – they simply aren't fair. I'm not so bad, now am I? I would never hurt you or your little friends, Phoebe – *never!* In fact, if you want to be angry and indignant at anyone..." Abaddon hesitated for effect, a feigned looked of wounded sorrow stealing across his face. "Well, I would suggest that it is *Cos-s-sain* at whom you should vent your annoyance – after all, *he* was foolish enough to drag you and your friends here to Mooar Mountain. He *really* should have known better – this is no place for mortals-s-s! You have no business being tangled up in a battle that is not yours. Who are *you* after all, Phoebe Wren? What makes you so s-s-special that you would imagine that the Atoner needs *you* or *any* of your kind to do anything? And why would you even think that He *cares-s-s* what happens to you mere mortals? No Phoebe, I am not the one at fault here. The Atoner has made a colossal blunder, and Cosain has put you all in danger – and for what reason? To feed his own ego, that is why! Foolish, puny, *vain* angel!"

For a split second, Abaddon's cool and controlled front was peeled away as the thought of the Atoner and His warrior angels riled him afresh, but in that fleeting instant Phoebe caught sight again of Abaddon's vile true nature and knew in her core that he was nothing more than a liar who would sell her any story she liked in order to lull her into a false and deadly sense of security. She tightened her grip on the arms of the huge chair and squashed down the growing sense of dread in her belly, then firmly set her resolve as she bravely addressed her captor.

"No, Abaddon," said Phoebe, her voice weaker than she would have liked it to be. She mustered her courage and willed herself to speak louder. "No, Cosain is neither foolish nor puny, and he is most definitely not vain. And the Atoner does not make mistakes – ever! He has a plan for me, a destiny, and it is *good* – in fact, it is tailor made and *perfect* for me, and I am going to fulfil it! You are not the victim of rumours or lies – you *are* lies! You are the *father* of lies! You *want* to see me *fail*, and you will do that by any means necessary. But I won't let you – Cosain won't let you..."

"*Cos-s-sain?*" Abaddon's fury had crescendoed in an instant and he no longer made any attempt to mask his true colours. Purple sinuous veins bulged and strained in his neck and across his forehead and his face was once again so close to Phoebe's that she could smell the sulphur on his breath. Abaddon's eyes were wide and crazed, his pupils dilated until both eyes resembled bottomless pools of purest black. "*Cos-s-sain won't let me?* Foolish child! Do you think he will have any *choice* in the matter? You will never see that ins-s-solent angel or his idiotic bumbling brothers again. You will meet your doom right here in my chamber along with those other two bothersome mortals. This is *my* domain, Phoebe Wren, mine! And here in the GuBrath Room *I* make the rules, *I* pass the judgements, *I* decide who lives and who dies! I am not under the Atoner's jurisdiction! You will soon see who is really in charge."

Phoebe was struggling to maintain her composure and out of the corner of her eye she could see that Schnither had backed right up to the great doors of the room and was pressed up against them, quivering in fear. The doors were barred and apparently impenetrable so Schnither could not make his escape, but he obviously felt the need to be as far away from Abaddon as possible. Phoebe gulped hard and could not help but wonder what hope she would have against the fury of Abaddon the Defiler if even the mighty Captain Schnither recoiled in terror from his furious wrath.

Despite her dry mouth and quivering lips, Phoebe mustered up the courage and defiance to speak once more.

"Yes, Abaddon," she said, her voice scarcely more than a terrified whisper. "You are right about one thing – we *will* see who is in charge, we will all see!"

The disrespectful impudence and insubordination of the mortal child was too much for Abaddon to bear and he roared his command at Schnither, who visibly jumped in fear and struggled to stand to attention. "Schnither! Bring this s-s-swaggering mortal to me," he roared as he strode across the GuBrath chamber. "I have the perfect spot for her where she will be just a little less-s-s vocal..."

Abaddon gestured towards the row of golden mirrors. "This one," he sneered in Phoebe's direction as he pointed to the mirror next to the one in which Demetrius was imprisoned. "This one has been reserved *es-s-specially for you*."

Any trace of the ethereal beauty from aeons past that Phoebe had glimpsed hidden beneath layers of rage and resentment and venom was well and truly gone, and Abaddon's face resembled a ghoulish mask of sheer hostility and wrath.

"No! No, I'm not going in there!"

Phoebe began to struggle as she felt Schnither loosen the molten ropes which had held her fast to the great chair.

"Please, Schnither – don't!"

She could think of no way out of this situation and in her desperation pleaded with Schnither in the hope that the Dark Captain possessed some tiny trace of compassion. But her pleas fell on deaf ears and Phoebe realised that appealing to Schnither's better nature was not even a possibility.

"*S-s-silence*, mortal child!" Abaddon's harsh voice hurtled across the room towards her and she was sure that had she been standing the very force of it would have knocked her off her feet. "You have said more than enough – it is time for you to be s-s-silent... *forever!*"

Phoebe punched and kicked as Schnither lifted her from the great chair in the centre of the GuBrath room, slung her unceremoniously over his shoulder and moved uncertainly towards Abaddon. He was trembling violently and his fear seemed to pass along his gnarly finger tips and infect Phoebe until she felt she may pass out.

"Hurry up you blundering idiot!" roared Abaddon, who very obviously no longer felt the need for feigned politeness. "Do you think I have nothing else to do but silence this child?" Phoebe felt Schnither quicken his pace and when they had crossed the great room he dropped her to the floor where her knees buckled beneath her and she sank to the floor. The rich red carpet which had been beneath her chair just moments before had somehow vanished and had been replaced instead with harsh cold stone which tore at her knees and cut her young skin until blood trickled down her left leg. Phoebe flinched in pain and tried to clamber to her feet, but her shaking legs would not allow it. She bit her lip in an effort to stop herself from crying, and the pitiful sight of the frightened fifteen year old mortal seemed to amuse Abaddon.

"Not quite so lippy now, are we?" he jeered. "I suppose I should give you your dues-s-s, Phoebe Wren – you evaded me for long enough, and you have been brave... if incredibly naïve and very, *very* stupid. Such a shame really – you could have been an asset to me you know... But it's just too late for that. S-s-schnither – prepare the mirror."

"Yes my Liege," said Schnither with a shaky voice and something akin to an awkward and almost laughable curtsy. He was obviously desperate to appease his Dark Master and was not entirely sure that he himself would make it out of the GuBrath room in one piece.

Quickly, Schnither reached forward toward the huge oval mirror and with the tip of his sword, he gently pressed the centre of the glass. For a brief moment nothing happened, but slowly the glass began to melt back towards the edges of the frame, revealing a space behind it that looked just big enough for Phoebe to stand.

"Get in, mortal," grunted Schnither, nodding towards the space as he sheathed his serrated blade. Phoebe did not move – even if she had wanted to obey Schnither's command, she was not sure that her jellied legs would support her weight. "Move it... *Now!*" Schnither raised his voice and tried to sound authoritative as he prodded Phoebe in the side with the toe of his black leather boot. Despite her fear, Phoebe swung round with bunched fists, lashing out wildly, but succeeded only in slapping Schnither's chunky knee, causing him to snort as he stifled a laugh.

"Ahh, she is a *feis-s-sty* little thing," jeered Abaddon with a twisted grin on his face. "Now tell me, would you like some help Schnither, or *do you think you can manage to get her where I've told you to all by yourself?*" Abaddon's voice rose sharply and Schnither did not have to be asked again. He grabbed at Phoebe's shoulder with his one remaining arm and pulled her painfully to her feet in a single deft movement. Phoebe resumed her thrashing and struggling and was about to deliver a swift kick to Schnither's shins when a quiet but unmistakable voice stopped her in her tracks.

"*Phoebe, take the weapon. Use it Phoebe.*"

Phoebe furrowed her brow and hesitated. Who was that? Was it Cosain? Had he somehow broken into this secret chamber? She glanced around the GuBrath chamber, her eyes darting from corner to corner in an effort to see who had called out to her. She could see no-one and realised that Schnither had momentarily ceased hauling her towards the open mirror, apparently confused by her strange behaviour.

"*Schnither's sword, Phoebe – you will know what to do.*"

There it was again – the most gentle, whispered voice Phoebe had ever heard, but at the same time the most compelling and unarguably authoritative sound. She still could not see whoever it was that had spoken, but she instantly felt courage rise up within her like a tide and simply knew that she could not ignore that voice. In a heartbeat Phoebe spun around, catching both Captain Schnither and Abaddon the Defiler completely off guard with her unheralded impetuousness. Her legs felt strong and trustworthy once more, and her focus was set. She reached out her steady right hand and caught a firm hold of Schnither's sword, pulling it from its sheath with equal amounts of ease and surprise. In that instant, the realisation of what was transpiring hit Abaddon and Schnither simultaneously and both sprang into action, arms outstretched, grasping at Phoebe as though securing their prisoner was the only thing in the world that mattered. Somehow – Phoebe could not say for sure how – she evaded their onslaught and slipped between her fearsome captors leaving them bumbling in her wake as she ran towards the two golden framed mirrors behind which Demetrius and Ella were trapped.

"It's okay Dem, I've got you now," Phoebe shouted as she raised Schnither's sword above her head and swung it in the direction of the mirror. The gnarly blade was heavy and cumbersome and Phoebe had no idea how she had been able to elevate such a formidable weapon, but just as she moved to bring the tip of the blade crashing down on the mirror glass, icy cold fingers coiled firmly around her slender wrist, halting the sword in its tracks. Phoebe jerked her head around in frustration and reeled in horror at the sight of Abaddon the Defiler whose lifeless eyes were flashing with fury as he held her in his iron grip.

CHAPTER 23

PHOEBE'S eyes were as wide as saucers and her breathing grew increasingly rapid as she stood, painfully suspended mid-strike, held fast in Abaddon's vice-like grip. She could see – if she needed any proof – from his taut jaw line that Abaddon was a ticking time bomb of fury, and although the teenager had come through some hair-raising moments since leaving Africa just a few short weeks ago, this was the first moment that it really occurred to her that her life could potentially end right here, right now, in the heart of Mooar Mountain. Abaddon was looking at his prey with unveiled contempt, while Schnither appeared more unsure and afraid than ever – he had definitely messed up this time, and he obviously knew it. Phoebe glanced quickly at Demetrius and Ella who were still entombed inside their glass sepulchres and could tell from the desperate look in their eyes that they also believed this to be the end of Phoebe Wren. She smiled weakly at her two best friends. The thought of having run out of time with them pained her greatly and made her wince. Abaddon tightened his grip on Phoebe's wrist and removed Schnither's sword from her powerless hand as if it weighed no more than a feather. The huge dark blade fell to the stone floor with a cacophonous clatter that resounded around the GuBrath chamber – '*some kind of odious death knell,*' Phoebe mused.

"*Enough*, Phoebe Wren," Abaddon breathed in a low menacing voice that made the hairs on the back of Phoebe's neck stand on end. He was breathing like a spent runner and Phoebe could tell that he would not tolerate her resistance any longer. "That is *enough*. I have been too tolerant for too long. This ends-s-s *now*. You have failed the Atoner, you will have to accept that. But more importantly, the *Atoner* has failed *you*." Abaddon paused, surveying Phoebe with inquisitive eyes, and for a fleeting moment she was sure that she glimpsed that same ethereal beauty of aeons past steal across his harsh yet undeniably flawless features. "Ah yes, I understand how *that* feels, mortal," Abaddon continued, "for the Atoner failed me too... Oh I know *His* take on events – He blames me for thinking that I could be like Him; He said that I became haughty, proud... Well, why s-s-shouldn't I be proud?" Abaddon's temper was rising again, and his grip on Phoebe tightened so that she grimaced in pain. "*Of course* I should be proud of myself – how do you think I got to where I am today? The Atoner certainly didn't recognise or promote my talents – so I took matters into my own hands-s-s. And what is more, I would do it again without hesitation! I am feared and respected, and rightly so for I am a force to be reckoned with... I am mighty... I am *in charge* here..." Despite his bravado and boldness, Phoebe could not help but think that Abaddon was in fact trying to convince *himself* of his own power and self worth. '*How very sad and just a little bit pathetic*,' she thought and flexed her jaw with disdain.

Bolstered by his ostentatious self-promotion, Abaddon turned his focus once again to Phoebe. "Now," he slurred. "What to do with *you*, pretty little mortal Miss Wren. I have prepared this *bijou* little space for you..." He gestured towards the large mirror whose glass had been peeled back to reveal a pliable interior that would take the shape of Phoebe's form and hold her fast once the glass was resealed. "To refuse to inhabit this little *snug* is, quite simply, just *rude*. So I think you should *get in*, don't you?"

Abaddon grinned a sickly smile at Phoebe that was half smirk, half grimace, then lifted her in his iron arms and began to lower her into the space in the mirror which had apparently been reserved especially for her from decades past. Phoebe felt a gnawing panic in her stomach as the gravity of the situation washed over her like a flood, but she knew that resistance was futile. Cosain had told her that her grandfather's time-stopping pocket watch would have no effect on Abaddon, but Phoebe was suddenly overcome with the longing to hold the little time piece in her hand once more because maybe – just *maybe* – it could buy her even a little more time... Besides, it was a connection with home, albeit a tiny one, and she wanted more than anything to be tangibly reminded of her family and home before the irreversibly deadly conclusion of her story was played out. Phoebe could scarcely believe that this was the end, and yet its inevitability was staring her squarely in the face.

Suddenly, from nowhere, a deluge of noise and activity and shattered rock exploded forward into the GuBrath chamber from beyond its dense walls, permeating Phoebe's senses with shock and confusion. So extensive and unexpected was this intrusion that even the apparently unmoveable Abaddon thrust both hands instinctively over his ears as he spun around to see what had transpired. In an instant that changed everything, Phoebe found herself dropped unceremoniously to the floor where she landed in an awkward heap at the base of the mirror whose gaping jaws still lay open and awaiting her arrival. She barely had time to register what had just happened, but her auto-pilot self took over and in a nanosecond she was in flight, half running, half tumbling across the floor, which was once again inexplicably adorned in thick, plush red carpet.

Phoebe did not dare to look over her shoulder but she could tell by the tortured screeches emitting from Abaddon's throat that whatever – or *whoever* – had just invaded his secret chamber was definitely not welcome. Phoebe scrambled on, regaining her senses so that she became entirely intentional in her escape effort. She pushed forward until she reached the back wall of the GuBrath chamber where the grand mahogany writing desk was positioned with its front leaf lying open. Abaddon had obviously been working at the desk in very recent times, and it occurred to Phoebe to wonder who on earth the Dark Master could be writing *to*. A large rectangular section of cream parchment lay half unrolled on the desk, and a great quill and pot of blood red ink lay neatly beside it. Phoebe was too frantic to even consider reading what had been written in beautifully flowing script on the scroll, but two words leapt off the parchment and hit her with immense force as she scrambled underneath the writing desk in search of shelter – '*Vincent d'Olcas*'. Why, even in the midst of the chaos around her, did that name ring a bell? Phoebe tried desperately to regain her composure and clear her mind as she crouched underneath the writing desk, her thoughts whirring and tumbling through her head as though they had been caught up in some kind of cerebral whirlpool. '*Vincent d'Olcas*' – Phoebe was certain that she knew that name, and even in the midst of the noise and frantic activity happening around her, it bothered her that she could not recall why. Suddenly, as if someone had switched on a light bulb in her head, Phoebe remembered where she had heard the name – back in her world, Vincent d'Olcas held a senior position on Arles Borough Council and had proven something of a stumbling block to Jack and Eva Wren as they had tried to advance plans for their venture, the Celtic Justice Organisation.

Phoebe recalled her mother's words very clearly now – '*There's something a bit... dark about him... I can't quite put my finger on it, but his presence unsettles me – he makes my skin crawl...*' Eva was not the type of person to speak ill of anyone, but she had taken great and instant exception to Vincent d'Olcas and suddenly it made so much sense to Phoebe.

Vincent d'Olcas – like Brother Clarence – must have been a Shapeshifter, a demon with the ability to look like an ordinary mortal, but who was in fact an infiltrator working for Abaddon the Defiler in the mortal realm. That would explain why his presence jarred so starkly with her mother's sensitive soul. As this realisation dawned fully on Phoebe, she wondered who else she had unwittingly encountered with a malevolent unseen agenda and hidden identity.

As her thoughts raced back to the situation at hand, Phoebe realised that this may be the only chance she would get at retrieving the pilfered section of the Key of Esse. She forced thoughts of Abaddon the Defiler and Vincent d'Olcas to the back of her mind and made herself concentrate on the small drawer in the front of the writing desk into which she had seen Abaddon put the key. She glanced around and knew that drawing any attention to herself could seal her fate, but concluded hopefully that everyone else in the room had more than enough to occupy them without worrying about her. She knew too that this could change at any second and without over thinking her actions she forced herself to her feet, spun around and yanked open the desk drawer in one deft movement. Phoebe scarcely dared look inside the little drawer, and her relief made her feel light headed as she spotted the section of the key still lying where Abaddon had tossed it. It occurred to her that he had been strangely offhand about the little piece of metal which carried with it such enormous implications for him and his dark forces. How arrogant the Dark Prince was! Phoebe scooped up the key with trembling fingers and shoved it as deep into her jeans pocket as it would go before dropping to her haunches again and scrabbling back underneath the writing desk.

Although it had taken only a few seconds for Phoebe to locate and secure the Key of Esse, she felt as though time was standing still. The furious noise of invasion shook her from her musings and she finally looked back in the direction from which she had just escaped. Abaddon and Schnither had launched into action and were relentlessly swinging their deadly swords in the direction of the intruders. Phoebe could have wept with sheer joy to see familiar faces – it was Cosain, Solas, Dilis, Trean, Neam, Lasair, Maelis, Keane, Lachlan and Ernan. She had never been so happy to see anyone in her life, and a rush of euphoria flooded through her being and made her soul dance despite her still precarious position. As she looked on, Croga and Cahir arrived from their posts on the outside of the Mooar Mountain, storming the GuBrath room through the remains of the decimated stone wall. The secret stone access door had been blown to smithereens, and Phoebe could see that the angelic warriors had blasted the thick wall apart so that it had shattered like glass. Shrieking demonic beings infiltrated the room at regular intervals through the gaping hole in the wall but as quickly as each entered, Croga and Cahir despatched them spiralling into the Abyss until the persistent stream of gnarly fiends began to dry up as the futility of their efforts slowly dawned on them.

Although Abaddon and Schnither were obviously outnumbered, they were certainly not going down without a fight. The indignation of losing an arm to the Captain of the Heavenly Host still weighed heavily on Schnither, and his desire for vengeance spurred him on with an intense and unrelenting fury. Abaddon was obviously incensed beyond any reasoning at having his private chambers infiltrated by such sickening *goodness,* and he rallied against his opponents without any consideration of how hopelessly he and Schnither were outnumbered. From her vantage point under Abaddon's writing desk, the outcome of the battle looked to Phoebe like a foregone conclusion, but if she had learned anything during the last few weeks it was that *nothing* is as clear cut as it may initially appear. Abaddon and Schnither were not about to concede defeat easily, and their combined indignation and rage made them a formidable force to be reckoned with.

The battle between the forces of good and evil raged on unabated for several minutes with neither side willing to give any ground. Abaddon and Schnither fought with unrivalled fury, and it was this same fury that seemed to translate into impressive swordsmanship and unparalleled drive so the Dark Master and his Captain were not easily overcome, despite the odds. They channelled their aggression and anger effectively and were more than worthy adversaries for Cosain and the angelic warriors. They may have been outnumbered, but Abaddon and Schnither displayed swordsmanship and agility that was as terrifying as it was impressive to behold.

As the battle raged on and Phoebe watched incredulously, she began to wonder whether Abaddon and Schnither might actually drive Cosain and the others back, but as the mêlée rumbled on she could see the Dark Master at last begin to wane, and Schnither was obviously struggling with only one arm for battle. When she was sure enough that the angelic warriors were on the brink of defeating their ferocious enemies, Phoebe mustered up enough courage to crawl cautiously from her hiding place and steal silently back towards the row of mirrors where Abaddon was keeping Demetrius and Ella. She stood shakily to her feet in front of her friends' glass sepulchres and spread the palms of her hands against the cold glass. "Don't worry guys, you're getting out of here – now!" Phoebe whispered, although she could not tell if her friends could hear her behind the glass. "I'll be back in just a second..."

Phoebe glanced over her shoulder. Yes, Abaddon and Schnither were still struggling hard against Cosain and his troops, but they were weakening by the minute, and Phoebe was sure that their demise could not be far away. She looked around for something – anything – that she could use to smash the glass in the mirrors and free Demetrius and Ella. Her mind was whirring furiously and she could barely think straight, but she was resolute in her intentions. She desperately scanned the GuBrath chamber for something solid enough to break glass, and her eyes came to rest on a little three legged stool lying idly on its side next to Abaddon's writing desk. She assumed it had been tossed there in the midst of the maelstrom happening within the room, and wasted no time in retrieving it. Although the stool was relatively small – a foot stool, she imagined – it was suitably solid and heavy, and Phoebe found herself obliged to grit her teeth and use all her strength to haul it back towards the wall of mirrors. She was aware that she would have to swing it with some effort to break the sturdy mirrors and yet was loathe to risk injuring either of her friends. Phoebe realised that she was dithering and time was of the essence, so without further hesitation she yelled at Ella over the noise of battle around her. "El, I'm gonna smash this mirror! I'll do my best not to hurt you – get ready... *Three... Two... One!*" With a gargantuan effort, Phoebe raised the wooden stool from the ground and swung it with all her might at the mirror. She held her breath in expectation as the little stool made noisy contact with the restrictive mirror.

Far from shattering however, the glass barely moved as the stool bounced backwards off it with such force that it almost knocked Phoebe off her feet. The teenager's face crumpled in frustration and disappointment, but she was in no mood to take no for an answer and swung the stool violently at the mirror again, and a third time. Phoebe was tiring very quickly so it was with great euphoria on her fifth attempt that the mirror broke and a jagged crack appeared, snaking upwards from top to bottom, then shattered outwards in a million tiny pieces. Phoebe threw her arms up across her face to protect herself from flying glass then quickly brushed herself down as Ella fell forward and gasped in air like a drowning swimmer surfacing for the first time. Phoebe wasted no time as she grabbed her friend, embracing her as she hauled her out from the broken tomb of glass.

"Phoebe!" Ella was panting like a spent sprinter. "You did it! Quick, we need to get Dem out too..."

Phoebe turned her attention to the mirror behind which Demetrius was trapped. Despite the burning ache in her weary arms, she hauled the wooden stool up off the floor and smashed it into the glass. Again. *Again.* As before, it was only on the fourth or fifth attempt that the mirror began to crack, a serrated fissure which snaked its way painfully slowly from the top to the bottom. The glass did not shatter as before so Phoebe raised the stool to strike it once again when she heard Ella's voice cry out. "*Phoebe! Look out!*" The unexpected shout caused Phoebe to spin around, dropping the heavy wooden stool to the floor. To her horror, Abaddon and Schnither were only inches behind her, and between them and the angelic troops a great dark vortex had opened up from the floor of the GuBrath chamber. Lightning sparked and flashed from its swirling depths and dark mists oozed out, spreading out around Phoebe's ankles like slime. This was the absolute antithesis of the vortex of light and the thought of where the dark portal might transport her horrified Phoebe.

"*No...*"

Phoebe scarcely had time to utter the word before Abaddon the Defiler lurched forward, grabbing her tightly by her shoulders. Schnither stepped back into the dark other-worldly portal with Abaddon and his captive hot on his heels. Time stood still as the Dark Master pulled Phoebe into the cold dark vortex. She had a weird sensation of surrealism and hideously reversed déjà vu as she peered helplessly back out towards Ella's terrified face and the angelic troops as they battled to pass through the sinister vortex and rescue her from Abaddon's clutches. Phoebe reached out her arms helplessly towards her friends and protectors, a look of pained disbelief on her young face. Time slowed to a crawl as the horrifying turn of events unravelled before those present, and Phoebe was sure that there could be no way back for her now.

As the dark vortex began to close around her, Phoebe was suddenly snapped back to the present as if someone had flipped a switch and time was moving at its regular speed again. At the very last second, right before the dark vortex twisted shut, a blinding blast of dazzling light exploded into the GuBrath chamber filling every inch of the room with ethereal brilliance. The room shone and glowed with a light that made even the brightest summer day seem dull by comparison, and to Phoebe's astonishment the dark vortex that had been swirling ever closer around her suddenly burst apart without explanation. Through confused eyes she could distinguish the dark forms of hundreds of gnarly bodies spinning and twisting outwards from the GuBrath room en masse. Cosain and his troops had suddenly ceased their battling and had fallen on one knee, where they were shielding their eyes from the blazing light that was flooding the room in its undulating brilliance. Phoebe could scarcely bear to look on the light but as she squinted her eyes she could distinguish a form striding purposefully towards them from its centre. Abaddon's guttural roar was loud and low as he burst out of the demolished vortex and back into the GuBrath room, with Phoebe still in his clutches. Behind them, the ominous vortex that had almost claimed Phoebe forever seemed to disintegrate and vanish taking a hugely relieved Schnither with it. As the furore in the room abated, the blinding light began to dim somewhat until Phoebe was able to look up without the need to shield her eyes.

"*S-s-so...*" It was Abaddon who broke the stunned silence that had descended on the GuBrath chamber. "*You came.* You actually came here. This mortal must be of great worth to you for you to so *grace us with your pres-s-sence.*"

Phoebe could almost feel the sarcasm and resentment dripping from Abaddon's lips, but she was aware too that his bravado was probably feigned and she was certain that his great form was quaking. "But I am afraid that your journey has been was-s-sted, for you cannot have her. *Finders-s-s keepers-s-s*, and all that... *Atoner*." Despite Abaddon's disrespectful audacity there was now no mistaking the trembling in his powerful hands, and with the mention of the Atoner's name, Phoebe realised why. Despite his ramblings to the contrary, Abaddon knew that he could not stand against the Atoner and in him, Abaddon had more than met his match.

"No, Abaddon, you are greatly mistaken. It is not 'finders keepers', not by a long stretch. Phoebe Wren is mine, she has always been mine. And I have come to take her back."

A tingle ran along Phoebe's spine as she heard for the first time the voice belonging to the One so often referred to by Cosain and the other angelic warriors. They spoke his name with the greatest reverence, and their genuflection reinforced the esteem in which they held him. The Atoner's voice was surprisingly low and entirely controlled, but his authority was unmistakable and beyond challenge. Phoebe did not doubt his ability to redeem the situation and she was sure that Abaddon did not either. Not even he could be so misguided.

Phoebe blinked in disbelief and dared at last to look directly at her would-be rescuer. She could not tell whether ethereal light surrounded him or in fact radiated from his very being, but beyond the outline of his impressive form she could not distinguish much by way of features or appearance. As her eyes wandered tentatively to his face, the glow around him seemed to pulse and undulate, but it was his eyes that stopped the youngster in her tracks. The Atoner's gaze met hers and at once Phoebe felt as if everything around her had melted away and she was entirely safe and secure in his presence. The eyes that held her stare were like none she had ever seen before – they were at once terrifying in their fiery intensity yet brimming with compassion and grace, and in that instant Phoebe had no doubt that the Atoner would have gone to any lengths to find her. She realised that she had never actually been in danger – not really, not when the

Atoner had plans for her. Why, she was not entirely sure, but in this instant, her rescuer's unspoken commitment to her was beyond doubt, and apparently oblivious to her bleak surroundings, she basked in his all encompassing presence and felt a contradictory peace like she had never known before.

CHAPTER 24

IN the stunned moments that followed the Atoner's unannounced arrival in the GuBrath chamber, no-one had dared to move. *No-one*. Any gnarly demonic fiend who had not already been despatched to the Abyss now exited the room with great haste, scrabbling furiously over and around each other, obviously thankful to escape with their pathetic lives. Cosain and the other warriors had arisen and flanked the Atoner on all sides so that Abaddon's sole potential escape route was entirely blocked off. Phoebe could not wrench her gaze away from the Atoner, and although her inability to distinguish any particular form confused and perplexed her slightly, the depths of tranquillity and peace she had found in his eyes mesmerised her so that she had almost forgotten about Abaddon the Defiler or the struggle for her survival.

"Abaddon the Defiler would seek to destroy you and Demetrius and Ella."

Phoebe realised that the Atoner's lips had not moved and he had not uttered an audible word, yet she could hear his voice so clearly.

"But I will not let him. I have chosen you and your friends for a purpose, and I will help you to achieve it. The organisation that your parents have established back home will be crucial – Celtic Justice Organisation will do more than feed the hungry and clothe the poor. Through it, justice and light will return to your homeland, and Abaddon's reign there will come to an end."

Phoebe blinked and frowned slightly. "*Why me?*" she wondered. "*What's so special about me?*" As if he had heard her unspoken words, the Atoner's knowing gaze rested on Phoebe and she heard his voice once more. "*You see what others do not see, Phoebe. You take the time to look, and as a result, you see. You believe. And your heart is braver than you give yourself credit for. You and your friends will return to Ireland and complete your mission. There will be further opposition, you can be sure of that, but Cosain and his troops will stay with you. Just trust them. And trust me.*"

Before Phoebe could even form the thoughts to utter a reply, Abaddon's grip on her was suddenly and unexpectedly released and she crumpled to her knees. Such had been his resolve to claim his prize that Phoebe had never expected Abaddon to let go of her, and her disquieting freedom momentarily bewildered her.

A sudden deafening roar echoed through the GuBrath chamber and Phoebe became aware of a dark shadow growing in height and width behind her as it slithered menacingly like insidious night across her kneeling form. Neither the Atoner nor any of the angelic warriors were looking in her direction now, and it was with a growing sense of dread that Phoebe slowly turned her head in the direction of Abaddon the Defiler.

What the young girl witnessed before her took her breath away. Where just seconds ago Abaddon had stood in all his dreadful enormity there now crouched a creature which caused Phoebe's jaw to fall open as her eyes grew wide. A gargantuan black beast was poised before her, his four massive legs tensed ready to pounce, bulging muscles taught and straining, and his fearsome claws fully extended. The creature had the appearance of an overgrown lion, although it was easily three times the size of an ordinary lion and more ferocious looking than any beast Phoebe had ever seen. His fur was glossy black and his impressive mane hung in sleek locks around his head like a darkly glinting halo. This could have been a creature despatched directly from the Abyss to come to Abaddon's aid, but it was the creature's eyes that confirmed his true identity. The furiously flashing orbs were unmistakable; they were flint grey and emotionless, and Phoebe knew that she was staring into the eyes of Abaddon the Defiler. Why had she not assumed that the Dark Master could morph at will? Of course she should have known! His creature of choice was this colossal and menacing black lion which had caused Phoebe to suck in her breath and hold it there before allowing herself to breathe out slowly, as if she was afraid of attracting the beast's attention. In truth, there was little need for Phoebe to be so cautious because the great black lion had her in his sights already, his piercing eyes locked on her trembling form as though she were some kind of target that he could not afford to miss.

'*Prey*', Phoebe thought and shuddered.

Despite the growing terror she felt in her belly, Phoebe forced herself to look away from the great black lion and back towards the radiant form of the Atoner. In a heartbeat, the light that had accompanied him and heralded his presence had returned to its undiluted brilliance, and she could not look directly at him.

"*Abaddon*," the Atoner's voice was louder now and remained uncompromising in its authority. "Stand down. You will not win. You *cannot* win. To defy me further would be most unwise."

Phoebe shivered as the Atoner's words washed over her. His voice and unyielding tone disquieted her even though she knew that he was on her side, and it occurred to her that Abaddon must be resolute in his pride and fury if he could hear the Atoner's direct command and still dare to disobey. '*Either that or he has taken leave of his senses*,' Phoebe mused.

"*Never-r-r,*" Abaddon's voice snarled unchanged from the great black lion's jaws as he bared his fearsome canines at the Atoner and the Heavenly warriors. "I have not come this far just to let you *take* the mortal. Did you really think I would just *hand her over?* No, she and her pathetic friends meddled where they have no business meddling, and I will not tolerate having my work interrupted by such puny creatures-s-s. The youngsters are mine. *She* is mine, Atoner... *mine.*"

With one ardour-infused bound, the mighty black lion pounced in Phoebe's direction with all the velocity and force of a runaway locomotive. In a fraction of a second, Phoebe saw the snarling jaws and ferocious fangs and closed her eyes tight as she threw her arms up protectively to cover her face. She tensed and braced for impact, fully expecting the unimaginable and wondering exactly how she hoped her feeble mortal arms could shield her. But the apparently inevitable attack never came and instead an unearthly light so vibrant and intense shot through the GuBrath chamber that it made her wince even through closed eyes.

As Phoebe cowered on the cold stone floor with her eyes closed, she was momentarily aware of a whistling sound which crescendoed rapidly until it became a roar like the sound of a rushing waterfall. A gentle wind began to flutter through her shoulder length brown hair, and gathered momentum until she was grateful that she was on her knees since the force of the gale that had culminated would have knocked her off her feet anyway.

Despite the elements crashing and tumbling around her Phoebe dared to open her eyes just a fraction. There before her like two immense and uncontainable forces of nature were what she could only assume to be the Atoner and Abaddon, represented not by instantly recognisable forms but respectively by brilliant light and darkness so dense that she was sure she could have reached out and touched it. Phoebe gasped as her eyes adjusted to the dichotomy of light and darkness and she could ascertain the forms of not one but *two* gargantuan lions. The beastly black form of Abaddon the Defiler was snarling at the Atoner's majestic white lion form with such venom that Phoebe thought he may choke on his own fury. This stand-off would be decisive, of that she was sure. Phoebe gave supreme effort to staggering to her feet, struggling hard against the wind and lightning that flashed unbridled around the room. Behind her, Demetrius's mirror had finally broken and Ella was helping him to step out from the glass prison. Phoebe pushed one foot in front of the other as she moved in the direction of her friends, forcing herself to proceed despite the strength of the unearthly storm raging around her.

Phoebe was tantalisingly close to Demetrius and Ella, so close that she could almost have stretched out her hand and touched them, when an unearthly cry reverberated around the walls of the GuBrath chamber. The storm gave one last insistent surge and an explosion of light broke through the swirling mist and wind, knocking Phoebe backwards. In her unsteadiness Phoebe caught her foot on the uneven stone floor and lost her balance, toppling back and hitting her head hard on the cold floor. She caught her breath and winced in pain, her head throbbing and her senses reeling from the fall. As she peered up at the furore that raged on around her, Phoebe made no effort to get back on her feet, and could only lie clutching her bruised head in her hands. The last thing she could remember before everything went black was Ella's frightened face and outstretched arms as she reached desperately towards her stricken friend.

CHAPTER 25

PHOEBE tentatively opened her green eyes and blinked several times in an effort to clear her groggy head. She had no idea where she was and the soft green grass beneath her only served to confuse her further. She pushed herself up gingerly on one elbow, and grimaced as pain shot through the back of her skull. She reached up with one hand and cautiously patted the throbbing site of the pain. A huge bump, painful to the touch, triggered a bell somewhere in the back of Phoebe's mind and as she struggled with swirling images and memories she realised that she was lying alone in the middle of a lush green meadow that strongly resembled... *No.* Could it be? Was this the field that sprawled out behind Ella's house? How long had she been lying here? Had she *always* been here? Had she imagined all of the fantastical characters and events that she had been so sure she had encountered in recent days? Surely not! She propped herself up further so that she could see above the tall grass and yes, there it was, the back of the Quills' family home. But that meant... If there had been no angels, no Cosain, no battles then... She could scarcely bear to acknowledge where her train of thoughts was taking her. If none of this was real, then she was still living with the Quills in Ireland and her beloved parents really were dead. This seemed to be the only sensible explanation and Phoebe's heart sank like a stone into the ocean of her soul. She involuntarily slumped her shoulders and chewed hard on her lip to stop the hot tears which were pooling in her weary eyes and blurring her vision.

Momentarily, like clouds drifting away from the sun, Phoebe's head began to clear and she realised that she was not alone in the meadow. As she strained her eyes to look across the landscape she saw a large figure striding purposefully towards her. This was not someone who was instantly recognisable to her and yet... And *yet* he had a comfortable familiarity about him that Phoebe could not quite explain.

As the man approached her, he did not speak a word but simply reached out his hand to help her to her feet. Phoebe hesitated for a moment before accepting the man's outstretched hand and clambering to her feet with just a little uncertainty. As she looked up inquisitively into the stranger's kind face, she was struck by the intensity and clarity of his bright eyes, which were brimming with compassion and loveliness. In an instant, memories flooded in and Phoebe gasped as her right hand shot up to cover her mouth. Those eyes; she had definitely seen them before... Could it be? Was there a mere chance that she had not been dreaming after all? As the strangely familiar figure spoke, all doubt was eradicated by the voice that sounded like the deepest ocean and Phoebe knew for sure who he was – the Atoner.

"It's okay, Phoebe. I am here. You are safe."

The Atoner's gentle voice washed over Phoebe like a tide, and the authority in his tone removed any confusion from her surging mind.

"You are *home*, Phoebe. Abaddon the Defiler has been subdued for now, but he will be back, and you must be ready. Your destiny as a Light Bringer will be fulfilled; I have plans for you, Little One – big plans, good plans. You will know what do."

The Atoner's voice soothed the deepest recesses of Phoebe's

soul and she knew that she could trust this individual in whose presence she felt peace and unparalleled security.

"Phoebe! *Phoebe!*"

The tranquil moment was gone as quickly as it had transpired as an unexpected call sounded across the open meadow, and Phoebe spun around to see Demetrius and Ella pelting towards her. She turned back to respond to the Atoner, but in the seconds it had taken her to look around he was gone and there was no trace that he had ever been there. Demetrius and Ella had finally reached her and both threw themselves at their friend with unbridled joy and gladness, almost knocking her off her feet again.

"Oh Phoebe," panted Ella, "I thought you were gone, I thought we would never see you again!" She grabbed her friend again in an embrace that threatened to squeeze the breath from her body, and Phoebe laughed as she wriggled free.

"Demetrius! Ella! It's so good to see you both again! *What happened?* The last thing I remember is hitting my head when I fell. And the wind... There was so much wind, and... and lightning? And the black and white lions – *were* there *lions?* And then it went dark. How did you guys get out? What happened to Abaddon? And where are Cosain and the others? Oh no... Please say they're alright..."

The need for information spilled out of Phoebe's mouth in a jumbled wave of questions, but every enquiry was suddenly silenced as a familiar voice spoke.

"We're fine, Phoebe, no need to worry about us."

Phoebe recognised the tender voice immediately: Cosain. She turned to find him standing close by with all eleven of the other angelic warriors and quickly ran to embrace the gentle giants.

"It was a close call, Phoebe," continued Cosain, "Let's just say I am very glad to see you here."

"You should have seen it, Bird," Demetrius picked up the thread of Phoebe's questions. "Abaddon – the black lion – pounced at you, I was sure he had you. But the – uh – Atoner lion had other ideas, and just when it looked like you were a goner, the room lit up and there was some kind of explosion – booming noises that made the walls shake, thunder, lightning... It was crazy, Phoebs. Anyway, a light vortex opened up from nowhere right below you and – *bam!* – you were gone. Abaddon went crazy but I think even he could see that he wasn't going to come out on top this time, so he threw open a dark vortex and vanished. The noise and light subsided and by the time Ella and I got ourselves gathered, we were alone in the GuBrath chamber with just Cosain and the others. No Abaddon, no demons, no lions – and no you. It was all so crazy, Ella and I didn't know what to think..." Demetrius grew silent, and Phoebe could see that unfolding events had shaken him.

"Demetrius is correct," Cosain confirmed the teenager's story. "Abaddon retreated and we were able to get out of the Mooar Mountain and return here to you. But..." The great warrior hesitated. "But we were almost overcome," he said with a sombre expression. "If the Atoner had not stormed the mountain..."

There was no need for Cosain to finish his sentence as none of the eclectic group was in any doubt about how things could have transpired had the Atoner not overruled.

"The Atoner," Phoebe said. "Where is he? Where did he go? He was here just now..."

Ella regarded her friend with dubious eyes. "Are you sure, Phoebe?" she asked. "You know, we were just here too and we didn't see anybody. You were alone when we got here. I think maybe that bump to your head is making you imagine things."

"Yeah," chipped in Demetrius, "There definitely wasn't anyone with you, Bird."

Phoebe was aware that she had banged her head quite hard, and the confusion of her friends made her wonder whether she had simply imagined her recent exchange with the Atoner. She felt a pang of disappointment in her belly and lowered her eyes. If she had just imagined the Atoner's presence, then maybe he wasn't all that interested in her after all...

"He was just checking that you were alright, Phoebe," whispered Ernan with a knowing wink, as if he could read the teenager's thoughts. "He *is* committed to you, as are we. He was here, for sure. He stormed the mountain to get you out Phoebe, don't you think he would stop by to make sure that you're okay?"

Phoebe nodded her relieved understanding; "*I knew it, I knew he came,*" she whispered under her breath. Her words were aimed at no-one in particular, but she found strength and hope in their reassurance.

Phoebe's thoughts turned again to the here and now. "So what's next?" she asked. "I don't imagine that the Atoner rescued us from Abaddon and the Mooar Mountain just so we could put our feet up? And if Abaddon and Schnither were able to escape, then I don't imagine that we've heard the last of them." Phoebe paused as some little memory rippled through her head. "Oh no," she sighed, furrowing her brow tightly. "What about the things Papa Augustus gave us? I dropped the watch back in the mountain. I lost it..." Phoebe's heart sank as she realised the implications of losing the little pocket watch and its magical powers. Her hand shot instinctively to the pocket of her jeans and she heaved a huge sigh of relief as she realised that the section of the Key of Esse was still there. "The key," she breathed, "At least I managed to hold on to that."

Far from being concerned, Demetrius smiled a wide smile and reached into his jeans pocket. "Don't worry Phoebe," he enthused, "I've got you covered. Don't you know by now that I've *always* got your back?" He pulled out his hand and Phoebe's heart leapt when she saw that Demetrius had retrieved the little gold pocket watch, which he handed to her with a respect that far exceeded its literal value. "And I've still got the map and the glasses and the mirror, so we're good to go."

Cosain allowed a slight smile to play across his lips. After everything that these plucky youngsters had just been through they were still ready and willing to complete the mission assigned to them. Such tenacity and bravery encouraged Cosain and he took note of the progress the young mortals had made. Nevertheless, he was all too aware of their humanity, and motioned to Dilis who gently touched the back of Phoebe's head with his sword. She gasped as she felt the weapon's regenerative and healing powers flow through her skull, and knew that the sizeable bump on her head had been removed. Demetrius and Ella watched in amazement, and the three friends shared an unspoken sense of awe at what had just transpired. "Thank you, Dilis," whispered Phoebe, as she tentatively felt the back of her head and found no trace of the injury she had sustained from her fall.

"You have done well," confirmed Cosain, "All of you. But we have much to do and a return to Darken Abbey is our priority. Schnither will undoubtedly have gone back there to rally his troops. He knows that we will make it our business to return to the abbey and lock him and his cronies behind the Geata Gate once and for all. We must rid this island of their interference for good and restore the natural balance. So, are you with me?"

Cosain looked at the three teenagers standing in front him and knew before they spoke what their response would be.

"Yes," answered Phoebe confidently on behalf of them all. "Yes, we are with you. And we will not stop until the enemy's plans are thwarted."

And without further delay Phoebe, Demetrius and Ella fell in behind the angelic troops as they set out for Darken Abbey.

CHAPTER 26

COSAIN and his troops hovered several feet above the ground as they made the short journey back to Darken Abbey. Firmly rooted on terra firma, Phoebe, Demetrius and Ella trailed a short distance behind their protectors and were quietly thoughtful for a good part of the short hike. In addition to the terrifying experience they had just endured, the teenagers were also sharing an altogether more human malady – they were *tired*. Drained. Zapped. Phoebe was inwardly glad that neither of her friends seemed to feel the need to discuss the details of what had just transpired, and for now she was quite content to simply walk and breathe and allow her thoughts to swirl around unheard inside her head. She allowed her eyes to flicker in the direction of Demetrius and Ella and could see that they too looked worn out.

"Hey," Phoebe started after a little while, keen to try and lift her friends' spirits. "That was some kind of crazy back there, huh? I really thought it might have been the end of the road for me..."

Neither Ella nor Demetrius slowed their pace or even raised their eyes from the gravel path in front of them, and Phoebe began to worry that perhaps both of her best friends had endured more than they could handle. After what seemed like an eternity Ella spoke. "Yeah," she said slowly and with much consideration. "I have to admit that I thought the same, I wondered whether we were all going to die, right there in that awful mountain. It was too close for comfort Phoebe..." Ella shifted her focus from her protracted march as she looked at Phoebe with weary eyes. "What if we hadn't gotten out Phoebe? What then? Our parents would never have found out what happened to us. They would have been left with a million unanswered questions and no closure, *ever*." Ella's musing obviously weighed heavily on her and the gravity of her words had a similar effect on Phoebe and Demetrius. The teenagers refocused again on the trail and continued to put one foot robotically in front of the other as each considered their own thoughts. Ella was right; it had been a very close call. Probably too close. If Phoebe had allowed herself to dwell on the notion, she was certain that she would have turned around and gone home without delay. But she was all too aware that they *had* gotten out, that they *were* alright, and that she, like Demetrius and Ella, had a job to do and a destiny to fulfil.

"You know guys," Phoebe came to a halt, causing her friends to walk a couple more steps before they stopped and looked round at her curiously. "You're right; this is *all* crazy and kids like us probably aren't meant to get ourselves into situations like this. But think about it – we've been *chosen* for the adventure. Of all the teenagers in all the world, *we* get to do this. I mean, would you swap it? Any of it? I know I wouldn't. We *are* safe, we are *okay*. And we have an incredible job to do. This is a once in a lifetime thing, and I don't know about you but now that I've seen just what Abaddon the Defiler and Captain Schnither are capable of, you can bet that I want to do whatever I can to stop them!"

Phoebe's renewed vigour and enthusiasm was infectious and as she watched she could see the life and verve slowly returning to her weary fellow travellers.

"You're right, Phoebe!" exclaimed Demetrius. "There's no way I'm gonna let those monsters win! This is *my* home now and I'm gonna fight for it!"

Ella looked pensive and Phoebe wondered whether her friend agreed with Demetrius or whether in fact she had other thoughts entirely on the matter. Slowly, Ella began to nod her head in agreement, although her expression remained sombre. As the friends stood now, just a few short minutes away from Darken Abbey, Phoebe knew that they were all in agreement despite their concerns and their tiredness. She looked up and realised that Cosain and the others had stopped a short distance ahead from where they had watched the teenagers' ponderings unfold. Phoebe gave him a weak smile as she and her friends began to move once again in the direction of Darken Abbey and their collective destinies.

★ ★ ★

Up ahead, unseen by humans or angels, two pairs of sneaky orange eyes were regarding the movements of the eclectic group with great interest. Twin demons Braygor and Graygor had remained in Darken Abbey while some of their larger and more ferocious counterparts had swooped to Mooar Mountain, battle ready and intent on eradicating the threat posed by Phoebe Wren and her bothersome allies. As they watched the mortals and angels approach from their vantage point in an ancient oak tree, it was very obvious that their fellow demons had not succeeded with their objective.

"See brother," sneered Graygor. "Being *big* and *scary* is no match for being *small* and *sneaky*. Malva and those other buffoons have not succeeded in removing the threat posed by the humans. I *knew* they would mess it all up! It looks like we will have to help them, show them how it's done." He snorted a prideful guffaw before settling back against a branch, letting go of the bunch of leaves through which he had been peeping. The small cluster of leaves and branches sprang round and slapped his brother curtly on the side of his head.

"Watch it you complete idiot!" snarled Braygor as he angrily swept leaves away from his face. The diminutive demon was arrogant in the extreme and since losing his tail to Cahir's sword he was particularly sensitive about anything that made him look daft. "Slap me with those branches again and I'll really give you something to crow about!"

Graygor surveyed his fuming twin with something akin to amusement. It crossed his mind to pull back another bunch of leaves and slap his brother again – just to see what would happen. But as the mortals and warrior angels drew closer he thought better of it and instead quickly changed the subject.

"You know brother," slurred Graygor. "The part we have played in getting these bothersome mortals here and back into harm's way has not been insignificant."

Braygor eyed him up with a mixture of contempt and intrigue – what was his twin inferring? "Go on..." he snapped.

"Well, it's just that it seems to me that Malva and Schnither and Craven think they're so very smart and accomplished, but actually if it hadn't been for *us* working behind the scenes, things could have turned out very differently. And I think that Abaddon owes us..."

"Graygor, *SHHH..!!*" Braygor sprang up from his perch and slapped a hand firmly across his lippy twin's mouth in one deft move. "Are you *mad?*" he squeaked, his eyes darting to and fro in panic. "If Abaddon hears you saying that..." The short demon puffed out his cheeks, hung his green tongue out the side of his mouth and with great drama and effect, drew a bony finger slowly across his throat from left to right. Graygor smacked his twin's hand away from his mouth. "I'm not *stupid*, brother!" he exclaimed. "*Of course* I'm not going to let *Abaddon* hear me! But still, don't you think we deserve some recognition for what we have done? Our input has been *invaluable* after all..."

Braygor stood down as the cogs in his head turned over and he began to realise that perhaps his gnarly twin had a point. "Hmmm..." he concurred eventually. "Perhaps you are not so misguided after all... Perhaps you do have a point..."

"Of course I do," said Graygor, his voice oozing self-righteous confidence. "And I think that if we bide our time and play our cards right, then we will finally get what we deserve..."

Graygor raised an eyebrow and smiled as a mask of devious glee slid across his twin's face. Yes, the sly little demons had done Abaddon proud, and they would make sure that they would not miss out on whatever reward was coming to them.

CHAPTER 27

THURSDAY 26ᵗʰ AUGUST
DARKEN ABBEY, IRELAND
PRESENT DAY

THE hefty Geata Gate almost flew off its ancient hinges as Captain Schnither blustered through from Mooar Mountain and up into the cold recesses of Darken Abbey. He was followed by a barrage of gnarly minions who slunk along behind him like reprimanded rascals. The motley crew had their metaphorical – and in some cases literal – tails between their legs and not one of them dared to utter a single sound. Schnither's arrival into the abbey was heralded by such clatters that even the fearsome Behemoth, the dreadful guardian of the gate, whimpered and scurried out of his road like a frightened puppy. Schnither stood until all of his cronies had hauled themselves up though the opening then slammed the Geata Gate shut with such force that the corridors in which the demons now stood shook and groaned, dislodging centuries of dust and debris, which fluttered over their fearful heads like snow.

"Is that everyone?" Schnither snarled in low raspy tones through gritted teeth.

"Uh... yes, Captain Schnither sir," stammered Bova whose emerald green eyes were clouded with terror and dread. "We're all here, I don't think anyone..."

"SILENCE YOU INCOMPETENT BUFFOON!" bellowed Schnither with such fury that drops of acidic drool were sent flying in every direction from his hacked lips. Yigno was unfortunate enough to be standing closest to the Dark Master and was unexpectedly showered in droplets of saliva. Despite the resulting fiery burning pain on his leathery skin, Yigno did not dare protest and worked hard at remaining unmoved. He clenched his jaw until the muscles popped and only when Schnither turned his back did Yigno dare to open his jaws in an unspoken *'ouch'* and frantically wiped the deadly acidic drool from his now blistering skin.

None of the assembled demons were in any doubt about the fact that Schnither would not think twice about removing their heads from their shoulders, and so each remained resolutely mute as they awaited their dark captain's command. Things had not gone to plan in Mooar Mountain by any stretch of the imagination, and to say that allowing Phoebe Wren and her scrawny friends to escape *again* had not pleased Abaddon the Defiler was a severe understatement. There were whispers and rumours amongst the legions of darkness that Abaddon had only spared Schnither's life when he swore to personally eradicate all three young mortals along with all of their angelic protectors. Furthermore, the gaping wound that now oozed yellow slime from Schnither's right cheek suggested that Abaddon had given him something to remind him of his oath.

With much huffing and snorting, but without another word, Captain Schnither led his troops up the dank staircase that wound from the bleak underbelly of Darken Abbey and out into the Great Hall. Their arrival was met by countless black creatures, all straining and eager to hear what had transpired in Mooar Mountain. As Schnither's beleaguered troops emerged into the Great Hall and made their way to the front of the huge room, some dared to shake their heads in warning at their fellow demons when they caught their questioning glances. It became apparent very quickly that the news coming from the mountain was not good, and those congregated instinctively knew not to ask any questions. Schnither stopped next to the stone altar at the front of the Great Hall. His cronies waited with baited breath as the Dark Captain appeared to draw in several deep breaths, apparently composing himself before he turned to face the assembled masses. Schnither's great shoulders heaved twice then he raised his terrible head and stood to his full imposing height before turning to face the sea of inquisitive faces. Even in humiliating defeat Captain Schnither's pride would not be quashed.

"Do not insult me by acting as if you have not all already heard what happened *down there*," snarled Schnither with scarcely concealed contempt and a nod towards the lower recesses of the abbey that housed the Geata Gate. "You have heard the rumours I am sure. The girl, Phoebe Wren, and her cohorts are no longer in our possession. We had them – ahh, we *had* them – but the *Ato...*" Schnither paused and curled his top lip as if he had tasted something sour. "The *Atoner* saw fit to meddle in things that he has no business meddling in, and he wrecked our best laid plans."

A beastly creature in the third row was apparently bemused by the news and dared to indulge in the slightest secret sneer. His overextended neck bore a proportionally tiny head with cold squinty eyes that glinted as he leaned forward and hissed in whispered tones to the equally fiendish demon in front of him; "What did he expect to happen? Did he really think the Atoner would just stand by and watch while they finished off the mortals? Pah! Idiots! I should have been there; I would have shown them how it's done!"

The ghoulish and reluctant listener bristled and moved his head away in a desperate attempt to disassociate himself with the brash creature who had deemed it wise to speak. But it was to no avail; Schnither had witnessed the hushed exchange and his simmering fury now erupted to the surface and spilled over as he lunged through the congregated demons in the direction of those involved, scattering lesser demons left and right as he surged forward. Both creatures instantly that they had been caught out, and cowered beneath Schnither's gargantuan frame. The first fiend opened his mouth to defend himself, but before he could utter a sound Schnither had run them both through with his deadly serrated blade, despatching them to the Abyss in an explosion of darkness and a swirl of orange mist. No second strike was needed. Nobody flinched; not one creature dared to move a muscle, and had there been gasps of horror or shock, these were skilfully muffled lest Schnither should decide to dole out the same punishment on anyone else. A hundred pairs of malevolent eyes had opened wide in disbelief and terror, and those congregated were left in no doubt that Schnither was in no mood for defiance. Not a trace remained of the two offending demons as the Dark Captain turned curtly on his heel and returned to his spot at the front of the Great Hall from where he surveyed the dark gathering with unveiled disdain.

"Anyone else?" he snarled slowly, surveying the sea of petrified faces before him. "Does *anyone else* have anything to say?"

The silence in the Great Hall was deafening and several fiendish creatures even held their breath in case the very sound emanating from their gnarly lungs would offend their dark captain.

"No? I shall take your silence as my answer. And let that little exchange be a lesson to you all – I will not tolerate impudence at any level! I *will* have your respect... And if I do not have your respect, *then I will have your life!*"

Schnither's stark warning was heard loud and clear, and understood by every beast gathered before him. None of them even dared to entertain the thought that his threats were devoid of intent. No, Captain Schnither did not joke, and his threats were seldom empty.

"Very well." Schnither's hulking body no longer shook with rage and his tone had settled to scarcely more than a gravely whisper. "We will regroup and formulate a plot. I have no doubt the Phoebe Wren and her stupid, *stupid* guardians will make their way back to Darken Abbey very soon – and we will be ready for them."

The still terrified onlookers could all tell from Schnither's voice that, despite his best efforts to the contrary, his pride had taken a severe bashing, and it was safe to assume that his self-belief had plummeted, but none of the wicked creatures possessed the bravery – or foolishness – required to mention this. Instead, they waited with baited breath as Captain Schnither began to unveil his heinous plans to the malevolent throng.

CHAPTER 28

OUTSIDE DARKEN ABBEY
IRELAND

PHOEBE paused as she and her fellow adventurers arrived just a stone's throw from the bottom of the gentle hill that housed Darken Abbey on its crest. She looked up at the imposing old building and could not decide whether its sinister appearance was the result of the quickly dimming evening light or the malevolent beings she knew to be inside its ancient walls. Scaffolding was still in place around the abbey's outer walls, a reassuring reminder that her that her parents were working hard to establish Celtic Justice Organisation. She tried to reassure herself that this perilous, ridiculous day would soon be over and normality could be resumed, but the harsh angular metal of the scaffolding only served to make the building look even more foreboding.

Cosain and the other warriors had congregated next to Phoebe, Demetrius and Ella, and the mighty Captain of the Host now stood surveying the scene pensively. For what seemed like an eternity, nobody uttered a single word. The eclectic group of angelic beings and young mortals were hidden by a little cluster of trees which had not yet started to shed their leaves for the fast approaching autumn season, and Phoebe was thankful for the veiled vantage point this afforded them. With the exception of the distant low rumble of a sporadic passing vehicle, there was little by way of sound or movement to disturb the quiet evening. It struck Phoebe that she could not even hear the comforting chirp of bird song, and she remembered with a shudder the stark silence of the wasteland outside Mooar Mountain, and grimly concluded that even the birds did not want to stay in a place where such evil resided.

Momentarily, Cosain spoke: "This is it," he said, addressing his troops and their young wards with a serious tone that put Phoebe further on edge. "We will make our ascent to the abbey under cover of invisibility as far as possible – but I do not believe that our entrance will be unexpected. I am certain that Schnither and his cronies will be awaiting our arrival. It is my assertion that he will have come directly here via the Geata Gate, which will have afforded him a head start on us. And he will be angry – *livid* – and absolutely determined not to suffer another humiliating defeat. None of us should make the mistake of underestimating Captain Schnither and his henchmen. This could prove to be the fight of our lives..." Cosain's voice trailed off as his golden hued eyes shifted from face to face, seeking out an assurance that each angel and mortal fully comprehended the severity of the situation. When he was satisfied that nobody was under any illusions about the gravity of what lay ahead, he continued; "We will enter the abbey via the main doors. Schnither's sentries will be posted at every access point, so we might as well take the direct approach. Once inside, there will be very little time – if any – for us to make our move before our enemies launch their attack, so we must be very clear about our course of action before we get there."

Cosain turned to Phoebe and her friends, and focused his attention very definitely on the nervous youngsters.

"Phoebe, I am assigning you, Demetrius and Ella the task of returning the missing piece of the Key of Esse to the Geata Gate to you. This will not be an easy task by any stretch of the imagination, but it will take our combined efforts in the upper level to stave off the onslaught from Schnither and his henchmen." He nodded towards the eleven imposing warriors gathered next to their captain. "I do not think that Schnither will expect us to allow you to carry out such a task by yourselves, but with the majority of the dark fiends busied with us in the Great Hall, I believe that the gateway should be... *relatively accessible*."

Cosain paused again and knew without asking that his words had sent a chill through Phoebe. '...*should be relatively accessible...*' The seemingly innocent phrase assaulted Phoebe's ears. Those four little words bore in them so many unquantifiable possibilities and reverberated around inside her head long after Cosain had uttered them. The Captain of the Host might as well have said '*impassable, impossible, don't even try it*', and Phoebe could not deny the forceful impact with which his words had assailed her.

Cosain surveyed Phoebe's horrified expression for a moment before he continued. "Yes, with Schnither and his cronies preoccupied in the Great Hall, I expect that the only person – *thing* – guarding the Geata Gate will be the Behemoth."

Despite the gravity of Cosain's words, Phoebe could not help herself and a wry little smile crept across her face as the sides of her lips twitched upwards. She clamped her teeth together several times in rapid succession then looked directly at Cosain. This was no time for levity, and she would not give voice to the nervous laughter that threatened to erupt.

"Cosain," she ventured, regaining her composure. "We have come this far, come through so much, and we aren't going to back out now, that is a given. But seriously... How exactly do you imagine that Demetrius, Ella and I are going to persuade the Behemoth to let us past him to get to the Geata Gate? Start a game of fetch?" As soon as she had uttered the words Phoebe regretted her sarcasm. She furrowed her brow and chewed on her bottom lip in annoyance, but, ever gracious, Cosain merely smiled at her and nodded his head.

"It won't be easy, I'll give you that," Cosain acknowledged. "But remember that you have powers to fall back on, you have tools at your disposal. These will be invaluable to you." Cosain hesitated just long enough to make Phoebe look up at him inquisitively. "And there is something else," he continued. "Like everyone and everything else, even the Behemoth has his Achilles heel."

"Go on..." said Demetrius, looking intrigued and terrified in equal proportions.

"Well," continued Cosain. "Legend has it that the Behemoth cannot bear the sight of his own reflection..."

As if a switch had been flipped in Phoebe's head, her face lit up. "Of course!" she exclaimed with the excitement of someone who had just discovered something of huge significance. "The little mirror we found in Brother Eli's room! No wonder he was so insistent that we bring it. And all this time I have been thinking that Eli got it wrong about the mirror."

"Exactly," concurred Cosain. "Brother Eli's mirror. I should imagine that he knew of the Behemoth's weak point. But..." Cosain paused, and his hesitation said more than his words. "But neither he nor Brother Bennett were afforded the opportunity to try it out before they were ousted from Darken Abbey."

As quickly as it had filled her with hope, the idea of using the mirror against the Behemoth suddenly seemed wildly irresponsible to Phoebe and her heart sank in unison with her shoulders.

"So... we don't know *for sure* that the Behemoth is afraid

of his own reflection?" The disappointment mingled with fear in Phoebe's voice was unmistakable.

"I'm afraid not," said Neam as he regarded the youngsters with concern in his clear blue eyes.

"But," interjected Dilis with all the enthusiasm and positivity of youth, "Don't forget that everything that we have heard about the creature to date has been correct – so there's every chance that this legend about the mirror is *more* than mere legend... Right?"

The young warrior's ability to remain upbeat and idealistic seemed to be infectious, and it was not long before angels and mortals alike were nodding in agreement as murmurs of, "*Dilis has a point, there **is** every chance that the legend is true, and if the Behemoth cannot look on his own reflection then we have a way to defeat him*" rippled throughout the group. Finally, Cosain held up his hand and a reverential hush fell as the Captain of the Host began to speak.

"I think we all know what we must do."

The commander's weighty bronze breastplate rose and fell as he heaved a deep sigh of responsibility. "We will attack the forces of darkness inside Darken Abbey head on, there can be no hesitation or shrinking back. Brothers, remain cloaked in invisibility until we have infiltrated the abbey; Demetrius, use the map to conceal your presence until we have engaged the enemy then you must move quickly to the Geata Gate."

There was no need for spoken responses; everyone knew their role and exactly what was expected of them. As Phoebe watched, Cosain and the other warriors drew their glowing swords before vanishing from sight. As was always the case, Phoebe was aware that the combatants could not been seen by other eyes, but they remained reassuringly visible to her. Demetrius pulled the magical map from his back pocket and opened it out to its unexpanded original width. He lifted the faded old document carefully above his head as Phoebe and Ella pressed in close on either side of him, partly in the desire to remain invisible and partly for the reassurance that being close to Demetrius afforded them. As Demetrius wrapped the map around himself and the girls, he marvelled again at the way in which the old parchment grew and expanded until it fit around their three forms as though it had been tailor made for them. Although suitably cloaked in invisibility, there was an undeniable air of trepidation as the angels and mortals made their way unseen up the hill towards Darken Abbey. Phoebe could not help but wonder whether anyone else could feel the electric jolts of nervous excitement that were coursing through her body as she considered with awe and horror what it meant to be part of the defining battle that would ensue.

CHAPTER 29

THE great front doors of Darken Abbey loomed ever larger as Phoebe and her friends made their way stealthily closer. Their ascent had been slow and cautious, but this had been necessary as the eclectic group wound its way carefully between shadowy demons stationed at intervals along the gravely pathway. Phoebe had held tightly to Demetrius's arm as they passed under the noses of the gnarly guards, and held her breath when the more astute beasts sniffed the cool evening air and furrowed their brows in confusion when they sensed an unfamiliar presence but could see nothing. On two occasions on the short journey to the brow of the hill Phoebe had been sure that her invisibility had been compromised when jittery black beings spun around unexpectedly in her direction, peering intently into the fading evening sky and only just avoiding bumping into her quaking form. Nearer the summit, Phoebe balked as she recognised several of the fearsome beasts – Bova, Eenu, Jarrda and Yigno had all been patrolling the parameters of the abbey, and Phoebe was sure she had caught a glimpse of the twisty twins Braygor and Graygor as they scampered around the abbey's grounds.

It occurred to Phoebe to wonder just how Bova and his cronies came to be here, since the last time she had seen them they had been securely bound by triple stranded angelic ropes, frozen solid by the magic of the pocket watch, and indelibly branded with the Atoner's crest by the tip of Solas's blazing sword. Several close but fruitless brushes with the enemy had reassured Phoebe of her invisibility and now, secure in the belief that she could not be seen, Phoebe dared to look longer and closer at the demons as she dodged past them. She could see jagged wounds on Bova's upper arm where the indignant beast had desperately tried to scratch away the Atoner's crest and imagined his fury as he willingly wounded himself in order to disassociate himself with the ranks of the Heavenlies. Ordinarily, being branded with the Atoner's seal would have rendered any dark beast instantly defunct in the realms of darkness, but Bova's relatively successful attempts to at least sully the mark if not remove it entirely, coupled with his presence here, suggested that Abaddon had rounded up all the dark creatures he could find, ready for some great showdown. Phoebe noted that Eenu, Jarrda and Yigno all bore similar freshly self-inflicted wounds to Bova, and she could have been tempted to pity the sorry creatures had she not witnessed firsthand their determination to snuff out all traces of good and light they encountered.

Cosain silently raised his left hand and signalled for everyone to stop just in front of the abbey's front doors. He turned to face his modest but fierce army, running his earnest eyes from one expectant face to the next until he was sure that each was ready for what lay ahead. Cosain nodded slowly and his lips twitched in the slightest smile of reassurance before the fearsome captain of the Heavenly hosts gritted his teeth and reached out to open the abbey's doors. Phoebe felt as though time slowed to a crawl as she watched the imminent battle begin to unfold. She observed Cosain's grip on his sword. The handle of the enormous blade was resting firmly in his right hand, and his knuckles were white from the intensity of his grip. With his free left hand, Cosain swung open the heavy doors to Darken Abbey as if they were made of paper, as the ancient wooden doorway creaked and groaned in protest. In an instant, time resumed its stride as the great doors slammed hard into the stone walls inside the abbey. Phoebe could just see inside past Cosain, and the hideous spectacle made her gasp. A sea of dark gnarly beasts spun around in the direction of the now open doors like an uneven Mexican wave that rippled throughout the Great Hall. Some of the creatures yelped in shock while others physically jumped in fright, jostling the dark beasts to their left and right and causing at least six demons to wobble and fall from their perches high up on the abbey's ceiling beams. The unfortunates who had been knocked off balance plummeted to the floor in tumbling masses of flailing arms and legs, and the resulting thuds as indignant bodies hit the floor sparked further confusion amongst the demons, who now turned their attention away from the doors and on to their fallen cohorts. Cosain seized the opportunity to work the confusion to his advantage and charged into the midst of the assembled creatures with eleven ferocious warriors and three unsure mortals close on his heels. Once inside, Cosain and his brothers materialised into visibility amidst irate howls and indignant screeches as the dark beasts realised that their ranks had been infiltrated. The demons that had fallen from the rafters were on their feet now as they joined their fellow monsters to face the angelic warriors.

Demetrius clamped his upper arms tighter to his body in an effort to ensure that Phoebe and Ella stayed close by his side, but he need not have worried. Both girls were clinging to Demetrius as though their very lives depended on it, and they stayed as close as they could to ensure that their invisibility was not compromised. Demetrius held the map resolutely closed over their heads as he moved quickly away from the battle that was beginning in earnest in the Great Hall. He did not dare run for fear that three sets of teenage legs would become entangled resulting in him and the girls tripping each other up and blowing their cover, but he was all too aware that there was no time to waste. Demetrius guided the girls across the back wall of the Great Hall, taking an unspoken lead that neither Phoebe nor Ella questioned. The teenagers moved quickly across the familiar room, each working hard to control the fear that was churning in their bellies. They were heading for the stone altar at the front of the great room and as they clambered ever closer, Phoebe found herself contemplating all that had happened in the last twenty four hours. She could scarcely believe that in the course of just one day, both of her best friends had been captured by Abaddon the Defiler and then rescued by Cosain and his troops. And they had all survived Mooar Mountain – that in itself was some sort of miracle. A crazy, surreal miracle. The magnitude of these thoughts was overwhelming and as they raced through Phoebe's head at an unbridled pace, they made her dizzy and somewhat nauseous. Phoebe forced herself to stop focusing on helter-skelter thoughts and concentrate only on the job at hand. *The job at hand.* The implications of *this* task were no less overwhelming than everything that had transpired to date, and Phoebe concluded that she should just focus on the moment in order to keep herself from being swallowed up by fear. '*Just breathe,*' she thought. '*That's all. Don't think. Just. Breathe.*'

Demetrius, Phoebe and Ella scurried along unseen until they neared the front of the Great Hall. Off to the right of the stone altar was the narrow doorway that led away from the abbey's main hall and opened on to stairs which wound downward into the imposing building's secret underbelly. Phoebe knew what lay below, and the dreadful knowledge made her want to turn on her heel and run as far and as fast as she could in the opposite direction, but she knew deep in her soul that this was not an option. Instead she paused just momentarily, gently pulling on Demetrius's arm so that he and Ella stopped and looked back in the direction of Phoebe's gaze. A bright and ferocious light had blazed through the Great Hall, flooding even the darkest recesses with an unearthly luminosity. Although the light burned her eyes and caused her to squint, Phoebe peered into it for as long as she could bear. She could make out the swirling silhouettes of myriads of gnarly demons all writhing and flailing furiously like stricken insects. They seemed to materialise from nowhere, thronging towards the epicentre of the battle from all sides as well as from above and below. But there in the very centre of the mêlée she recognised twelve familiar and beloved forms: Cosain, Ernan, Solas, Dilis, Trean, Neam, Croga, Lasair, Maelis, Keane, Lachlan and Cahir. The warriors were fully engaged in battle, their flawless forms easily distinguishable from the twisted, broken bodies of the demonic horde. The angels were outnumbered by perhaps twenty to one, but this did not appear to be having a negative impact on Cosain and his brothers as they sent demon after screeching demon to the Abyss in a barrage of blows from their fiery swords. The stench of sulphur was overwhelming as demonic beings threw themselves recklessly at their assailants only to meet their doom at the end of an angelic blade. Shadowy creatures were disintegrating into plumes of smoke all around the Great Hall as the warrior angels' swords met their mark time and again.

Just as Phoebe was about to turn away and descend the stairway out of the Great Hall, Cosain looked up and caught her eye from the centre of the battle. It was a microsecond in time but as the youngster's gaze locked on Cosain's his golden hued eyes relayed a thousand unspoken words of calm and reassurance, and an unearthly peace flooded over her that entirely contradicted her circumstances. In that instant, Phoebe knew that she was exactly where she was supposed to be. She was a Light Bringer and she was on her way to fulfilling her destiny. The deep and undeniable consciousness that *all would be well* washed through her jangled soul leaving its soothing mark long after the moment had passed. She smiled as she looked away, and when she returned her gaze Cosain was locked once more in deadly battle with several hideous beasts. Neither Demetrius nor Ella had witnessed this brief exchange between mortal and protector, but both felt the marked shift in Phoebe's boldness as she urged them on towards the stairway and – ultimately – the Behemoth below.

As the teenagers made their way on to the stairs and began their descent into the abbey's lower recesses, they gradually left the noises of battle behind them as the eerie quiet from the abbey's substratum snaked its way up to meet them. But the tiny exchange between Cosain and Phoebe had not gone unnoticed by everyone in the Great Hall, and in the huge and violent space above, Braygor was retreating unnoticed from the furore. He had caught the fleeting look in Cosain's eyes and if his suspicions were correct, those troublesome teens had been in the Great Hall. Oh, he hadn't actually *seen them,* but he was certain that they were here, *somewhere* in the abbey. The diminutive demon could scarcely disguise his glee as he slunk unnoticed away from the raging battle and made his way to the front of the abbey, headed assuredly in the direction he was certain the bothersome mortals had gone. If they *were* in the abbey, then Braygor was going to find them and make them sorry that they ever crossed his path.

CHAPTER 30

PHOEBE, Demetrius and Ella fumbled their way down the cold stone staircase in pitch darkness. Only when they had descended a good distance from the Great Hall did Demetrius dare to lower the map, leaving the teenagers in plain sight. He folded the invaluable document once again and returned it to the back pocket of his jeans.

Although they were now clearly visible, the friends stayed close together with only one stone step between them at all times. After everything that they had been through in the Mooar Mountain, none of them was in any doubt that sticking together was by far their preferred option. They descended cautiously, partly because the stone staircase had been dampened and made slippery by the chill that hung in the air in the deeper levels of the abbey, and partly because they knew what awaited them in the abbey's clandestine lowest level.

The teens were only a few steps from the bottom of the staircase when the slightest flutter in the air around them caused Demetrius to bristle and stop abruptly. It may have been nothing more than a hunch, but it was enough for Demetrius to shove the girls unceremoniously back against the dank stone wall as he scrambled to pull the old map from his back pocket. There was no time for either Phoebe or Ella to question Demetrius's actions and with mere seconds to spare he thrust the open map in front of them as five shadowy black beasts swooped around a corner and shot up the stairs past the shaking teenagers. The last one to pass by – an ugly winged beast with a twisted back and green leathery skin – was apparently more astute than his terrible colleagues and he paused momentarily just two steps up from where Phoebe and her friends stood motionless and invisible. The creature turned and peered back down the staircase that he had just ascended, his yellow eyes straining into the murky darkness. He sniffed the dank air several times, his great nostrils flaring and emitting orange gas as he did so, then craned his long leathery neck so close to Ella that she had to hold her breath for fear that the creature might feel the warmth of her breath on his hideous visage. Seconds passed and still the suspicious creature stood, peering and sniffing, until eventually he turned and, realising that his cohorts had gone on ahead without him, he snorted an irritated '*pah*' noise and began his climb up the staircase after his long gone cohorts. Just as the creature was about to disappear from sight, a short and sneaky looking demon lurched down the stone stairway towards him, travelling too fast to be able to stop, and collided with the irritated and much larger demon.

"Braygor," snarled the retreating beast. "Watch where you're going you idiot! What are you doing here anyway? Where are you going? You should be upstairs, helping our brothers to finish off those stupid angelic warriors."

Phoebe, Demetrius and Ella held their breath as they recognised Braygor's diminutive form, and realised that he must have followed them from the Great Hall. They could only watch silently to see how the encounter would transpire.

"What's it to you?" snarled Braygor in response as he attempted to squeeze past the inquisitive demon who was blocking his downward descent. His prickliness was met with a stinging slap to the back of his head, and Braygor yelped in pain and indignance. "*Oww!*" he howled. "Hey, what did you do that for?" The incensed little demon rubbed his head and regarded his offender with loathing.

"I asked you a question, little monster," retorted the yellow eyed creature. "And you're not getting past until you tell me what you're up to."

Braygor sighed so deeply that the hidden teenagers could see his jagged ribcage rise and fall as he resigned himself to the fact that given his tiny size, it would probably be in his best interests to respond politely.

"I saw the mortal children leave the Great Hall..." Braygor started before he was rudely interrupted.

"What?" exclaimed his tormentor. "You *saw* the Wren girl and her friends? They're *here?*"

"Yes," exclaimed Braygor in exasperated tones before pausing and reconsidering his response. "Well, that is... I didn't *actually see* them – but I know they were in the Great Hall and that they were headed this way."

The words had barely left Braygor's mouth when he was rewarded with another humiliating slap from the much bigger demon who was now blocking his route downstairs with his hulking body.

"You snivelling little idiot," snarled the demon. "You were trying to *escape*, weren't you? You didn't see the mortals any more than I did! You were just too scared to stay and fight alongside your brothers! You're a disgrace, Braygor, I ought to send you to the Abyss myself!"

Braygor started to protest, but was curtly silenced by the much bigger demon, who grabbed him by the ear and began to march him back up the stairs towards the Great Hall.

"I've just come up this way you sneaky little fibber!" the bigger demon shouted. "There are no mortals down here! Do you think I'm an idiot? Let's see what Captain Schnither has to say to your insubordination..."

The fuming yellow eyed fiend hauled Braygor unceremoniously back upstairs and out of sight as the little demon kicked and protested in vain. Demetrius waited until he was certain that the last of the advancing beasts had gone before he deemed it safe to lower the map, and he, Phoebe and Ella dared to breathe out a long and unanimous sigh of relief.

"That was close," whispered Demetrius, who was folding up the map with noticeably shaking hands.

"Way *too* close," agreed Phoebe as she turned to look at Ella. "How on earth did Braygor know that we were up there in the Great Hall? I can't even bear to think what might have happened if he had followed us down here and caught up on us!" She paused and rubbed her forehead then looked at her friends. "You okay, El?"

Ella's already pale complexion had drained of any colour it may have possessed and she stood now quaking with fear and so deathly ashen that she looked almost iridescent. Ella swallowed hard and bit her lower lip. She could not quite find the words to reply and merely nodded her head at Phoebe who gave her hand a quick and reassuring squeeze.

"It's okay, we're almost at the bottom," Phoebe offered, then stopped suddenly and fell quiet as she realised that her choice of words probably offered little by way of comfort or reassurance to her terrified best friend.

Demetrius resumed the lead as he and the girls began to move again, and Phoebe could not be sure whether it was their close encounter with the five dark fiends or the thinning air in the substratum of the abbey that was making it difficult for her to regulate her breathing. She worked hard to slow her breathing and resolutely began to refocus on the task at hand.

With a last downward step, the three friends exited the stone staircase and arrived in the foreboding lowest level of Darken Abbey. They were surprised to find a few dimly glowing oil lamps scattered at irregular intervals along a dark and forbidding corridor. It would seem that even the darkest beings from the Abyss still needed just a little light. It occurred to Phoebe that the corridor ahead of them seemed to be the sole point of entry and exit on this level. She could not be sure whether the same thought had occurred to her friends, but decided it was best not to draw any unnecessary attention to the fact. There was nothing they could do about it at any rate, and highlighting the issue would probably only serve to put an already nervous Ella even more on edge.

"Looks like we're going this way," whispered Demetrius. "I guess the Geata Gate must be down here."

"Yeah," said Ella in hushed tones. "And if the gate's down there then so is the Behemoth." Her pretty face was wrinkled and contorted with fear and Phoebe could see that it was taking every ounce of courage for Ella to just hold her ground.

Ella's observation had an instantaneous sobering effect on all three teenagers and they stood in silence for a moment before making their next move. Finally, Demetrius inhaled deeply and slowly began to proceed along the dull and intimidating corridor. Not wanting to be left behind, Phoebe and Ella quickly fell in behind Demetrius as he crept ever further along the corridor and away from the only escape route out of this deep and brooding level of the abbey.

The friends were glad of the light afforded them by the sparse oil lamps. Even though their glow was paltry, it permitted the youngsters some degree of warmth and reassurance. Phoebe shuddered to think how all encompassing the darkness would have been but for the insipid light of the weakly glowing oil lamps. As it was, even with the light, the darkness felt as though it was crawling over her skin, clinging to her outline like some formless sticky weed that would squeeze the breath from her body if it was given half a chance. She shuddered again and shook her head and shoulders as if to free them from the grasp of the dark and cold as she followed her friends into the unknown.

After some time, Demetrius came to a halt. He and the girls had been negotiating the corridor for what felt like a very long time, and the unspoken realisation of just how deep into the abbey's belly they had journeyed was not lost on any of them. They were cold and hungry, and tiredness was creeping up on them all making everything seem so much more difficult than it already was. Phoebe had no doubt that the air was perilously thin down here and she had to force herself once more to regulate her breathing and refuse to panic or give in to the claustrophobia that threatened to overwhelm her.

Up ahead, the teenagers could hear snorting snuffly noises that reminded Phoebe of the sound a pet dog might make as he lolloped around in his owner's garden. But she knew all too well that *this* dog was no pet, and he definitely would not take kindly to the notion of having an owner. The snorting noises were dimmed somewhat by an altogether more sinister sound that Phoebe just could not put her finger on. Phoebe felt the blood freeze in her veins as she silently listened to the strange swooshing noises emanating from the direction of the Behemoth's lair. It took her a few moments to recognise the sound, but suddenly words from Brother Bennett's journal flooded into her mind – '*perhaps the creature's most terrifying feature was its tail, the tip of which blazed with scorching fire which illuminated the entire chamber*'. Of course. That was it. The swooshing sound she could hear was the sound of the Behemoth's fiery tail flicking off cold stone walls as the beast patrolled its territory. So it was not asleep as Phoebe had dared to hope. Far from it, judging by the noises echoing back along the sparsely lit corridor. '*Why couldn't it be his nap time?'* Phoebe wondered in frustration as she scowled into the darkness.

"This is it," Demetrius's tone was thick with trepidation as he voiced what the girls were thinking. "The Behemoth is just up ahead, that's him making the noises. We've got to distract the beast, lure him away, and use the mirror to unnerve him enough to let you get in there and lock the gate, Phoebe."

"*Me?*" Phoebe's response was louder than she intended, and the three friends held their breaths, terrified that their cover had been blown. The Behemoth's snuffling and swooshing stopped momentarily, but recommenced without further investigation from the gnarly creature, and Phoebe thankfully closed her eyes as she blew out a sigh of relief.

"Me? Why me Dem?" Phoebe asked in lowered tones. "Don't you think *you'd* be better to lock the gateway? I mean, what if it's rusty or stiff and I can't get the missing piece of the Key of Esse to fit?" Phoebe could feel her heart beating faster inside her ribs and she really began to doubt that she had what it would take to complete her mission.

"You can do it, Phoebs. I know you can." Demetrius smiled at his jittery friend as he took her hand, and Phoebe felt herself relax immediately. How did he do that? Demetrius just had the knack of calming Phoebe down and making her return to herself. "You're much smaller than me so you'll be able to get closer to the Geata Gate before the Behemoth notices you."

"Oh great," exclaimed Phoebe in a hushed tone, but with renewed agitation in her voice. "So I get up close and *then* it sees me! What then, Dem? Throw something and hope it wants to go fetch it?"

Despite the gravity of the situation, Demetrius grinned mischievously at his best friend's indignation. "Look, you've just got to *trust me* Bird. Ella and I will do what we can to get the big dog away from its post. I'm not sure how it'll react to its reflection in the mirror, but what else can we do? We've got to try, right? *Right?*"

"Yeah," sighed Phoebe with an air of unavoidable resignation. "You're right."

Demetrius nodded at his friend as he stepped closer and pressed a cold length of metal into her palm – the missing piece of the Key of Esse. Phoebe shivered involuntarily as she thought of what Demetrius had referred to as the '*big dog*'. Big dog? That made the slobbering beast sound like some giant puppy who just wanted to play. '*I'm not sure I fancy playing with that monster*', Phoebe thought but she kept her reservations to herself and decided to trust Demetrius. He was usually right, after all. *Usually...* She gripped the section of the Key of Esse in her clammy hand and swallowed hard.

CHAPTER 31

THE nervous teenagers knew that the task ahead of them would require all the strength and courage they could muster and with this in mind they determined to give it their best shot. The thought of letting Cosain and the others down was not something they wanted to have to experience. They inched their way closer to the source of the beastly sounds until just one jagged corner separated them from the reality of the Behemoth's claws. Demetrius paused once again and looked from Phoebe to Ella. Their faces told him that they were as ready as they would ever be and with a solemnity that contradicted his youth he pulled out the map with all the ceremony of some official occasion. Phoebe took a deep breath then nodded at her friend with a look that said '*it's now or never*'. Ella pressed in closer to Demetrius as he unfolded the ancient map which extended to a suitable size as he wrapped it closely around the two of them. Phoebe watched as her friends disappeared from view. She knew that trying to watch where they went was a fruitless exercise, but she strained her earnest green eyes nevertheless in an effort to follow their movements as they moved away from her and closer to the Behemoth. Phoebe recalled the last time she had been separated from Demetrius and Ella in Mooar Mountain, and the memory made her shudder. She pushed the thoughts to the back of her mind then began to inch cautiously along, pressing her back firmly against the cold stone wall as she edged just far enough round the rocky corner to be able to see what was happening without being noticed.

With her heart in her throat, Phoebe turned her gaze in the direction of the Geata Gate, not wanting to look and yet propelled to see what fate awaited her. As her eyes locked on the fearsome Behemoth, Phoebe's hand flew involuntarily over her mouth as her jaw fell slack. The creature that was guarding the gateway truly was like something that had just stepped out of a nightmare and into her reality. His huge hulking body seemed to fill the room and his powerful frame bulged with muscles that jumped and flexed as he moved. The beast's head did indeed resemble the 'big dog' to which Demetrius had referred, but was perhaps three or maybe even four times bigger than even the largest natural dog Phoebe had ever seen. His enormous mouth hung open, revealing apparently endless rows of terrifying fangs from which dripped great rancid droplets of drool. The beast's six muscular legs carried his giant frame with ease as he patrolled his territory, and his powerful flaming tail swished back and forth. It would undoubtedly incinerate anything that came into contact with it. Phoebe could feel the hairs on the back of her neck bristle as she realised that she could not afford to connect with *either* end of this horrible beast. '*Oh wonderful,*' thought Phoebe. '*Not only is he awake but he's on high alert!*' She sucked in a sharp breath as she briefly looked away then took a moment to steady her breathing and steel her jangling nerves. When she dared to look back, her heart missed a beat as she realised that the Behemoth was glaring in her general direction. His terrible black eyes were scarcely discernible against his coarse black fur but as they rolled crazily in the beast's head Phoebe realised that he was not in fact looking at her but merely scouring his territory for anything untoward. The fact that she had not been spotted reassured Phoebe somewhat, and she gritted her teeth and began to watch for just the right moment to proceed. She ran her finger over the little gold pocket watch in her pocket and felt a sudden pang of home sickness. It felt like aeons had passed since she had seen her parents or her grandparents, when in fact not even a full day had transpired. How she wished that the watch's time-stopping powers could be used right now, but she remembered her Grandfather's words of warning, "*the watch is powerful, but it's power is not without limit. It will have no effect on certain enemy forces – including the Behemoth*". Why did the Behemoth have to be exempt from the watch's power? It would have made things so much simpler if he could just have obligingly fallen under the watch's spell!

A few moments passed and Phoebe continued to watch and listen for any sign that she should make her move. She was not entirely sure what she was watching for, but she did not have to wait long to find out. Peculiar *meowing* noises began to fill the air in the underground chamber, barely audible at first, but increasing in volume until they reverberated off the cold stone walls and bounced crazily around the room. Phoebe shook her head and the corners of her mouth twitched in a wry smile that remained unformed as the source of the curious noises dawned on her. Demetrius had referred to the Behemoth as a big dog, so of course it figured that he would attract its attention by making *cat noises*. '*Silly, crazy Dem,*' Phoebe mused. Her eyes were fixed on the overgrown black dog and she hoped desperately that he would take the bait. The monster seemed puzzled by the persistent noise at first and after sweeping the room with his black eyes and finding nothing, he plonked down on his backside and scratched his ear with one of his six powerful legs. The great beast looked almost vulnerable as he sat there looking confused, but Phoebe knew better than to underestimate his ferocity. Undeterred by the beast's lack of reaction, Demetrius continued to make the ridiculous cat noises until the Behemoth could no longer ignore them, and he stood to his feet looking angry and perplexed. Phoebe watched as the beast sniffed the air, his giant head moving back and forth until he apparently caught a scent. The beast's coarse black fur bristled and a low growling noise rumbled from his belly and up his throat. The thin air was suddenly thick with foreboding and Phoebe put a hand against the cold stone wall to steady her head, which was beginning to spin.

The Behemoth glared into the half light. He knew that there was something out there and he was not amused. Slowly, the huge black beast began to move menacingly across the expansive chamber. He was obviously agitated but not afraid. Phoebe didn't imagine that the Behemoth feared anything. The hulking monster crouched low as he moved, the muscles in his powerful legs retracting so that he was ready to pounce on whatever had invaded his space. Phoebe watched and waited, biding her time until the exact moment when she would make her move. There would be only one chance, Phoebe knew that. She could not afford even the slightest error. Time seemed to crawl along as Phoebe watched intently while the scene unfolded. Her heart was thumping inside her chest so loudly that she was sure it was only a matter of time before the Behemoth heard it and turned to seek *her* out. Thankfully, the beast kept moving in the direction of the noises that Demetrius and Ella were making, and Phoebe knew that her moment was at hand.

Suddenly, and without any warning, Demetrius threw off the map that had been keeping him and Ella hidden from view, revealing their feeble mortal forms pressed in one corner of the room.

"Phoebe! *Now!*" Demetrius's shout was clear and unequivocal, and in a heartbeat Phoebe sprang to life. The Behemoth spotted Demetrius and Ella at exactly the same moment as Phoebe did, and as she bounded out from her hiding place, heading fast for the Geata Gate, the Behemoth exploded like a runaway train in the direction of her two best friends. Phoebe's head was spinning and she felt that she may throw up. Her heart was thudding so hard in her chest that it actually hurt, and she barely knew what her feet were doing, but as she hurtled towards the Geata Gate she could only assume that they were doing what was expected of them. Phoebe did not dare to look sideways at the Behemoth or her now fully visible friends, but focused on the gate as she bounded towards it, moving faster than she ever had in her life, and yet slower than she would have liked.

It took only seconds for Phoebe to reach the Geata Gate although she felt as if she had just run several miles. She was aware of the swishing sounds of the Behemoth's fiery tail and the enraged howls emitting from his terrible mouth, but still she did not dare to look in the beast's direction. Panting and shaking like a leaf, Phoebe forced herself to focus as she regarded the gate and the enormous Key of Esse which was protruding from the lock. She grasped the key firmly in her fist before realising that her hands were clammy and unreliable. She wiped them feverishly on her jeans before returning her attentions to the key. Phoebe was relieved to find that, despite its years and layers of rust, the Key of Esse slid freely from the lock. At least something was straightforward. With her other hand, Phoebe grabbed the bottom section of the key and attempted to twist the two sections apart. Her heart fell as she realised that separating the key was apparently going to prove more difficult than removing it from the lock, but she was determined, and she sucked in a quick breath before trying again.

As Phoebe wrestled with the key, she glanced up in the direction of Demetrius and Ella. Her friends had succeeded in attracting the Behemoth's attention, but now the great beast had realised that he had been duped and he had turned to catch Phoebe standing with the Key of Esse in her hand. With a howl that sent shivers down Phoebe's spine, the Behemoth turned in her direction. His obsidian eyes locked with Phoebe's, and in that second she could see that the monster had no intention of letting her escape. Her heart was racing at a crazy pace and the old key in her hands was showing no signs of coming apart. Far from bounding over and pouncing on her, the Behemoth had lowered his gait and was approaching her with slow deliberation. The beast had hunkered down so that his belly was almost touching the stone floor, and Phoebe was sure that a heinous grin was playing at the corners of his enormous mouth. She felt for all the world like an injured deer sitting helplessly in the path of a predator, and having the Behemoth's sights trained on her was not helping her to focus on separating the Key of Esse.

Phoebe swallowed hard and forced herself to realign her thoughts. Just when she feared that she may never succeed in splitting the key, the two sections snapped apart with an angry pop. Phoebe wasted no time as she grabbed the missing piece of the Key of Esse that Grandfather Augustus had given her and twisted it into the top section. She frantically screwed in the final piece then scrabbled to slide the key back in the lock.

Just a moment too late, the Behemoth realised that he needed to pick up his pace and as he shifted from preying on Phoebe to preparing to pounce, Demetrius dived in front of the gnarly beast with the small mirror gripped tightly in his hand. The Behemoth was caught completely off guard and as the great beast reeled back in surprise it looked first at Demetrius and then at the little mirror. Phoebe held her breath as she watched, desperately wanting the mirror to be the Behemoth's Achilles heel, but barely daring to believe that this could be so. She need not have worried. As the Behemoth caught sight of itself in Demetrius's mirror, the huge beast lurched sideways as if he had lost the power in his legs as an almost pitiful howl burst forth from his throat. The Behemoth shook his head frantically as if trying to rid himself of the image he had just seen, but Demetrius was not giving up. The plucky teenager pursued the monster as it staggered and floundered, holding the little mirror aloft and forcing the beast to look again.

"Quickly Phoebe!" yelled Demetrius over the pained howls of the Behemoth. "Open the gateway!"

Phoebe used both hands to twist the Key of Esse in the lock. She heard the locking mechanism inside the Geata Gate creak and clunk as the lock slid open. Phoebe hauled on the round iron ring that should have opened the gate, and her heart crashed into her boots as she realised that she simply could not budge it. She was about to allow her dismay full access when a soft voice spoke.

"Together, Phoebe," Relief flooded Phoebe's soul as she realised that Ella was standing by her side, shaken but resolute. "If we do this together we can get the Geata Gate open."

The two girls stood side by side as they grabbed hold of the great iron ring on top of the Geata Gate. The gate was old and heavy, made from an ancient and solid wood and fitted with heavy hinges. "After three," cried Phoebe, not even daring to look towards Demetrius and the Behemoth. "One... Two... *Three!*"

Phoebe and Ella hauled together at the heavy wooden gate with all their combined might. The old wood crumbled and small pieces broke away, jagging splinters into their soft hands but they did not care. Together they continued to use all the strength they possessed until the Geata Gate groaned and protested but finally began to open. An eerie grey light began to seep out through the opening and the girls felt as though the gate was being pulled down again despite their best efforts, but they knew all too well that Demetrius was depending on them, and so with renewed vigour and determination they continued to haul the gate upwards. In a sudden abrupt movement, the Geata Gate shot open as if whatever had been holding it shut had just been removed. Phoebe and Ella toppled over backwards at the unexpected release and from the cold stone floor they looked up desperately in the direction of Demetrius and the Behemoth. They expected to find their friend still wrangling with the monstrous dog, but Demetrius was standing completely still.

His arms had dropped by his side, and the mirror was still clasped tightly in one hand. The girls followed his gaze and were aghast when they witnessed the Behemoth suspended several feet above the ground, his back arched and his six powerful legs scrabbling furiously as he tried to avoid the inevitable. The great beast was being pulled slowly towards the open gateway by an unseen force from which he could not escape. The formidable guard dog appeared terrified and unwilling to go near the Geata Gate, but the force that was drawing him ever closer was far more powerful than he was, and the creature had no choice in its fate.

Suddenly, the dank room was flooded with ethereal light, and the unexpected and stark contrast to the gloom caused Phoebe and Ella to cover their eyes.

"Dilis!"

The girls lowered their hands from their eyes and squinted into the light when they heard Demetrius's voice, and were overjoyed to see Dilis's imposing form in the room with them.

"Quickly!" There was an urgency in Dilis's voice that told the teenagers not to question his instruction. "The map. Open it Demetrius, get the girls behind it!"

Demetrius ran towards Phoebe and Ella, pulling the map from his back pocket as he moved. He hunkered down on the stone floor next to the girls, and drew the map close around the three of them. From the safety of their map cocoon, Demetrius, Phoebe and Ella watched in awe as events unfolded before their eyes. A gentle, almost imperceptible, breeze began to blow in the chamber, scarcely noticeable at first, but building in intensity until every oil lamp was extinguished and even the Behemoth's chains were being rattled by the force. As the Great Wind that had blown up continued to swirl and thrash around the room, screeching demons began to appear in its flow, sporadic at first but more and more appeared until a steady stream of hideous, furious black beings were being pulled towards the open Geata Gate. As the wind continued to howl through the room the evil beasts all did their utmost to avoid being sucked through the gateway. They were suspended above terra firma with arms, legs and wings flailing as some tried to run while others tried to swim through the air and away from the pull of the Great Wind. There was no escape for the vast majority of the demons, although a small handful of the larger beasts clung desperately to protruding sections of the stone wall and ceiling and were able to avoid the gateway, for the time being at least.

Phoebe gawped in shock and horrified awe from beneath the safety of the map. Within its embrace, neither she nor Ella nor Demetrius could feel so much as a breeze on their faces. They were entirely protected from the elements and from the flailing demons who were at the mercy of the Great Wind. For what seemed like an eternity, the wind raged on unabated pulling demon after howling demon down from the upper level of the abbey, along the stone corridor, and through the Geata Gate. Phoebe knew that the dark beings were all being returned to Mooar Mountain, but as to what fate might await them there, she had no idea.

The steady stream of furiously screeching demons began to subside eventually until the last stragglers had been caught up by the Great Wind and forced through the Geata Gate. Dilis, who had been pressed securely against the back wall of the Behemoth's lair, moved from his secure spot as the wind began to subside.

"Phoebe," Dilis's voice was quieter now but the sense of urgency remained. "You need to lock the Geata Gate shut now. There is more to come."

More? More what? Phoebe wondered what Dilis meant, but did not question his instructions. Demetrius released the map from around the friends as Phoebe began to move towards the Geata Gate. The Great Wind had died down now, but a gentle breeze still danced along the stone corridor, making her hair flutter across her face.

Phoebe stood over the gateway. She did not dare hesitate too long for fear that any bolshie demon might see its chance and make a dash for freedom back up through the open gateway. But she simply had to look and so with trepidation making her pulse quicken, Phoebe glanced into the opening. An eerie grey light continued to emanate from the open gate and as Phoebe strained her eyes to look further, she gasped at the sight that awaited her. A swirling vortex of grey led downward towards the depths of the Mooar Mountain. She could not see the bottom, nor did she wish to, but she could hear the roars of the newly imprisoned demons. Some roared in fury while others howled in anguish, but all protested loudly against what had just transpired. The noises made Phoebe's skin crawl, and she stood to pull the gate closed and lock it forever. As Phoebe straightened to her full height and reached for the wooden gate, a twisted hand with grey leathery skin suddenly shot upwards from the murky depths and grabbed her wrist in a vice like hold. Phoebe uttered a shocked scream and pulled back away from the Geata Gate. In an instant, Dilis was by her side and with one deft blow from his sword he had severed the demon's hand. The incapacitated monster howled with rage as he fell back into the depths of Mooar Mountain, as Dilis threw the creature's still twitching hand after him.

Phoebe did not hesitate one more second but slammed the heavy wooden gate shut and turned the Key of Esse in its lock. She felt the locking mechanism slide into place and heard the old lock fasten with a satisfying clunk. Without further ado, Phoebe withdrew the large heavy key from the catch and felt a weight lift from her shoulders as she held it tightly in her clasped fist.

Phoebe looked at Dilis and wondered whether she had done enough, but there was no time for discussion as the angelic warrior was bustling Phoebe back underneath the map, along with Demetrius and Ella. Phoebe realised that whatever was about to happen would be treacherous, and would require the covering and protection of the map. The realisation made her shudder as she huddled closer to her friends and waited for the inevitable.

CHAPTER 32

IN the Great Hall above, Cosain, Ernan and their troops were regrouping in the middle of the huge and now largely empty room.

"Is everyone okay?" asked Cosain with a solemn voice and concern clouding his golden eyes. One by one, the angelic warriors all confirmed that they were alright, although torn garments and bruised bodies told the tale of a battle which had been no walk in the park.

"Most of the enemy's number have been taken by the Great Wind. But there are always stragglers," continued Cosain solemnly. "We will need to take cover while the Great Fire finishes the job here."

Further explanation was not necessary. Cosain and his troops had all experienced this before. The eleven fierce warriors moved quickly to the sides of the Great Hall; some took shelter behind stone pillars while others pressed themselves into the natural contours and crevices of Darken Abbey's strong stone walls. *All* encapsulated themselves in their powerful wings, drawing them together in front of them and creating secure individual cocoons.

To an onlooker, the sight of numerous Heavenly warriors sheltering in an empty hall with their wings closed around them may have seemed somewhat preposterous. But Cosain knew exactly what was about to transpire and the safety of his troops was of the utmost importance.

As the angels huddled and waited, a whistling sound like a distant wind began to grow once again within the Great Hall. The whistling crescendoed and grew as a tiny lone spark ignited right in the centre of the enormous room. As the little spark glowed and brightened, the wind whistled around it, breathing life into the ember until it was a great flame that blazed and danced. What was feeding the flame was not apparent, but as the wind blew and the fire grew, the Great Hall came alive with light and heat and dancing shadows. In an instant, a Great Fire had filled the entire room and it began to undulate and move throughout the reaches of Darken Abbey. It burned ferociously as it travelled until not one inch of the abbey had been left untouched, from the Great Hall right down to the substratum and the Behemoth's now empty lair. Those dark creatures who had believed themselves to be terribly clever for outsmarting the Great Wind were now despatched to the Abyss by the Great Fire, which burned away all the dross until there was not one dark fiend left within the walls of Darken Abbey. The flames were ruthless and unrelenting, leaving no room for escape.

Behind the protection of their great wings, the angelic warriors were all protected and unharmed, and in the lower recesses of the abbey, beneath the incredible sheltering force of the map, Phoebe, Demetrius and Ella watched as the Great Fire raged around them, but left them untouched. The friends had never seen such an inferno, let alone be caught up right in the middle of one, and each began to wonder whether the fragile looking little map would succumb to the flames, leaving them to an unimaginable fate. But the map did not burn up, and the teenagers huddled beneath it were none the worse for their ordeal.

After a time, the Great Fire began to subside, its fury slowly abating until nothing remained except a dully glowing ember in the centre of the Great Hall from whence the flames had originated. The wind had died away and a semblance of normality returned to Darken Abbey. Phoebe, Demetrius and Ella waited until Dilis stood and unfurled his great wings from around his body, then Demetrius cautiously unwrapped the enchanted map from around them and the three friends stood up. For a moment, no-one spoke. It was as if the enormity of what had just transpired was only just beginning to sink in for the adventuring friends, and each was lost in their own thoughts for a time. Eventually, Demetrius blinked himself back to full consciousness from his shock-induced reverie, and began to sniff at the cuff of his tee shirt.

"Dem," said Phoebe, curiously perplexed by her friend's bizarre behaviour. "What on earth are you doing?"

"No smoke, Bird," replied Demetrius, making very little sense to the girls. "We were just now sat right in the middle of the wildest fire I have ever seen, and my clothes *don't even smell of smoke!*"

Phoebe and Ella found themselves smelling their own tee shirts and were stunned to realise that Demetrius was absolutely right. Phoebe grabbed Ella by the shoulder and spun her round. It was as she expected – there was not so much as a singe mark on her friend's clothes. Crazy. As Demetrius examined the old map, the friends were incredulous to find that the delicate parchment had not been damaged in any way. Just how such a thin and fragile document could have offered them any form of protection from the fury of the Great Fire was beyond Phoebe's comprehension, but if she had learnt anything during the last few weeks, it was to second guess nothing and be ready for the unexpected.

Dilis smiled at the teenagers as they marvelled over their shared experience. "The enemy cannot withstand the Great Fire," he said by way of brief explanation. "The Atoner designed it specifically. But provided we are duly diligent, it causes us no harm. The Great Fire will not destroy the light, it is drawn to darkness and wherever it find darkness, it carries out its purging work."

"So what now, Dilis?" enquired Phoebe, her green eyes eager and expectant.

"First," replied Dilis, "We must find Cosain and the others. You have the key, Phoebe?"

The Key of Esse had been in Phoebe's vice-like grip since she pulled it from the lock of the Geata Gate, and now she clenched her fist tighter just to reassure herself that it really was still there, and was heartened by the feel of the old metal key in her hand. She nodded at Dilis, then fell in silently with Demetrius and Ella as they started back along the stone corridor with the youngest of their guardians taking the lead. The little group progressed quickly to the end of the dark corridor and back up the stairs which led them out into the Great Hall. Cosain and the other warriors met them halfway across the room and despite everything that had just transpired, there were shouts of relief and jubilation as the angels and mortals were reunited and began excitedly sharing their experiences. Phoebe had never seen the angelic warriors anything other than composed and matter of fact, and the jubilant scene before her made her smile.

After a few moments, Cosain held up his hand to silence the animated chattering and summon everyone's attention. The angelic warriors regained their composure in an instant on their Captain's command, although the teenagers had to work harder to stifle their adrenalin-fuelled excitement.

"Brothers," Cosain's voice bounced off the stone walls and around the lofty ceilings of Darken Abbey. "We have secured a major victory today here in the abbey, there is no doubt about that, and you are right to celebrate. But..." The ethereal Captain's face dropped just perceptibly, and it was enough to make Phoebe's skin crawl. "But a small pocket of resistance remains."

"What do you mean, Captain?" enquired Lachlan, his sapphire blue eyes clouded with concern. "Surely between us, the Great Wind and the Great Fire, no demons could possibly have escaped... Could they?"

Cosain sucked in a deep breath, his battle-scuffed bronze breastplate rising sharply as he did so. "Yes, Lachlan, that is precisely what I mean. You all fought valiantly and of the enemy hordes gathered here today, many hundreds fell by our swords. But before the Great Wind and the Great Fire finished off what we started, I witnessed Schnither and several of his cronies make their retreat. They must have realised the inevitable outcome of the battle and decided not to risk staying. I could not break away from combat to pursue them, but I am certain that Schnither realised that I witnessed their retreat. He will be back, of that there is no doubt. But we have won significant ground here, and we will be ready for him."

Cosain's words seemed to settle angels and mortals alike, and for now at least they were content to appreciate their victory while remaining watchful and ready for whatever would invariably come at them next.

CHAPTER 33

FRIDAY 27th AUGUST
IRELAND
PRESENT DAY

THE joyful twitter of bird song danced through the crisp morning air and stirred Phoebe's senses as she wakened from a deep and grateful sleep. Sallow autumn sun was streaming into her bedroom through not quite closed curtains and as she blinked and stretched underneath her cosy duvet, Phoebe furrowed her brow in confusion. What day was this? *What* had she been dreaming? *Had* she even been dreaming? As the new day and the realisation of exactly what transpired yesterday dawned on her, Phoebe sat bold upright in bed. Slow motion animations of demons and gargoyles and angelic warriors replayed through her head and it took her several moments to still their skipping and prancing before she could fully grasp the reality of the here and now.

"Wow," Phoebe breathed the word out loud although there was no-one around to hear or respond. She rubbed her forehead thoughtfully and whispered again, "*Wow*". For now, it seemed that she could think of nothing else to say, and as she clambered slowly out of bed and pulled on her snugly purple robe and matching slippers, she began to wonder how she was going to manage a shift back to normality on time for Monday's return to school.

With everything that had happened since leaving Johannesburg first time round, Phoebe had given little thought to starting school back in Castletown. She had not attended school in Ireland since she and Ella had become best friends at Arles Primary School over a decade ago. Settling back into Irish school life would probably have been challenging enough *without* all the drama that had occurred during the last few weeks, but now Phoebe wondered how she, Demetrius and Ella could possibly go back to being 'just' school kids and not demon battling Light Bringers.

Phoebe sighed as she began to descend the stairs towards the family kitchen, and resigned herself to the belief that everything would work itself out – *somehow*. The smell of freshly brewed coffee snaked its way tantalisingly up the stairs to greet Phoebe, and as she breathed in the pleasant aroma, she was thankful to be safe in her own home.

Jack Wren had an early shift at Castletown Hospital, and Phoebe knew by the absence of his silver car from the driveway that that her dad must have already left for work. She rubbed the last of the sleep from her eyes as she entered the kitchen where her mother, Eva, was sitting at the breakfast bar reading the morning newspaper. "Hey mamma," yawned Phoebe, pouring herself a mug of hot coffee and pulling up a stool next to Eva.

"Good morning sleepy head," smiled Eva, setting down her newspaper and regarding her daughter over the top of her reading glasses. "I was gonna wake you, but I took pity on you considering it's back to school on Monday. I thought you might as well have a little lie in while you still can."

Phoebe gave her mother an exaggerated roll of her eyes and groaned. "Yuck! School... Please don't remind me!"

Eva chuckled. "Let's think positive here Phoebs – maybe you'll really enjoy it? Castletown Academy has a great reputation. And you never know who you'll meet up with from years ago at Arles Primary School." She paused for effect before continuing in a knowing tone. "In fact, Ella's mum was telling me that Brady Toms has moved on to Castletown Academy with Ella. Apparently, he asks after you all the time..." Eva's voice trailed off as she peeped at her daughter from lowered eyes, eager to gauge her reaction. She raised one eyebrow and a hint of a smile played at the corners of her mouth.

"Oh *ple-e-ease* mum," Phoebe sighed in feigned exasperation, although in truth the mention of Brady's name had caused her tummy to do a funny little flip. "Seriously, last time I saw Brady Toms he was about six and was trying to pull the legs off an angry bee. Luckily for the poor bee, he failed miserably and got stung on the thumb instead. Served the silly boy right."

Phoebe shook her head in fake disdain, but smiled fondly despite herself at the thought of six year old Brady with his crop of untameable black hair, and his green eyes that sparkled with mischief at the thought of what trouble he could get into next. He had often received a scolding from a young Phoebe or Ella for pulling their pigtails or pinching them in the playground, but somehow Phoebe had always retained a little soft spot for the interminable Brady Toms. They had contacted each other once or twice via social media during Phoebe's time in Africa, but really their friendship had drifted so much, and Phoebe found herself nervous at the prospect of encountering Brady again after such a long time. As she let her memories drift back in time to the funny little school boy, Phoebe realised that she was smiling softly to herself and quickly wiped the sappy look from her face. But it was too late. Eva had that motherly knack of detecting little hints and clues in her daughter, and Phoebe's secret smiles for Brady Toms were no exception.

"Oh yeah," Eva smiled as she picked up her newspaper

and resumed reading. "He was just a silly little boy alright."

Phoebe knew there was no point in trying to persuade her mother that she had gotten the wrong end of the stick, and so she sipped at her coffee and tried to hide her blushes in the steam rising from the hot liquid. Eva allowed herself an unspoken little '*Aha! So I was right about Brady Toms*' gloat before alleviating her daughter's awkward blushes with a seemingly offhand remark.

"You were late home last night, sweetheart."

Eva's observation sounded as though it required a response, but Phoebe was reluctant to get into the details about how her day had been. How could she possibly hope to explain *yesterday* to anyone? When she had finally returned home last evening, she had been utterly exhausted and had made only the bare minimum amount of conversation with her parents before falling gratefully into bed.

"Yeah," Phoebe offered sheepishly. "I guess me and Dem and Ella just kinda, eh, lost track of time." She glanced up at her mother, whose head was still buried in her newspaper. "There's still so much to show Dem," Phoebe added, just to be sure that her reasons sounded authentic.

"He'll soon feel right at home here, I'm sure," replied Eva, and Phoebe was glad that her mother didn't seem to need any more information right now. She hated not telling her mother the whole story. Phoebe had always been so open and honest with her parents, and now she felt as if she was deceiving them somehow. But to try and explain the whole crazy adventure to them at this stage would be madness, Phoebe knew that.

"Has he not appeared yet this morning?" asked Phoebe, suddenly realising that Demetrius must still be fast asleep.

"He came downstairs earlier just before Dad left for the

hospital and had a cup of coffee with us. But he looked so tired that I sent him back up to bed, and I haven't heard a peep from him ever since. Whatever adventure you've been taking him on must have been pretty intensive!"

"Yeah," mumbled Phoebe, "All that exploring definitely takes it out of you..."

Phoebe got up to pour herself another cup of coffee and toasted some bread which she slathered with peanut butter before sitting back down at the breakfast bar opposite her mother. She sipped carefully at the hot sweet coffee, appreciating both its warmth and the satisfying crunch of the peanut butter much more than she had done yesterday morning. *Yesterday morning.* A mere twenty four hours had passed, and yet Phoebe felt as if she had lived a little lifetime in the space of just one day. She puffed out her cheeks and blew out her breath as yesterday's surreal craziness washed over her anew, and the sound caused Eva to set down her newspaper and look up inquisitively at her daughter.

"What is it, Phoebe? You've been a million miles away lately. What's on your mind, Love? You can tell me you know."

Eva's eyes were clouded with concern and her brow was slightly furrowed, and Phoebe realised that she had not been as good at keeping her thoughts to herself as she would have liked to have been. She and Eva had always shared a wonderfully close bond, and part of her desperately wanted to just blurt out the entire story to her kind and compassionate mamma right now over breakfast. But Phoebe was all too aware that it was not just as simple as that. There really was *no way* she could just hit Eva with the full insane story, it was just too ludicrous. And even if her mother did believe her rather than worrying that she had lost the plot, Phoebe didn't want to draw Jack and Eva in too deeply. She figured that the less they knew, the safer they would be, and Phoebe much preferred muddling through all this with Demetrius and Ella than putting her parents at risk. She just could not risk losing them a second time.

"Ahh, it's nothing Mum, honestly. I think it has all just been a bit overwhelming, you know? I mean, we've only been home a few weeks, and everything is still pretty new to me. I'm nervous about starting Castletown Academy and seeing all those faces that I haven't seen in over a decade – that's a *lo-o-ong* time, Mum. And then there's Dem. I mean, if it's taking me some time to readjust, imagine how crazy this new life must be for *him!*"

Phoebe realised that she was beginning to babble, and not wanting to sound like she actually *did* have the cares of the world on her shoulders, she decided that changing the subject would be beneficial.

"How are things with Celtic Justice, Mum?" asked Phoebe, trying her best to sound carefree and interested. "I guess you'll be starting to see the old abbey beginning to take shape in the next few days, eh?"

Eva's pretty face brightened at the mention of the abbey and her beloved project. Phoebe's diversion tactics had the desired effect, and she was glad to be out of the spotlight. Eva set her newspaper down on the breakfast bar as she animatedly began to tell Phoebe about the progress they were making with the organisation. With Jack so busy at the hospital, Eva had shouldered the majority of the responsibility for CJO, but it was a task she relished and Phoebe knew that her talented mother was more than able to cope with the demands.

"It's all coming along so well, Phoebe," Eva enthused. "There's quite a lot of work to be done to the interior of the building, but we've made so many changes and improvements to the exterior. The scaffolding is still in place, but the builder tells me that the abbey is now structurally sound and we should be able to get the team of decorators in next week. The council has been very good, especially Celeste McGill and Brent Atwood – they're so supportive, and I don't imagine that they had an easy time talking that Vincent d'Olcas round to their way of thinking. I really can't think why he would be so opposed to CJO. I mean, it's not like we would be treading on his toes in any respect... Peculiar man, *really* peculiar."

The mention of Vincent d'Olcas, who was the treasurer at Arles Council and chief advisor to the mayor, Mr. Bradbury Jones, caused Phoebe to bristle, and she cast her mind back to the moment she had seen his name penned on parchment on Abaddon's writing bureau. Phoebe was certain that d'Olcas had some allegiance with Abaddon the Defiler, and it was her best guess that he was an elusive shapeshifter, strategically placed in Arles Council to thwart her parents' plans for Celtic Justice Organisation.

Phoebe realised that her mother was still deep in conversation, and tuned back in to what she was saying.

"The whole thing is pretty exciting, sweetheart!" enthused Eva. "You should take Dem and Ella up to Darken Abbey when you get a minute just to see how it's all coming on – I bet you won't recognise the old place. But don't get too close, Sweetheart, I definitely don't want any of you getting hurt when there's renovation work going on."

"Sounds amazing, Mum," Phoebe smiled a genuine smile at her mother's enthusiasm and the unintentional irony of her words: "*Don't get too close*"...

"If only you knew, Mum, if only you knew..."

CHAPTER 34

A N hour later and Demetrius had finally surfaced and finished his breakfast. Phoebe was dressed and ready to go. She was eager to regroup with Ella to mull over the events of yesterday, and she really wanted to make the most of their last few days of free time before school started back on Monday.

"Oh *come on*, Dem," Phoebe complained, tired of waiting for her friend to get himself gathered so that they could meet up with Ella. "It's gonna be Monday by the time you get out at this rate!"

"*Relax*, Bird," Demetrius teased his impatient friend. "After all, I hung around long enough yesterday waiting for you..."

Phoebe caught the mischievous twinkle in Demetrius's eye and realised that he was referring to how long he and Ella had been encapsulated inside the mirrors in Mooar Mountain before Phoebe had arrived to set them free. She raised one eyebrow then grinned despite her growing impatience and punched him gently on the shoulder.

"Okay smarty pants," she conceded. "I got there as fast as I could, given the circumstances..."

Demetrius winked at Phoebe then grabbed his jacket as the pair headed out through the back door. They chose not to travel along the main road and set out instead along the little country lane that was a short cut to Ella's house. Within minutes, they arrived at the Quills' welcoming green front door, and were greeted by the perpetually smiling Rose Quill.

"Hello my dears," she beamed as she gave Phoebe and Demetrius a quick hug. "It's nice to see you both looking a bit brighter than you did when you left Ella home last night. What a day you all must have had! Ella never stirred all night and don't tell her that I told you, but she isn't long out of bed this morning!" Mrs. Quill winked at Phoebe and Demetrius as Ella appeared into the hallway from the kitchen.

"Hey guys," she said with a weak smile. Ella's lack-lustre greeting caused a little flutter in Phoebe's belly and she worried that Mrs. Quill might probe her daughter on why she was so unusually quiet. But she need not have worried. Mrs. Quill simply chuckled as she pulled her daughter in for a quick embrace before tousling her sandy hair.

"You'll not get much chat out of this one today I'm afraid," Rose said with mock concern. "She's exhausted! One good day's exploring and my little girl needs her sleep." Rose seemed content that Ella was simply tired, and Phoebe felt relief flood over her that they had avoided any more probing questions.

"It was a pretty full day for sure, Mrs. Quill," replied Demetrius. "For a small town there's definitely a lot to take in."

Rose Quill smiled at the three teenagers. "Off you go then," she said. "Go have fun, and enjoy the last few days of summer. I'll see you later, Love," she said with a smile in Ella's direction. "Have you got your 'phone?"

"Yes Mum, I've got it here, I'll call you later so you know what time to expect me home," said Ella in a considerably brighter tone. She obviously realised that she had come across as distant and didn't want to worry her mother or prompt any awkward questions. "See you in a while, Mum."

Rose Quill waved the three friends off before shaking her head and smiling to herself. '*Kids today, they just can't hack the pace*' she mused as she took the vacuum cleaner from its cupboard and set about sprucing up her cosy home.

For a little while, Phoebe, Demetrius and Ella walked in silence. They had no particular agenda for the day, and nobody had suggested a destination, so for now they were just content to be together and strolled along in easy silence, following the direction the road was taking them. After everything that had happened and all that the friends had experienced, it was very likely that they were all mulling over the same thoughts, but if this was the case, then each chose to keep their ponderings guarded for the time being, and the events of yesterday were not spoken of. They continued like this for quite some time and before any of them realised it, they had arrived in Castletown and were almost at the gates of the high school. The friends surveyed the imposing building in front of them, and it was Phoebe who broke the comfortable silence.

"So after the *major* day we had yesterday, we've got another *major* day to survive on Monday as well," she sighed, hoping that her jokey comparison would be well received, but with just a hint of anxiety in her voice nonetheless.

"Yep," concurred Ella. "Back to school. Always a fun day..." The irony in her voice was not lost on Phoebe or Demetrius, who both smiled at their friend in an '*I feel your pain*' kind of way.

"It can't be *that* bad," suggested Demetrius. "In fact, I really quite enjoy school." He paused and when neither of the girls spoke up in agreement he continued in a wry voice; "And besides, Bird, you'll get to catch up with *Brady*..."

Ella's head bobbed to attention. "Have you been talking about Brady, Phoebe?" she asked with great gusto. "*Brady Toms?* I knew it! I *knew* you had a thing for him. Fancy telling Dem though instead of me – uh, no offence Demetrius! Now I can't *wait* until Monday!" Ella was grinning from ear to ear now, and Phoebe, who had not been afforded the opportunity to disagree with her friend's assumptions, shook her head in mock despair.

"I do not have any sort of a *thing* for Brady Toms, Ella, you know that full well! And Demetrius, how did you even hear his name? I'm sure that I never mentioned Brady to you – why would I, after all?" she added, anxious not to sound too interested. "Were you eavesdropping on me and my mum this morning?"

"Ooh, so you were telling your mamma about him then?" squealed Ella. Apparently, there was no derailing her enthusiasm when it came to the matter of Brady Toms.

"*Ella!* You're as bad as Mum! I wasn't telling her *anything*, really. She *suggested* that maybe I'd be glad to see Brady again after all this time... And, as it happens, she was wrong, I'm not bothered in the slightest..." Phoebe did her best to appear disinterested, although she was fairly certain that her success was limited. "And besides," she added. "I'm sure Brady has a girlfriend already..."

"A girlfriend?" Ella's voice had almost gone supersonic. "Who mentioned anything about girlfriends?" she teased.

Phoebe could see that she was fighting a losing battle, and decided that it was best just to stop trying to convince them of her indifference towards Brady Toms. In truth though, she was not indifferent about him; the mere mention of his name had caused nervous little flutters in her belly, let alone the thought of actually meeting him again on Monday.

"I imagine there will be loads of old faces to get reacquainted with," suggested Phoebe, desperate to change the subject. "I only hope that I can remember them all, it's been a *lo-o-ong* time."

"I don't imagine there'll be any problem for you and Brady, I imagine you'll recognise each other instantly," Ella teased, obviously not willing to let the subject drop just yet. "In fact, given how many times he asked after you the last few years, I would guess that he'll actually be looking out for you..."

Phoebe found herself at once embarrassed and delighted by the thought that Brady Toms had missed her and remembered her after all these years, but she desperately wanted to keep any interest she may have to herself.

"I'm sure he won't be looking out for me Ella, why would he do that?" ventured Phoebe, secretly hoping that Ella might elaborate. But if Ella caught the double entendre in Phoebe's question, she was not taking the bait, and instead changed the subject, this time much to Phoebe's frustration.

"Do you think we'll see Cosain and the others again?" Ella asked to no-one in particular. The simple question replaced all thoughts of Brady Toms and Castletown Academy with memories of events from the last few days, and a sombre silence fell over the three friends. Each now seemed obliged to acknowledge their thoughts about events which had transpired yesterday in Mooar Mountain, and with this acknowledgement came a sobering reality check.

"I really don't know, El," replied Phoebe tentatively after a few seconds. "I mean, I don't think that Cosain could just leave it like this, could he? Surely there needs to be some kind of, uh, debrief or something, you know – so that we all know where we stand."

"Yeah," agreed Demetrius. "Although I reckon that our part in the whole crazy story must be finished now... Right? I mean, we did our part, didn't we? We returned missing piece of the Key of Esse, made sure that anyone – *anything* – that didn't belong in Darken Abbey got sent back through the Geata Gate, and we locked up that doorway good and tight!"

"Yeah, and we even made it home in one piece – just about," added Ella dryly with a shudder.

Demetrius nodded. "So surely Cosain will pay us a visit, if only to alleviate us of our duties?"

Phoebe could not help herself and smiled wryly at Demetrius's serious tone and military imagery. "*Some army we turned out to be,*" she mused, although she kept her thoughts to herself for fear of offending Demetrius. She allowed events and images from yesterday's battle to skirt about in her mind for just a moment longer before flipping her long locks over her shoulder and linking arms with her two friends. There was a niggling thought in the back of Phoebe's head, but for now she did not want to give it voice. She could not help but think on the fact that Captain Schnither and a few of his minions had evaded the Great Fire and the Great Wind – surely if he was still alive and kicking out there somewhere, then she and her friends probably had not heard the last of him and his havoc wreaking ways? Phoebe felt sure that Schnither would be back, but for now she just needed time to breathe, and so she kept her concerns to herself.

"Let's not stew on it, eh?" Phoebe said with a levity to her tone that she did not entirely believe herself. "It has been a crazy, *crazy* few days, there's no denying that... But it's all over, we made it, and on Monday our lives will return to normal and we'll all be regular school kids with nothing more to worry about than algebra, grammar and the periodic table." She paused and looked from Ella's face to Demetrius's, searching for their agreement. When she found their unspoken acceptance of her ponderings, Phoebe continued, "I reckon that we need to take a vow of silence – the stuff that we have all just come through should be kept between us – *just us*. Nobody else needs to know. *Nobody*." She laboured the point, knowing in her very core that none of them could afford to discuss any of their bizarre adventures with anyone else. No-one else *needed* to know. And besides, who in their right mind would believe them? Angelic warriors? Demonic foe? A gigantic rabid six legged dog bent on destroying them? It was almost too fantastical to be believed by Phoebe and her friends, and they had lived through it all.

Demetrius and Ella did not have to be asked twice. Both nodded their heads in wholehearted agreement, their stern faces indicating that neither of them had any intention of telling another soul their outlandish tale. Phoebe loosened her hold on Demetrius's and Ella's arms and slowly extended her right arm with the palm of her hand facing down. Demetrius and Ella followed Phoebe's lead, placing their hands solemnly on top of Phoebe's. "Agreed," they said in unison with all the solemnity of someone taking the strictest oath. Phoebe wondered if her friends felt the relief that this straightforward act had just permitted her to experience. The simple promise to tell no-one, coupled with the knowledge that Demetrius and Ella would always share her secret, afforded Phoebe a sense of well-being and safety. Somehow, she knew that, for now at least, all was well and she had played her part in an incredible adventure which had ensured the safety of her family and friends and everyone living in the surrounding area.

Phoebe sighed deeply as the reality of it all washed over her anew, and somewhere in the deepest recesses of her consciousness she had to acknowledge again the gnawingly persistent thought that maybe Demetrius was wrong and the whole '*crazy story*' was in fact far from being over. For the time being, though, she did not want to consider this possibility, and contented herself instead with the acceptance that *for now* she and her friends were safe, *for now* Darken

Abbey had been made secure from the infiltration of dark forces, and *for now* she would simply regroup and get on with life, one day at a time.

"Coffee?" Phoebe suggested hopefully, eager to diffuse the pensive mood that was quickly descending.

"Ahh, you read my mind," smiled Demetrius.

"The Bean House?" suggested Ella, as the three friends set off instinctively in the direction of Ella's favourite coffee shop.

"Sound good to me," smiled Phoebe. She was pleased to find a genuine peace and contentment settle on her soul despite the many questions which remained unanswered. Phoebe had come to recognise this calm, and knew from experience that it tended to herald the presence of Cosain and his heroic brothers. She glanced quickly around, half expecting to see a tell tale flutter in the nearby trees, or the glint of a fiery sword, but there were no clues suggesting Cosain's proximity. Phoebe smiled to herself nonetheless. *'Cosain knows what he's doing,'* she mused. *'If he's not here, then I guess we'll see him when we need to see him.'*

CHAPTER 35

PHOEBE, Demetrius and Ella made their way into the quaint old township of Castletown and headed directly for the Bean House coffee shop. The cosy little establishment was always a welcoming haven, and the trio followed the warming scent of freshly brewed coffee as they found themselves a secluded booth near the rear of the shop. The girls settled into their seats while Demetrius went to purchase drinks and treats for them – lattes for him and Ella, while Phoebe splurged on a hot chocolate with whipped cream and marshmallows. The friends made the most of this free time and lingered in the Bean House for an age. They had no agenda for the afternoon, and were happy to simply spend time together, chatting and laughing. This afternoon, they were not Light Bringers or demon battlers, they were just three friends hanging out together. This normality had been starkly lacking during the last while, and Phoebe in particular was incredibly thankful to be able to enjoy time with her best friends, secure in the knowledge that her parents were safe and all was well with her little world.

Three hours and copious amounts of coffee and cocoa later, Ella stretched and yawned. "Oh boy," she said stifling another yawn, "All this sitting around talking definitely makes you sleepy, eh? I guess we should make a move for home."

Phoebe and Demetrius chuckled and nodded their agreement. "Yep, it's the coffee that does it," grinned Demetrius. "Definitely the coffee and not the death defying escapades in strange other worlds catching up with us…"

Ella took his point, and the trio enjoyed a giggle together as they stood up to leave. As Demetrius rose to his feet, something slid from his jacket pocket and clattered on to the hexagonal wooden table. It was Grandpa Augustus's deceptively unexceptional looking glasses. The sight of the glasses stopped Phoebe and Ella in their tracks.

"Wow," whispered Demetrius. "I actually can't believe that I had forgotten about these."

"Yeah," agreed Phoebe. "Me too. And the other stuff – I still have the pocket watch."

"I can't believe Dem found that little watch in all the confusion," exclaimed Ella. "You made a pretty hasty exit from Mooar Mountain, Phoebs, and I was sure the pocket watch would have been lost in the chaos."

"Ahh, no problem to me," joked Demetrius with an exaggerated bravado. "And I still have the map and the mirror too," he added.

Remembering the peculiar objects which had been of such importance to the friends served to pull a sombre blanket back over the teenagers, and for a moment each was lost in their own thoughts. Finally, Phoebe broke the silence.

"Let's just hold on to them, eh?" she suggested. "That's not to say we'll ever need them again – but better safe than sorry I guess. What's that old saying? Better to have and not need, than need and not have."

"Agreed," said Demetrius, and as Phoebe caught his eye she realised that he too must be thinking that their shared story may not quite be over.

Demetrius and Ella both seemed satisfied with Phoebe's reasoning, and Demetrius gathered up the glasses and stowed them safely back in his jacket pocket. As the friends made their way out of the Bean House, they resumed their apparently carefree chatter about what the weekend held in store and how weird it might be to catch up with old faces on Monday at Castletown Academy. But the reappearance of Grandpa Augustus's glasses had unsettled Phoebe, and the persistent niggle that perhaps she and her friends had not fully completed the task set out for them reared its head once more. For now, Phoebe chose to shake it off and followed her best friends out of the coffee house as they made their unhurried way home.

★ ★ ★

In a dense little copse of trees on the outskirts of the town two diminutive demons were beside themselves with rage. The gnarly little monsters were no strangers to this area – indeed, they knew the town like the backs of their leathery hands, having stalked its streets for aeons past. Twin demons Braygor and Graygor had been amongst a small number of black fiends to escape yesterday's angelic onslaught in Darken Abbey. The twins were wily and shrewd, and both had experienced enough of the frustratingly victorious ways of the Atoner to know that they would have to make their escape from the abbey quickly if they wanted to survive. Braygor and Graygor had hissed their frantic warning to whichever of their brothers at arms would listen as they raced to escape the battle that raged in the abbey, but few had heeded their counsel. It was not loyalty or nobility that had kept the other demons locked in battle in Darken Abbey, but rather a stubborn unwillingness to concede defeat and an erroneous pride which had assured them that they could outsmart and defeat Cosain and the angelic troops. Braygor and Graygor had not loitered in the abbey to try and persuade anyone – no, they had issued their warning on the wing, barely pausing to see who would follow them, much less caring who took their advice. Were they their brothers' keepers? Certainly not! And they would not be held responsible if the other demons were too stupid to take good advice. Still, it had been a crushing defeat, and the diminutive twins were not entirely unaffected by the enormous losses.

Once outside the abbey, the dastardly twins had found a secure perch on an ancient oak tree that offered them prime views of what was unfolding within the abbey without any of the risk of being caught up in the inevitable end. They had watched aghast as the Great Wind swept through Darken Abbey, and knew that the vast majority of their evil cohorts would have been caught up in the gale and swept back to their dark headquarters through the Geata Gate, which undoubtedly had then secured and irrevocably locked. Their already slack jaws had drooped further as they witnessed the ferocity of the Great Fire which raged unabated through the abbey, undoubtedly annihilating any dark stragglers who had been fortunate enough to evade the Great Wind. Or *unfortunate enough*, as the case may have been. When the whole terrible scene had been played out in its entirety, Braygor and Graygor had pressed themselves further back into dense foliage of the oak tree and remained hidden as twelve blazes of furious ethereal light had departed from the abbey – Captain Cosain and his angelic brothers, undoubtedly bound for the Celestial City to report back to the Atoner. The diminutive twins had watched while the aggravating mortal child, Phoebe Wren, had run from the abbey with her two equally infuriating friends Demetrius and Ella, and had almost passed out with indignation at not being able to hunt them down and eradicate the mortal nuisances. But they had known that they dare not risk being seen; Cosain and his ridiculous brothers were not far away, and if the twins had been spotted, it would have spelled immediate annihilation for them. And what hope to wreak havoc *then?* No, for all their thick-headed ways they evil twins knew that sometimes you have to pass up on the good in order to be able to fulfil the great – and finishing off the three mortal youths *would* be great...

When the dust had finally settled around Darken Abbey, Braygor and Graygor had taken stock of all that had transpired, and the enormity of the humiliating defeat suffered by the dark forces had been a particularly bitter pill to swallow. The heinous twins took some comfort in the discovery that several of their cruel collaborators had heeded their warnings and followed them out of Darken Abbey, thereby evading the angels' blades, the Great Wind and the devastating Great Fire. Malva, Krake, Craven, Jarrda and Yigno, along with Schnither, Captain of the Dark Army, had escaped from the abbey along with a small handful of furious demons, and Braygor and Graygor gloated in the fact that their gruesome colleagues owed them their lives. In the moments that followed Captain Schnither had wasted no time in vowing revenge. The furious Dark Captain had reluctantly acknowledged the need to bide his time, and to this end had ordered Braygor and Graygor to keep an eye on the mortals. Spurred on by venom and pride, the odious twins had deployed immediately, and in the interim had been keeping close watch on Phoebe and her friends.

And now they sat, unseen by an unsuspecting town on which they would soon unleash their unbridled fury. Troublesome Phoebe Wren may have won this battle – but they would see to it that she would never win the war. And by the time they were finished with her, she would rue the day she chose to meddle in things best left alone...

Phoebe Wren
And The School Of Secrets

CHAPTER 1

MONDAY 30th AUGUST
PRESENT DAY, IRELAND

7:30am on Monday morning came far too quickly for Phoebe Wren's liking. The fifteen year old had very mixed emotions about beginning student life at Castletown Academy. Part of her was cautiously excited at the prospect of getting reacquainted with old faces from her distant past, faces of friends she had left behind over ten years ago when her parents had moved from Ireland to Africa. But another part of her was terrified by the same thought – what if no-one remembered her? Or – *worse* – what if they did remember her, but time and circumstances had created a gap that could never be crossed? What if she wasn't welcome now? What if everyone had *moved on* and left her in the distant past..?

Phoebe looked at her own image in the full length mirror in the corner of her bedroom – Castletown Academy's compulsory uniform wasn't so bad as far as school uniforms went, and she felt reasonably comfortable in her new attire.

The school's smart uniform consisted of a modest grey knee length skirt trimmed with red, black shoes, grey knee socks, a white shirt and a striped tie bearing the school's motif. Her dark navy blazer was well tailored and somehow made her feel older than her fifteen years. On the small pocket at the front of the blazer was the school's logo of a white dove with a branch in its mouth, wings outstretched, surrounded by the motto, '*Fidelitas: Honor: Observantia*' – loyalty, honour, respect. Phoebe felt sure that she had learned more about these qualities during the last few weeks than she had in the entire rest of her life, and the thought made her smile.

"Phoebe! Demetrius! It's way past time that you two were up and at 'em!"

Eva Wren's voice broke through the tumbling thoughts that were bouncing around in Phoebe's head.

"Come on now, you don't want to miss the bus on your first day at your new school!"

"*Oh thanks Mum,*" thought Phoebe. "*As if I wasn't nervous enough already...*"

Phoebe met her lifelong best friend Demetrius on the upstairs landing and the two of them bustled downstairs together, although it was very apparent that Demetrius was by far the most eager of the pair. Since moving from Africa to Ireland to live with the Wren family, Demetrius had been intent on making the most of every opportunity afforded to him, and today was no exception. As he had done with every other day since his arrival in Ireland back in July, Demetrius had grabbed hold of this new day with gusto, and despite his slightly irksome eagerness, Phoebe was so glad that he was here, sharing their first day at a new school together.

"Ahh, don't you both look so smart?" beamed Eva, smiling proudly at her daughter and Demetrius, who she regarded as being entirely part of the family. Phoebe felt suddenly self-conscious, and kicked at the corner of the large red floor rug with the toe of her shoe. She knew that she was letting nerves get the better of her, and willed herself to calm down. Apparently oblivious to his friend's nagging discomfort, Demetrius grinned excitedly back at Eva.

"Thanks Mrs. Bird," he smiled, referring to Eva with the same pet name he used for Phoebe, derived from her unusual surname. The simple and familiar phrase made Phoebe smile despite her nervousness, and instantly she felt her shoulders drop as she reminded herself to just relax. Demetrius had always possessed the inexplicable knack of making Phoebe feel safe and comfortable, and it was a trait she never took for granted.

"I actually can't wait to get to Castletown Academy and get started," Demetrius enthused. "There's just so much more I want to know! I still can barely believe that I'm here in Ireland with you guys and about to start high school with Phoebs – it's all like a dream!"

There was no denying that Demetrius's enthusiastic babble was infectious, and Phoebe found herself chuckling along with her mother, who pulled Demetrius close in an affectionate embrace. He was the son that Eva and Jack never had, and Phoebe had looked on him as her unofficial big brother since they were very little.

"You'll love it, Dem," enthused Eva with a smile. "And so will you, Phoebe," she said gently to her daughter, obviously aware that Phoebe was nervous. Phoebe smiled at her mum and nodded; she had never been able to hide much from her perceptive mother, which had made the events of the last few weeks particularly difficult.

Phoebe and Demetrius made their way into the warm and welcoming family kitchen where they hastily made themselves breakfast which was quickly demolished.

"Right mum," Phoebe called in the direction of her mother's study as she pulled on her coat and grabbed her already packed schoolbag. "We're off, see you later."

Eva reappeared from her study, pulling her reading glasses off and sliding them on top of her head as she drew first Phoebe and then Demetrius in for a quick final hug.

"Have you got everything you need kids? Books? Money? Bus passes? Right, off you go. Have a great day you two, and tell Ella I said so too."

"We will mum, see you this afternoon," Phoebe waved over her shoulder as she and Demetrius closed the front door behind them and set off in the direction of Ella Quill's house just a few minutes' walk away. Fifteen year old Ella completed the trio of comrades, who had become inseparable since they were reunited just a few short weeks ago. And if joyous friendship was not enough to underpin the strong bond that existed between them, then the unimaginable adventures that they had shared certainly cemented it. Phoebe and her friends had lived through the most incredible time of their lives, and as she prepared for the adventure of a new school and new faces, she could not stifle the notion that there was more in store.

* * *

Back inside the house, Eva Wren smiled to herself and dabbed lightly at her dewy eyes with a tissue. It was a big day for her little girl, and the start of a new chapter in her life. *'Ahh, if only she could stay my little girl forever!'* Eva mused wistfully, shaking her head at her own sentimentality, but she knew that Phoebe was growing up and the marked maturity and boldness in her daughter during the last few weeks was unmistakable. Actually, now that she thought about it, Eva realised that Phoebe had changed a *lot* since the family had returned to Ireland... *'Wow,'* Eva pondered the changes in her daughter. *'I knew being home in Ireland would change her, but I never anticipated just how much.'*

A little pang of sudden guilt stabbed at Eva's heart as she considered just how busy she and Jack had been during the last few weeks. Work on Celtic Justice Organisation had been rather all-consuming, and Jack had been back in full swing in his senior post as a surgeon at Castletown hospital. Maybe they should have given more consideration to their daughter and how she was settling back into life in Ireland? Eva tucked the thought away in the back of her head, then brewed herself another cup of coffee and returned to the study to continue her work. She and Jack, her husband, were getting ready for the launch of Celtic Justice Organisation, the project that they had returned to Ireland to establish. Building work on nearby Darken Abbey, the establishment's new headquarters, was moving along at a pleasing pace, and Eva knew that it wouldn't be too long before the organisation was ready for its official launch. Yes, it had been a hectic few weeks, and the Wrens had definitely hit the ground running when they touched down on Ireland's green shores just a short while ago, but Eva had no doubt about the validity of the project that she found herself heading up. She had no regrets about putting her career as a surgeon on the back burner, and was excited about the direction that CJO would take. And, she concluded, Phoebe did seem to have settled very well into life back in Ireland, so perhaps the little pangs of motherly guilt were misplaced... At least, Eva hoped this was the case.

Eva Wren's musings simultaneously excited and daunted her, and she knew that theirs was a mammoth task, but she believed wholeheartedly that CJO would prove to be invaluable in Arles, Castletown and beyond. *"Don't put any limits on CJO, Eva,"* she chided herself, *"You just never know where this thing's gonna go!"* The thought sent butterflies of anticipation and possibility whirring through Eva's belly, and she set about her work with renewed gusto, smiling to herself at the thought of her lovely daughter and the new adventures on which they all found themselves. Yes, coming back to Ireland had been the right move for her family, and Eva was excited for the journey ahead, even with all its potential bumps and hiccups.

★ ★ ★

Outside the Wrens' home, two small and snarling twin demons turned to each other and grinned so widely that their purple lips sustained new hacks. Braygor and Graygor loved nothing more than wreaking havoc on unsuspecting mortals, and could scarcely contain their glee at the thought of what they were about to unleash on Phoebe Wren and her nauseatingly perfect family.

"Aww, poor naïve Mummy Wren," snorted Braygor, the more juvenile of the gnarly brothers. "She thinks life is so good back here on this sickeningly green island. Ha! We'll make her think again, won't we brother?"

Braygor hopped down from his perch on the branch of a tall maple tree and proceeded to perform a freakish dance around its trunk, flinging his legs wildly about this way and that like a deranged ballerina.

In the branches above him, Graygor curled his top lip in disdain and rolled his eyes at his idiotic twin. He wondered how such a pathetic creature could actually be his brother... Maybe there had been some mistake? No matter. He had more than enough cunning and skill for both of them.

"*What* are you doing you buffoon?" snarled Graygor in the general direction of his hopping and skipping brother. He couldn't bear to look at him any longer.

"What am I doing? *What am I doing?*" slurred Braygor as though the question was the most ludicrous he had ever been asked. "I'm *Irish dancing* you idiot! *When in Ireland,* and all that." The diminutive demon continued with his awkward jig while his brother pouted in disgust in the tree above. *He* had no time to waste larking about like his ridiculous twin. No, the terrible twosome had been assigned a very specific task and Graygor intended to carry it out, even if Braygor was going to be more of a hindrance than a help.

"Come on you clown," Graygor snapped. "We've got work to do."

And with that he leapt down from his branch, deliberately landing on Braygor's shoulders and sending him sprawling in an indignant heap across the grass. Graygor was on his feet before Braygor could regain his composure and took to the sky, flapping his black leathery wings furiously and keeping ahead of his twin despite Braygor's angry attempts to get his own back.

"Wait, brother, *wait*," Braygor hissed the words out with jolty breaths – the little demon was more out of shape than he had imagined and was having trouble catching up with his twin.

"I don't have time to hang around waiting for you, Braygor!" snapped Graygor indignantly. "Now get your backside in gear or go back to Mooar Mountain. We have work to do and if you don't move it, we'll lose sight of that annoying girl and who knows what *good* she might get up to? We can't have *that* now, can we?"

Despite his prickliness, Graygor had slowed just enough to let Braygor catch him up and now the two travelled side by side. "I suppose you're right, brother," Braygor concurred as he drew alongside his agitated twin. "But just because I agree with you on this matter doesn't mean that you don't deserve this..." Braygor drew back his fist and smacked the unsuspecting Graygor square up the side of the head, causing him to career wilding off his flight path, narrowly missing a tall tree. Braygor shot off into the skyline, cackling with glee as Graygor gathered himself and resumed his travels. It would seem that he was going to have more to consider on this mission than merely upsetting the quiet life of Phoebe Wren...

~ ABOUT THE AUTHOR ~

Julie Timlin was born in Lisburn, Northern Ireland, in 1974 and grew up in the countryside near Lurgan on the shores of Lough Neagh. She has an honours degree in English from the Queen's University Of Belfast, and taught English and Religious Education for several years before quitting teaching to work alongside her Dad in family business, Norman Emerson Group. Julie is married to Marty and they have two daughters, Caitlin (13) and Ella (11), a cocker spaniel named Lincoln, and a bearded dragon called Buddy.

'Phoebe Wren And The Mystery Of Darken Abbey' is the second book in the Phoebe Wren Series. Book one - *'Phoebe Wren And The Vortex Of Light'* was published in June 2014 and is available from most good online retailers.

 www.facebook.com/phoebewrenseries

 @JulesTimlin